Odds
ON THE
RAKE

SOFIE DARLING

OLIVER-HEBER BOOKS

The Race of the Century

The thrill! The pulse-pounding exhilaration!

Hark ye!

Attend, one and all! The most anticipated and electrifying Thoroughbred contest of this century -Nay, of all time!

Only and Exclusively this Season's Winners of The 2,000 Guineas, The 1,000 Guineas, The Oaks, The Derby, and The St. Leger shall vie for the prize of

£10,000

To Claim the Mantle of Greatest Champion

SATURDAY 22ND OF SEPTEMBER

IN THE YEAR OF OUR LORD 1822

EPSOM DOWNS

Published by Oliver-Heber Books

0 9 8 7 6 5 4 3 2 1

✿ Created with Vellum

CHAPTER ONE

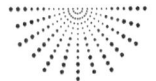

SUFFOLK, ENGLAND, MARCH 1822

*G*emma squinted up at the time-beaten sign swinging above the coaching inn's entrance, shoulder braced against her brother's heavier weight, and couldn't help marveling that months of running had led them here—an inn called The Drunken Piebald located in the nether regions of Suffolk.

It wasn't the name of the inn that put her off, but rather the knowing smirk on the horse's mouth as he held up a tankard in jolly toast.

Unnerving, that horse's smile.

"Whoever heard of a drunk horse, anyway?" she said to make light conversation for her brother whose face was stretched into a pained grimace.

Liam gave a dry snort. "Old Featheringham gives his Thoroughbreds biscuits and canary wine on race day." He winced as she carefully maneuvered him across the inn's threshold. "Watch how you go, sister," he groused under his breath, a bead of sweat running down his cheek.

In the cramped receiving area, the fug of the inn's taproom met them full in the face—spirits gone sour and ale gone stale mixed with the sweat of unwashed bodies, both past and present. It was a smell Gemma and Liam had come to know well over the last year as they'd moved from one inn or stable loft after the other.

They never stayed long in one place. It was how they hadn't been caught.

But soon that life would be behind them.

Soon, they would be able to plant their feet in one place— which was what had brought them to Suffolk.

Liam frowned and attempted to ease a measure of his weight off Gemma as she swiped the perspiration from her brow. Hobbling around with a brother whose leg was broken above the knee presented more difficulty than she'd expected, truth told.

From his place behind a high oak desk, the cool-eyed innkeeper of The Drunken Piebald sat, unmoved and unmoving, and observed the two strange auburn-haired brothers as they approached step by shuffling step.

How much more askance would he be viewing them if he only knew the scrawny brother with two good legs was, in fact, a sister.

Well, he wouldn't know.

Gemma had long since discovered that was what trousers, chest binding, and a slouch hat were for.

Still, if she'd been dressed as a woman, he would've been left with no choice but to assist them. But two lads staying in the cheapest room on the ground floor? They were left to get on beneath their own steam.

She dug into the pocket of her dull brown coat and pulled out a pouch, which gave a muted clank when it hit the oak surface.

"Half, as agreed," said Liam through gritted teeth, as if the words cost him more than what was in that pouch.

He always spoke for them, making it easier for Gemma to pass without much notice in public places. Tonight, a light sheen of sweat coated skin that had paled with the journey up from London. He needed to lie down.

"And the other half at the end of the month," he finished.

The innkeeper's mouth widened incrementally—what passed for a smile on those thin, stingy lips, Gemma supposed—as he tested the weight of the purse before peering into its contents. Satisfied, he nodded and tucked it away.

The tension in Gemma's shoulders released an increment. One obstacle overcome. The Drunken Piebald was the nearest inn to where they needed to be—and the cheapest.

The innkeeper swept around the front desk. "If you'll follow me," sounded in his wake, the syllables as clipped and efficient as his feet.

Gemma and Liam met one another's gazes with lifted eyebrows. They didn't need much more than that to communicate. It had ever been so since they'd emerged from their Mam's womb seven minutes apart—Gemma being the elder, as she liked to remind her brother when he needed it.

"You'd think *he* was paying *us*," muttered Liam as Gemma dug a shoulder beneath his armpit.

"Ready?" she asked, the weight of his long, lanky person settling onto her slighter form, though she was lanky too. Lanky enough she could pass for a lad of seventeen years.

"Toward the promise of a bed?" he asked, hobbling forward. "Aye."

One six-inch step at a time, they negotiated their way through the cramped foyer. "It'll be hard and lumpy, you know," she said, again trying for lightness.

He snorted. "Not anything I'm not already used to."

Now, it was Gemma who snorted.

Liam wasn't complaining—and neither was she. They might be sleeping on hard, lumpy beds, but they were living a life of their own forging.

What were a few hard, lumpy beds compared to that?

Through the near-empty taproom they shambled, one unbalanced step after another toward a—*blessedly*—short corridor, at the end of which stood the innkeeper with an exasperated frown, room key grudgingly extended. He seemed to be having second thoughts about accommodating this motley duo of lads. Gemma snatched the key away before he could change his mind.

"If that will be all," said the innkeeper as he pushed around them, the words trailing in his wake.

Left alone, Liam lifted a single, silent eyebrow, and Gemma inhaled a chirrup of laughter as, together, they took in the room. A single, narrow bed filled one corner, the stand for a jug and washbasin the other. A table and chair were positioned beneath what looked to be a sizeable window. Thank goodness for small miracles as that pane of glass would provide Liam's only view beyond these four walls for the next month.

"Ah, blessed bed," he said, crossing the distance on a few short hops before lowering himself and swinging first his good leg onto the hard, lumpy surface, and then the broken leg more gingerly.

The surgeon had told him he'd been lucky the fall from the Thoroughbred hadn't broken the bone clean through. From what the man had been able to tell by pressing and digging into the wound with his fingers, the bone was fractured, which still needed ample time to heal, but Liam wouldn't be permanently lamed—as long as he stayed off it and didn't injure it further. A directive that Gemma had been struggling to enforce.

While Liam settled upright onto the bed, Gemma got to the business of transforming the room into her brother's home for the foreseeable future. She dragged the jug and washbasin stand to position it within easy reach. Same went for the chamber pot beneath the bed. All he'd have to do was lean over to reach it.

Liam was tall for a jockey. Everyone commented on it, but still he'd been making a name for himself as a rider with his sensitive hands and light touch with the bit. Until he'd been thrown from one particularly surly beast and landed at an angle just wrong enough to break his leg.

Wrong enough to nearly break every single one of their dreams.

Except Gemma wasn't about to let that happen.

So, they'd journeyed to the wilds of Suffolk anyway—to be near the Duke of Rakesley's famed racing estate, Somerton, as they were being paid to do. Even though Liam couldn't exactly try for a jockey position in Rakesley's stables with a broken leg.

It was a problem.

But not an insurmountable one.

Gemma was determined.

She dragged the room's only chair next to the bed and took a seat. "All set?" she asked.

"As much as I can be," her brother groused, shifting his bottom an inch this way, then that, until he eventually settled. His gaze landed on Gemma, and a stubborn light entered his eyes— one she'd come to know well this past week. She readied herself for a battle.

"Now, Gemma," he began.

She held up a hand to stay the words in his mouth. *"Don't."*

But of course, he continued. "I don't see the purpose of us being here."

This...*again*. "We were hired for a job—"

"*I* was hired for a job," he corrected.

"—and," she continued as if he hadn't spoken, "we're here to see it through."

"Deverill hired *me*, Gemma."

She shrugged. A minor detail, that. "Deverill wants information about Rakesley's stables." She spread her hands wide. "*I shall provide it.*" She shifted forward, rigid with determination. "This is our chance, Liam. We can't walk away from the money Deverill is offering."

£50.

It was a lump sum of money that only came along once in a lifetime—if one was lucky.

Life-changing money…and they both knew it.

But only if one had the guts and gumption to seize it.

"There's too much at stake to walk away," she said.

Liam wanted to believe her. She saw it in his eyes.

But he didn't.

She saw that too.

He shook his head, slowly, as if to let her down easy. "Somerton's head groom, Wilson, won't hire you on. He's a known hard arse."

"And why not?" she hissed when she wanted to raise her voice. "No one knows their way around horses better than me. Not even you."

That last bit had been to needle him.

Liam remained unamused and unmoved. "Because you're a woman, Gemma."

She pinched at her trousers and tugged her ever-present slouch hat. "No one knows that when I'm wearing these."

He heaved an exasperated sigh. "You wouldn't fool them for long, and girls don't get jobs in stables. You know that."

Gemma did—and it frustrated her no end. But she had considered the possibility that Liam might be right, and another idea for inveigling herself into Rakesley's household had—reluc-tantly—occurred to her.

An idea she didn't like—not one bit.

"I know how I can get a position."

With limbs suddenly made of lead, she retrieved her valise and removed a garment she hadn't worn in a solid year.

"You know you are about the most stubborn—"

Gemma held up the garment and let it unfold.

A dress.

And it stopped the remainder of Liam's sentence dead in his mouth.

"I could get work as a scullery," she said.

The wind left Liam's sails, and his brow crinkled with concern. "We made a pact, Gemma."

"I know, but—"

"Our pact was that neither of us would ever work in service, and particularly not as a scullery." The sudden intensity of his gaze held her in place. "You won't be safe."

"I know how to stay safe."

Liam shook his head, unconvinced. "But *lords*, Gemma. They don't know what the word *no* means."

Gemma didn't like it, either. Women in service were vulnerable to a lord's whims and desires. They both understood it too well.

"I'll be alright, Liam."

"Damn this broken leg," he exclaimed in a sudden burst of frustration.

Gemma placed a calming hand on top of his and held his eyes of the same hazel hue as hers. "Just one month, then you'll be healed, and we'll have Deverill's blunt to go to New York with our Cassidy cousins, like we've been planning." She sensed her brother's resistance slipping—or perhaps he was simply exhausted from the journey. "Only a few weeks," she whispered, sensing an opening.

He slid down the bed to lie flat on his back. "We can talk more about it on the morrow," he said on a yawn, his eyes drifting closed.

Gemma stood and made for the door. "I'll just go and inquire about a mat and blanket for myself."

"Mmm," was all she heard at her back as the door clicked shut behind her.

Instead of returning to the front desk, however, she scanned the taproom—which had acquired a few more patrons—and located the side door that led to the stables. She tugged her slouch hat down her forehead, hunched her shoulders, and made straight for it, careful not to draw attention to herself. She'd gotten good at that this last year.

Outside, a breeze whipped sharply about her. She inhaled deep and long. Life in London didn't afford one air like this. It almost made her miss the country estate where she'd spent her childhood.

Almost.

There wasn't any true reason for her to venture into the stables. She and Liam didn't have a horse of their own to board. But if there was a stable—any stable—nearby, she liked to pop her head in and see how the horses were being tended. Though in a coaching inn like The Drunken Piebald, it was likely to be full of coach horses, resting up for the next leg of their stage journey. Perhaps a hack or two for the lords who would be traveling through to Newmarket.

Newmarket...horse racing...

Her and Liam's reason for being here.

For the last year, they'd been bouncing between various stables in and around London. Liam had been steadily climbing his way up the ladder—starting as a stable lad, then as a groom, and more recently as a jockey. As Liam's silent, younger "brother," Gemma had been able to accompany him everywhere— stables, racecourses, and even Tattersall's once.

And it was all because she wore trousers, bound her breasts, tucked her hair away, and kept her mouth shut.

But the thing she'd noticed—as a woman—about being a lad...

It felt safer out in the world as a lad.

Besides, she loved to ride and never did have any use for all that sidesaddle nonsense.

She wasn't a lady.

Even if their father was an earl—an accident of birth, that— their mother had been a cook from Ireland.

In other words, no one gave a fig if Miss Gemma Cassidy wore trousers and called herself a lad.

"A strange pair," she'd heard whispered about the two of them.

But neither of them cared. She and Liam had always stuck together—and they always would.

In the stable warm with heat from the horses, it was as she'd suspected. In the first few stalls, overworked coach horses were in various stages of being brushed, fed, and watered after their stage journey. A Cleveland bay extended his head over the gate of the fourth stall she came to. She reached inside her pocket for a chunk of carrot. She always carried a bit of carrot, turnip, or apple. The bay gently took it off her palm, and she stroked his black mane and cooed a bit of nonsense into his ear. To a one, these horses were used poorly, and their working lives totaled to no more than three years. Most were sold on for farm work after that. She could hardly stand to see it.

A sudden, loud racket came from the very last stall. Gemma glanced around at the stable lads. They appeared to be daring each other to see about the animal—and neither seemed keen on taking the bet.

While she was pretending to be a quiet lad, she couldn't give them the dressing down they very much deserved. Instead, she made her own way down the center aisle to investigate, her curiosity up. With each step she took, the racketing continued. The horse sounded quite intent on kicking his stall door down. When she reached the last stall and peered inside, the breath caught in her chest.

Before her stood a dapple-gray gentleman's hack, not an inch below fifteen hands. From his size and evident musculature, she put the stallion down as five or so years. "Aren't you a proud, handsome fellow? I'm sure all the fillies in Hyde Park whinny when you trot past."

He stepped forward enough so his head arched over the stall door. He nudged her shoulder with his muzzle. This proud, handsome fellow wanted a treat. "Was that what your tantrum was all about?"

She dug into her pocket for a chunk of carrot. While he took it, she stroked the white star on his forehead. Her hand moved along to his black mane, a striking contrast to his light gray coat. She'd never met a horse she couldn't woo, and her streak wasn't about to end today with a high-spirited stallion with no small amount of Thoroughbred blood in him.

The Drunken Piebald's lazy stable lads, notwithstanding, this was a much-cared-for animal, even if he wasn't as sweet tempered as he could be.

She shook her head.

Stallions.

She dug out another treat for him—a turnip. When he took it softly from her palm, she experienced the familiar thrill of triumph—but not of conquest. Horses weren't meant to be conquered, but made into family. Why was it so many people couldn't understand that?

"He doesn't allow just anyone to do that," came a man's voice behind her.

Gemma didn't startle. One didn't show high emotion around a horse. They required a calm, settled atmosphere.

Before she turned, she already knew a few facts about the voice's owner. With the deep, cultured tone and particular intonation of his syllables, he was a gentleman. A lord, even.

And he was the owner of this horse.

Slowly, she pivoted, careful to keep her face pointed toward the ground. Lords expected as much. Black boots buffed to a mirror shine, that was the first thing she noticed about this lord.

Unable not to, her gaze continued upward, over tan buckskin riding breeches—and noted the muscular thighs beneath. Up farther, her gaze couldn't help traveling across his tall, rangy form—hunter-green jacket fitted perfectly across broad shoulders...white silk cravat knotted neatly at his throat...square jaw and dimpled chin...angular cheekbones that caught the flickering light of the lantern...thick black hair that just curled at the ends from beneath his black hat.

But it was the endless black pools of his eyes that drew her in and held her in thrall. Those eyes could see into a soul—if one wasn't careful to guard it.

She needed to lower her gaze. It was an impertinence for a lowly lad such as herself to be meeting the eyes of a nobleman in the first place.

A single black eyebrow lifted in silent question, and the spell broke. Her gaze fell to her feet—where it belonged.

Why was her heart racing in her chest so?

It wasn't as if she'd never met a nob.

But...she'd never met a nob as devastatingly magnificent as the one presently lifting the gate latch and readying his horse to ride.

Checking the saddle straps, he said over his shoulder, "I thought all the lads at this coaching inn stayed clear of Moonraker."

"*Moonraker,*" she found herself repeating when all that was expected of her was a noncommittal grunt. Really, though, what a wonderful name for this horse with his light grey coat.

The lord cast a speculative glance in her direction. "You like the name?"

She nodded, gaze on her feet, and muttered, "I do."

Then it struck her: Contrary to what Liam thought, she could pass herself off as male without him. For this lord clearly thought her a lad. Fragile possibility lifted its head...

"*Rakesley,*" came another cultured voice.

Gemma's head whipped around to find another tall, impeccably dressed lord entering the stable. But where the one before her was dark and rangy, this one was blond and massive. Rather like a Viking, she couldn't help thinking. But a Viking with kind, laughing eyes, she could see from here.

Yet that wasn't what had her heart galloping in her chest.

Rakesley.

The Viking lord had called this lord...*Rakesley.*

Sudden, irrefutable fact walloped Gemma over the head— she'd been conversing with the Duke of Rakesley.

Careful to remain unobserved, she stepped away until her back met the stall gate on the opposite side of the aisle while the lords readied their mounts to leave. From beneath the brim of her slouch hat, she took Rakesley's measure.

Here was the man with the most renowned racing estate in all of England.

Here was the man she was being paid life-changing money to spy upon.

She'd formed an idea of Rakesley based on the Thoroughbred-owning, turf-obsessed lords she'd come across in London stables and at Tattersall's over this last year. Men not nearly as stunning as the beasts they owned, to put it nicely.

But *this* Rakesley...

He was stunning—full stop.

Here was no bumbling, inept lord, but very much a capable duke.

She couldn't help wondering if Deverill understood that.

She couldn't help thinking he didn't.

Rakesley and the Viking lord—Rakesley called him Julian— led their stallions from their stalls, and Gemma snapped to. Here was opportunity slipping away from her...walking his mount down the center aisle and into the stable yard.

No, no, no.

"Your Grace?" she called out, desperation seizing her as her feet kicked into a run to catch him.

Without answering, Rakesley mounted Moonraker before turning so man and mount stared down at her, twin arrogant expressions on their faces—if a horse could be arrogant.

The man certainly was.

"What is it?" he demanded, his dark, bottomless eyes narrowed on her. Rakesley didn't like to be kept waiting.

A useful fact to know about a man—particularly if one was being paid to spy on him.

Gemma's mind went suddenly blank. "Would…would…" she stammered, searching for the words that had been suspended on the tip of her tongue mere seconds ago. "Would your stables be needing a lad?"

Her question was met with not an iota of surprise. "What about your employ here?" he asked, utterly indifferent.

Gemma shrugged. "It's nothing."

Which was the truth. She wasn't employed by The Drunken Piebald.

In fact, she was employed by Rakesley's rival.

All of which, she'd be keeping to herself.

Tetchy nerves jangled through her. He was bound to see with those eyes of infinite darkness that she was no lad at all. "I don't allow just anyone into my stables," he said. "Do you have experience beyond broken-down coach horses at a third-rate coaching inn?"

It wasn't his rudeness that gave Gemma pause. It was the way he was utterly unyielding—and arrogant and condescending.

The point was this—one wouldn't want this man for an enemy.

And if she somehow gained a position in his stables, that was precisely what she would be making of him.

An enemy.

The lord called Julian broke in. "What's the harm, Rake? The lad clearly knows about horses and has a way with them."

Hope sparked through Gemma. She'd been correct in thinking the Viking lord had kind eyes.

Rakesley's gaze coolly assessed Gemma, as if he were evaluating a questionable piece of horseflesh. She wouldn't be at all surprised if he asked to check her teeth.

Now, there she'd be in trouble, for she wasn't a lad of seventeen years but a woman of twenty.

Just when she'd convinced herself that he wouldn't relent, he said, "Be at Somerton's stables at seven o'clock tomorrow morning—*sharp*. I do not tolerate laggards. Ask for Wilson."

All the nerves held in check within Gemma released in a rush, "I'll be there at six."

The Viking lord laughed, and Rakesley said, unsmiling, "Let's not get carried away. Seven will do."

The lords rode out of the stable yard, leaving Gemma alone, the *clip-clop* of horse hooves fading into the night. Tempering the feeling of triumph currently streaking through her came a chill. The instant she stepped foot inside Rakesley's stables, she would make an enemy of that magnificent, capable duke.

But what choice had she?

Her future, and Liam's as well, was at stake.

And there was nothing she wouldn't do to secure it.

Liam would resist, of course.

But she would prevail.

Mainly because Liam was confined to a bed.

Well, one had to take one's luck where one found it.

She had this under control.

Except...no one controlled the Duke of Rakesley.

No matter. She wasn't planning to control him. She would only gather information about the operation of his renowned stables and send it along to Deverill in agreed-upon regular missives by post.

When viewed from that angle, it was practically a crime without a victim. No one would be getting hurt. It was simply the passing on of information. If she didn't do it, someone else would.

And someone else would get that life-changing fifty pounds.

She made her way across the stable yard, and the wind caught at her slouch hat, a tendril of hair slipping from beneath. By the time she entered the inn, the errant lock was securely tucked away before she stopped to secure an extra blanket and pillow. It wouldn't be the first time she'd slept on a floor.

Nor the last, she suspected.

Inside their room, she nudged Liam awake and recounted the happenings of the last half hour, leaving out not a single, solitary detail.

He let her finish, then said, "It won't work."

She puffed out an irritated breath. "Why is that?"

Liam didn't rise to it. "Just look at you, Gemma."

"I know what I look like."

His eyes rolled toward the ceiling. "You're a woman," he explained slowly. "Truly, the man must be blind." Another thought seemed to strike him. "Or a complete dolt, like most lords."

It was only established fact. Most lords were self-centered dolts.

But Rakesley...

She wasn't sure what he was—man or mythology—but one thing she was sure he wasn't.

This duke wasn't a dolt.

She shook her head. "He's neither blind nor a dolt."

Liam sucked his teeth. He didn't like that answer.

"You know, I'm very much the size of a lad," she continued. "The binding on my, *erm*, chest keeps it flat enough, and I've learned how to hide my privy habits around the stables in London."

Liam pointed an accusatory finger square at her face. "Not a hint of fuzz on your upper lip."

"Some lads don't have any until later." She could only hope she didn't sound as desperate as she felt. "I'll smudge dirt into my skin. No one will notice me."

"Your hair," stated Liam, as if those two words were enough said.

"What about my hair?"

"Tucking it away works when I'm around to vouch for you. But I won't be there, Gemma."

The worry was apparent in his eyes. They'd always protected one another, and with her up the road at Somerton and him here with a broken leg, he wouldn't be able to.

"Your disguise might suffice for ten minutes, in the dark, but not every hour of the day. Your hair is silky. Like a woman's."

"I suppose I am a woman," she admitted, grudgingly. "Beneath it all."

"And won't the Duke of Rakesley know it?"

Gemma removed her hat and took a long look at herself in the mirror. A riot of thick red-gold curls. That was her untamed hair—a force to be reckoned with. And in combination with the delicate features of her face...

Liam was, of course, correct.

Rakesley, with his fathomless black eyes that pierced and assessed, would see through her sooner rather than later.

An idea stole in. A bold idea...

Who was to say she had to keep all this hair, anyway?

She wasn't some ingenue about to make her debut with the intent of securing a lord for a husband.

She was a bastard on the run, trying to secure a future free of fear for herself and her brother.

Was there anything that woman wouldn't do?

Right.

She turned on her heel and made straight for the door.

"Where are you going now?" Liam called out to her back.

"To procure a pair of scissors."

CHAPTER TWO

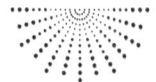

SOMERTON MANOR, NEXT MORNING

*R*ake stepped inside the breakfast room drenched with morning sunshine at precisely seven o'clock—as he did every day.

The first to arrive, too—every day.

His was an ordered life. It was the same for any man who ran a successful stable. Horses—particularly Thoroughbreds—thrived on structure and had a keen distaste for disorder.

He took his usual place at the head of the gleaming mahogany table that sat a modest twelve—this wasn't the dining room, after all—and settled back into his chair, allowing the servants to perform their jobs: one footman placing the morning papers and correspondence to his left, another pouring coffee to his right, and yet another footman setting his breakfast before him—a plate bearing fruit, two boiled eggs, and a bowl of honeyed porridge. The same meal every morning.

Rake shuffled the turf newspaper to the bottom of the stack and began flipping through letters while he sipped his coffee, on the lookout for one missive in particular. It wasn't there. In fact, this was the fifth consecutive day he'd been expecting the letter and it hadn't arrived.

The Dowager Duchess of Acaster was playing the tease.

A ploy he could respect.

Her deceased husband, the Duke of Acaster, had been in possession of the second finest racing stable in England—second to Rake's, of course. A year had passed since the old lech's death, and Rake didn't like the idea of all those fine Thoroughbreds sitting around and going to fat—or worse, being sold off in a Tattersall's dispersal sale, which widows were prone to do with their deceased, horse-mad husbands' stables.

Rake would write her again today. She had a five-year-old mare named Silky Sadie he was keen to have for Somerton. Silky Sadie was descended from the Darley line and had won at Doncaster as a three-year-old. No matter their lineage, Rake only bred mares who were race winners, which was how he maintained the excellence of his stud.

At least, that would be the surface of his letter to the duchess. In truth, he was considering taking her to wife. The two of them were of an age, and she was a fine-looking woman to boot. It had been her bad luck to have had an ambitious father, willing to sell her off to a decrepit old duke desperately in need of a legitimate heir after a lifetime of licentiousness. The old roue hadn't succeeded, which was Rake's gain. He wouldn't have to worry about raising another duke's duke.

Most importantly, however, there was the duchess's second-best stable to consider. No matter he and she had only spoken once—more than a decade ago at a ball when she'd been a debutante on the hunt for a duke and he'd been a duke with no interest in being caught.

Not after the mistake he'd made with Felicity.

But ten years was a long time, and he was in a different place in life. As a man approaching his thirties—a mere six months away, in fact—he had heirs to consider and a bloodline to continue. An alliance with a woman like the Duchess of Acaster was the ideal solution. Neither of them would hold any illusions about marriage or that love need be involved. Two people couldn't have been more perfectly matched.

Movement at the doorway caught the edge of his eye, just as a familiar voice rang bright, "A good morning to you, brother."

His sister, Lady Artemis, strode into the breakfast room with a wide smile on her face. Younger than him by a year, Artemis was the cheeriest person he knew. "Artemis," he returned by way of greeting.

She lowered her tall, willowy form into her chair while her breakfast plate was set before her. Every day, she went for the full English, with eggs, blood sausage, mushrooms, stewed figs, and toast. She speared a mushroom and reached for a turf rag. She was as horse mad as Rake. "About Dido," she said. Determination shone in her eyes.

This, again. "You know my feelings about racing her," he said, neutrally.

She canted her head and dipped a round of sausage in egg yolk. "Worried she'll win?" she asked with a smile. "She's a three-year-old now. Just in time for the Two Thousand Guineas."

Rake shook his head. They'd been over this. "Wait until later in the season," he said, reasonably. "You'll get more out of her. She remains immature and prone to startling."

Artemis spread the turf newspaper between them and stabbed her forefinger into the center of the page. "But I would have her qualified for the Race of the Century sooner than later." She settled back and took a sip of her morning tea. "I've never seen a girl more ready than Dido. She can take the prize. I *feel* it."

Rake knew that feeling. How certain horses got inside one's mind and became an obsession. There would be no convincing his sister.

Though they shared the Somerton stables, Artemis did as she

pleased. Just as he was the son of a duke and a duke himself, she was the daughter of one duke and the sister of another. She not only knew her mind, but could do whatever she liked and no one would dare naysay her—not even her brother.

"Why don't you at least try her out on a different track?"

Artemis stared at him as if he'd sprouted another head. "And let the Ring catch wind of her?" she asked, utterly befuddled. "I'd have to set up a cot and sleep in her box every night to keep the blacklegs away."

She had a point, even if she was being dramatic. The blacklegs were in the employ of the Ring, and the Ring had a very serious and vested interest in ensuring the horses with the best odds to win, won.

Rather than minimizing risk by hedging their bets against a fancied horse, the Ring was known to use methods more certain to stop that horse from winning—like bribing jockeys, laming horses, and poisoning troughs with arsenic. Blacklegs would stop at nothing to see their favored horse win—and collect the tens of thousands of pounds at stake.

The winning purse at a racing meeting was nothing to the obscene amounts of blunt collected and disbursed—but mostly collected—by the Ring.

"With her temperament, a few false starts will do her in on race day," continued Rake. False starts were another favored method the Ring used to spook horses. "Bring her to the Two Thousand Guineas, but don't run her. Get her accustomed to the atmosphere, then race her the next day in the One Thousand."

Artemis wagged a finger and shook her head with a knowing smile. "You simply don't want her to beat your Hannibal, as the One Thousand Guineas is fillies only and he can't run it."

Rake exhaled a resigned sigh—Artemis would do as she pleased, of course—and pivoted the conversation. "Have you yet submitted your colors to the Jockey Club?"

"I have."

"And what are they?"

"Rich saffron and light ash."

Rake snorted. "Yellow and gray not poetic enough for you?"

"Not at all." She speared a stewed fig. "And you're staying with spring green and midnight blue?"

"Yes, green and blue."

Artemis smiled. "You know, brother, someday, something or someone will inspire poetry in you so strong it will be all you can speak."

Rake shook his head. "I know a curse when I hear one."

A massive figure filled the doorway. "What's this about poetry?" said Julian, taking his place at the table.

Rake chose to ignore the question. "Any interesting news this morning?"

Julian took a testing sip of coffee. "Aye, the location for the Race of the Century has been announced."

"And?" asked Artemis, moving forward in her chair.

"Epsom," said Julian.

Rake nodded. "I'd hoped for Goodwood." It was, in his estimation, the best racecourse in the country.

"The race is being promoted to all London, so Epsom's proximity to Town is likely the reason for the location." Julian snorted. "Besides, I can't see the Duke of Richmond tolerating a swarm of the masses soiling his beloved Goodwood."

"Why is it being called the Race of the Century, anyway?" Artemis seemed to be gearing up for one of her quasi-philosophical discussions.

"It had to be named something grandiose, I suppose," said Julian.

"Except," began Artemis, her chin propped on her thumb, her forefinger tapping her cheek, "we're only twenty-two years into the century. How can one know if it will be the Race of the Century?" She sat back and spread her hands wide. "There are still seventy-eight years to go."

The men met her observation with a blank silence.

Julian shrugged. "Either way, my Filthy Habit will win it." He wasn't one for philosophical discussions. More a man of action.

"He'll have to get through my Hannibal first," said Rake, his tone light, the words serious.

"Have you found anyone he'll let on his back yet?"

Rake grunted noncommittally. This was a current sore spot. *Hannibal.* What was he to do with the blasted beast?

"Anyway," said Artemis, "we'll all have to get through Clifford's Little Wicked." Her eyes screwed up to the ceiling. "Oh, wait, she doesn't belong to Clifford anymore. That chancer Deverill won her off him after a night of Macao." She waggled her eyebrows. "Some say it was his devilish plan all along."

"Who is this Deverill?" asked Julian.

"No one to concern ourselves with." Rake was met with twin looks of disbelief. "What?"

"Ah," said Julian with a knowing smile.

"*Ah?*" asked Rake.

"Still miffed about that, are you?"

It was no secret Rake had been trying to get Clifford to sell him Little Wicked since she'd been a yearling. And now this had happened—the filly had gone to a man who had no business owning her—all because of a gaming debt.

"What does a man who made his fortune from the manufacturing of steam engines know about horses?" groused Rake.

"As opposed to a man who made his fortune by being born into it?" asked Artemis conversationally.

Julian chortled. "She has you there, old chap."

"Little Wicked comes from the Godolphin line. She belongs in a proper stable."

There. Indisputable fact.

Artemis canted her head. "Does Little Wicked like cats?"

Both Rake's and Julian's brows lifted in question.

Artemis sighed. "Everyone knows Godolphin harbored deep affection for a stable cat named Grimalkin."

Both men nodded slowly, and Julian gave her an encouraging, "Ah."

"Anyhow," continued Artemis, "that Deverill is one to pay attention to. He's hungry. I'll write Beatrix to wheedle more information about him."

Lady Beatrix St. Vincent was the only legitimate child of the wastrel Marquess of Lydon and Artemis's bosom friend since their come-out years ago. She spent more time on racecourses than Rake—if that was possible.

Anyway, Rake had a full morning ahead of him. He came to his feet and addressed Julian. "You're returning to Nonsuch today?"

Nonsuch Castle was the family seat of the Ormonde marquessate. As Somerton and Nonsuch were little more than five miles apart, it wasn't much to ride between estates.

"Aye." Julian popped one last chunk of bacon into his mouth. "I'll see you soon, no doubt."

"Safe journeys," said Rake, already on the move. On any given day, he didn't spend much time seated.

As he made his way through the house—which would've been better named *palace* or *castle*, given its grand scale—and toward the east wing that opened onto the stable side, Hannibal was on his mind.

Truly, what was he to do with the beast?

He'd purchased the horse at a Tattersall's auction, having long heard tales of the blazing speed of the colt. And all had gone to plan until Rake had received the animal. *Spirited*, that had been a word used to describe him. A word that hadn't put Rake off. Who didn't want a Thoroughbred with a little spirit? He could only see it as a good quality.

Then other words began to be whispered. *Foul tempered.* That one came after Hannibal had bit two stable lads.

Still, Rake hadn't been put off. The horse had only just been transferred to Somerton. He needed time to settle.

Then a week on, another word had begun making the rounds.

Unrideable.

Hannibal wouldn't allow anyone to mount him.

That was a problem.

And, as Rake wasn't a proponent of training methods that beat horses into submission, it was a sizeable one, at that.

However, Rake hadn't bought Hannibal only to put him to stud. He'd had plans for the three-year-old this racing season. Plans that were very much in doubt, now.

Blast.

Hannibal had to have been mildly drugged at the sale. That was the only explanation for the sweet-tempered animal Rake had purchased last month.

Outside, the morning was soft with dew and the sun shone mellow morning orange through a stand of oaks, enlivening the air and light. His boots clicked sharply across the cobbles as he passed beneath the stable yard's arched entrance, the clock tower striking half past seven. He nodded a good morning in the direction of the grooms and stable lads hustling to and fro with various morning tasks, and a stray thought wandered into his mind.

Had the lad from The Drunken Piebald arrived?

If so, Wilson would've already been putting the lad through his paces to see if he was up to snuff, for Rake only allowed lads possessed of a certain temperament into his stables. *Calm. Patient. Steady. Sure.*

Even if Rake himself didn't exactly possess those qualities in abundance, anyone working with his horses did.

Still, he supposed it didn't matter whether the lad had arrived or not. Somerton had close to thirty lads and grooms. What was one more lad?

Yet for some reason he couldn't fathom, that lad had become stuck in his mind.

There had been a glint of something in his eyes. *Determination* and…something else.

Something that puzzled Rake.

Something he wanted to put his finger on and couldn't quite…

Desperation.

That was the something else.

The lad had been *desperate* for a position at Somerton.

Which wasn't too difficult to understand. Who wouldn't rather be employed in a duke's stable than that of The Drunken Piebald?

At Somerton, a future could be had for a lad possessed of a talented, sure hand with a horse—which the lad had certainly demonstrated with Moonraker.

Wilson fell into step beside Rake and immediately began updating him on the state of each and every horse in the stable— as he did each and every morning.

Consideration for a single, solitary stable lad was pushed aside as Rake sank into the comfortable familiarity and routine of his day.

CHAPTER THREE

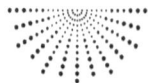

*T*here was an art to mucking out a stall.

A fact most stable lads didn't appreciate.

And, like most arts, it required patience and a method.

First, the horse had to be short racked to the side of the stall and given a bit of hay to keep him occupied. Then the dung and wet straw were skipped out before the remaining clean straw was stored below the manger so the bare planks could be properly swept. After a bucket of water was sloshed across the surface, fresh bedding was returned and banked against the stall walls. A bit of litter on the floor would encourage the horse to urinate—which would also be mucked out—and thusly was a stall made clean.

For the moment.

The process would be repeated in the evening.

And Gemma didn't mind it one bit.

She loved the sights, sounds, and smells of a stable—especially one run as tightly as Somerton. Every horse had a stable lad assigned to him, and that lad's sole job was to tend the needs of his horse from grooming, feeding, and watering to mucking out the stall and checking hooves for stones. In the course of a day, a single horse had myriad needs.

Mucking out was the only task the sharp-eyed, terse-tongued Wilson would entrust to her until he'd spoken directly with his master. If she proved her worth, she would be allowed in the same stall as Moonraker.

It was only right by Gemma's way of thinking. Wilson wouldn't yet know if the slight, lanky stable lad who tugged his hat low on his forehead and refused to meet his eye and called himself "Gem" knew a horse's forelock from its tail.

Gemma estimated Somerton housed fifty horses between all the carriage, hacks, and hunters, with the Thoroughbreds being housed in an exclusive, separate wing. Spacious and airy, with its soaring, timbered ceilings and large, high windows that let in light fit for a cathedral, this stable's glory must surely be unsurpassed in all England. Even the stall she was presently mucking out was larger than most, and it was only for a carriage horse. She could only imagine what the Thoroughbred stalls would be like—except they wouldn't have been stalls, but rather boxes. She was sure of it.

Magnificent.

Like everything associated with the Duke of Rakesley, she was coming to understand.

Like the man himself.

"So, yer the new lad, I reckon?" came a voice. "Gem, is it?"

Gemma glanced around to find a groom leaning an indolent shoulder against a post and chewing a length of straw.

"Aye," she grunted and busied herself with folding a blanket.

Here was her first genuine test of authenticity as Gem. She'd only met Rakesley in a dark stable, and Wilson had hardly glanced at her, but she'd be working with the grooms and lads all hours of the day. It was best to establish a hard-working, taciturn reputation from the outset.

"I'm Cal," continued the groom. "Anything ye want to know, ye can ask me."

Gemma nodded and grunted—as if there was any chance of that happening.

Then Cal was gone, and Gemma's heart could slow.

The disguise was holding.

Of course, it had to have helped that she'd taken scissors to her hair last night. To be safe, she'd wanted to cut it an inch short all around her head, but Liam had protested so vociferously that, instead, she'd sheared it just above her shoulders, so she was able to wrangle the thick mass into a blunt queue at the nape of her neck.

Another tactic of evading close scrutiny had occurred to her on the two-mile walk to Somerton this morning. *Dirt*, liberally applied. So much dirt that any potentially curious pair of eyes would immediately glance away in distaste. To that end, she was considering not washing for her duration here.

Not a soul would suspect a woman beneath a slouch hat and dense layer of aggressive filth.

Her head canted at the sound of voices approaching. Not loud voices, but voices in mild conversation. Directives given with authority and accepted with deference. Rakesley and Wilson. Within the flash of a second, they strode purposefully past the stall. She supposed a man like Rakesley—a *duke*—wouldn't know how to walk any other way.

But within that flash of a second, an occurrence happened. Rakesley's head angled, and his bottomless gaze met hers for an instant.

An instant long enough to make the breath catch in her lungs.

Then, in a blink, he was gone, and Gemma could breathe again.

Intuitively, she understood it a mistake to meet that man's gaze. And yet…

Somehow, she couldn't *not*.

The duke's gaze held a pull. It demanded to be acknowledged —and one stood powerless against the demand.

She gave her head an annoyed shake. What absolute rot. One couldn't be powerless against a *gaze*.

She returned to her work, now focusing her efforts on the carriage horse himself. She picked up a hoof pick, and her mind wandered as she tended the horse's hooves.

This work would do for now, providing enough information on the running of Somerton for a few missives to Deverill. But she had to finagle her way into the Thoroughbred wing. Only there would she find the information that would provide life-changing money for her and Liam.

A figure appeared in the periphery of her vision and planted itself in the gate's opening. Before her mind could register the person's identity, her body did. Her heart kicked into a full-tilt gallop, and her mouth went dry, as her gaze subtly slid over and confirmed the identity of the tall, imposing form.

The Duke of Rakesley.

Watching her at work.

Nay, not *her.*

Gem.

She would do well to remember that.

A few too many beats of silence loped past, and Gemma released the horse's foot and straightened. He would see through layers of wool, cotton, and the linen that bound her chest, down to skin, and on through to bones and the very cells of her being.

A woman...not a Gem.

Eyes inscrutable, he opened his mouth and said, "Follow me."

And he was gone.

Gemma blinked, and her breath released. The meaning behind his command at last penetrated, as her feet scrambled to catch him. Perhaps he'd seen through her disguise and meant to march her out of his stables and off his estate.

But if that were the case, they were marching in the wrong direction.

Nay. He was leading her down the center aisle and deeper into the stables, then across the cobbled stable yard, the clock tower bell striking nine o'clock.

It suddenly occurred to her where they were going.

To the Thoroughbred wing.

She tried not to gawk as they entered, but that proved impossible. She'd been mightily impressed by the carriage horse stable, but it was nothing to where the Thoroughbreds were housed. From the red-bricked floor stood polished oak partitions and stone columns that supported the vaulted ceiling. As she'd suspected, there were no stalls in this stable, but boxes, each larger than any of the London quarters she and Liam had shared this last year.

Well, the Duke of Rakesley's Thoroughbreds would never suffer cramped quarters in all their indulged days.

Following the duke at a distance of ten or so feet, Gemma poked her head into each box. To a one, whether black, bay, or gray, the duke's Thoroughbreds impressed. It was little wonder Deverill wanted information about the operation at Somerton. Gemma wasn't sure even the royal stables were better outfitted.

Rakesley came to a stop before the last box in the row. Gemma sidled only near enough so she could poke her head around the gate post.

Several feet away, Wilson and Cal had positioned themselves to either side of a stunning black Thoroughbred who was shaking his head and stamping a front foot. From the sweat trailing down the men's cheeks, they were having the devil of a time with this horse who easily stood sixteen hands tall.

"Hannibal," said Rakesley, firm and direct.

The horse's ears perked forward, and he went still, though his nostrils flared and his eyes showed white, as he assessed this new interloper.

"Can't even get a curry comb on 'im to get the field muck off," said Cal with a swipe of his brow.

Concern tinged with no small amount of anger flared through Gemma, and ill-considered, impetuous words were flying from her mouth. "What sort of operation are you running here? Clearly, this horse has been mistreated."

The box went dead silent, Gem's words settling into the air and making themselves uncomfortable. Wide-eyed and befuddled, Wilson and Cal stared at the new stable lad. Even Hannibal quieted.

Heat crept through Gemma, and she stifled a groan. That would be her flushing crimson from head to toe. The curse of the red of hair.

Why, oh, *why* had she spoken? She was here to keep her pert mouth shut, observe, and report back to Deverill. That was all. Now she was sure to lose a position she'd been lucky to get in the first place.

And Rakesley... The duke regarded her with a cocked eyebrow. "What is your name?" He didn't seem particularly offended, rather mildly taken aback.

"*Erm*, Gem," she said as gruffly as possible.

"*Gem*, this is Hannibal, and he's a recent acquisition. It was only after he arrived at Somerton that we were able to apprehend the particularities of his nature," he said. "No horse raised from birth at Somerton behaves so."

This was a clear point of pride for the duke.

Gemma nodded, chastened, but her attention remained fixed on Hannibal. He was filled with fear and lashing out. This horse was suffering.

Instinctively, she stepped into the box.

"Watch yourself, lad," said Wilson in a warning voice.

She held out her hand to Cal. "I'll take that curry comb."

Wilson opened his mouth again, and Rakesley gave a barely

perceptible shake of the head. "I must caution you about approaching the beast."

"He isn't a beast," returned Gemma. "He's a horse in pain."

"In the weeks we've had him, he's only let me near," said Rakesley without a return of emotion. "Which is the problem."

"Why is that a problem beyond the obvious one that he's in crisis?" Gemma asked without thinking.

She was the by-blow of an earl, not a true daughter—not a lady. She didn't have the right to be questioning a duke.

And yet this duke didn't appear to mind.

Stables had a way of rendering all on a somewhat equal plane.

"Because I intend to race him."

Gemma took another small step forward and left that fact in the back of her mind for future reference. For now, her concern lay with this animal—*Hannibal*—who showed no damage of the body, but rather of the mind.

Of the two, it was the latter wound that could be more debilitating. She'd seen it many times in various stables and racecourses around London.

She made a shushing sound as she approached, slow and careful, her hands held respectfully open before her. "See?" she said low. "Nothing to fear here."

Warily, Hannibal allowed her into his space until she was close enough to reach out and lay a hand on his withers. But she didn't—not yet. "What was done to you, my friend?"

She always addressed horses as her friends. They could sense her sincerity and respect. They knew her as a friend.

She slipped the curry comb into a pocket. She wouldn't use it now. Her only goal for the moment was for Hannibal to allow her to rest her hand on him. That was the place to start. Perhaps in his entire life no one had ever laid a kind or comforting hand on this animal. He needed to know he was safe.

Calmly, she stood inches from him, whispering bits of nothing, until he angled his head toward her. Gemma went still. The moment could go either way. He could bite her shoulder and let her know he wasn't having it—or he could nudge her arm, let her know what she was doing was all right.

Which was what he did.

Gently, she placed her palm on the strong bend of his neck, feeling the heat and banked strength through his glistening ebony coat, allowing a connection to form between them at this single point of contact. Her hand moved, slowly stroking along the muscular curve. "In your chest beats a good, brave heart, doesn't it, my friend?"

She felt the last bit of tension ease from Hannibal and took the comb from her pocket. She placed it on his withers, lightly swiping it across his coat, which would be lustrous once she finished grooming him—*if* he allowed her to groom him.

All eyes, silent and observant, watched her finish currying and take the whisp to remove the dust raised by the curry comb. Then it was on to brush and linen cloth. It was a lengthy process, but everyone understood the necessity that every step was followed. This was the first step toward Hannibal being healed. The other men in this box might not see it that way, but Gemma did.

"This fellow could win a host of races," she said, finishing up with his mane. "What a glory he is."

"Aye," agreed Rakesley. "But first, he has to let someone ride him."

Ah.

And there it was.

Rakesley saw Hannibal as a three-year-old colt whose best season was only months away. He saw him purely as an investment—and one that might not pay off.

Gemma didn't know this man beyond the few words they'd exchanged, but she understood it would be an embarrassing failure if he couldn't get Hannibal to perform.

And, like that, she had information to pass on to Deverill.

As if on cue, a compact man who looked entirely composed of dense muscle and who could only be the jockey intended for Hannibal swaggered into the box. He had the calm, but nervy, way about him particular to all jockeys.

The problem was that the instant Hannibal saw the man, he tensed. Gemma seemed to be the only one who noticed as the men greeted one another.

Wilson spared a glance for Gemma. "That will be all, *erm*—" His gaze searched the rafters as if he would find her name there.

"Gem," she supplied.

"Cal, take Gem over to—"

"Gem stays here," said Rakesley.

Everyone stopped. It would've been comical had not all gazes shifted and landed directly upon Gemma. Hers found her feet, her heart in her throat, as she willed the men to look somewhere —*anywhere*—else.

"Assign the lad to Hannibal's box. He clearly has a way with the animal." The duke looked in higher spirits than she'd yet seen him.

Wilson nodded. "You heard His Grace," he said to the side of Gemma's face. "You can muck out while they take Hannibal out for his paces."

Gemma gave an incoherent grumble and stood aside. These men acted as if she'd solved the problem of Hannibal, and she understood it didn't work thusly.

From beneath the brim of her slouch hat, she watched the inevitable disaster unfold as Cal attempted to place a saddle onto Hannibal's back. For his reward, he got a nip on the shoulder.

With a shake of the head, Gemma slipped out to the tool room to fetch a shovel. From what she'd observed, Rakesley ran a peaceable stable, so he wasn't accustomed to this type of Thoroughbred. Gemma, on the other hand, had seen plenty around various stables and racecourses over the last year. Sellers gave them mild sedatives for showing, just enough to fool potential buyers into thinking the animal possessed of a good temperament, which couldn't be further from the truth. By the time the new owner discovered this fact, it was his problem.

Gemma certainly had something to report in her first missive to Deverill. Rakesley intended to make a run at the Race of the Century—with an unrideable horse.

And yet...

While she was at Somerton, Gemma knew she wouldn't be able to let Hannibal go. In fact, she was already working out a plan of attack and woo.

A good wooing of an irascible horse began with a lump of sugar.

CHAPTER FOUR

A WEEK LATER

It was just this side of sunrise, and the world was still and quiet in the fading gray of pre-dawn air, when Gemma took Hannibal's reins in hand and led him from his box.

As she had for the last five mornings.

The only sound was the clatter of shod hooves echoing down the red-brick aisle as she led him out of the stable and into the south paddock. Somerton had a few paddocks, but she'd chosen this one for a very good reason.

It couldn't be viewed from the manor house.

No dukely eyes would look out of one of the hundred or so windows and happen upon her stealing time with the estate's prize colt.

Actually, Hannibal wasn't yet viewed thusly, but he would be.

Gemma was determined.

One person, however, had noticed what she'd been doing every morning—Wilson. Like her, the man was an early riser, and he'd seen her returning Hannibal to his box three days ago—the day the colt had allowed her to place a saddle on his back. Wilson would've noted it, and she suspected that was why he was permitting her to proceed. A saddle on Hannibal's back was the right sort of progress. It spoke to the trust she'd built with the animal.

And today she would earn more.

Today was the day she would mount this splendid Thoroughbred. Not in conquest. That was where so many owners and jockeys got it wrong. They wanted to break and conquer the animal to get it to do their bidding. But that sort of brutish handling wasn't only unnecessary; it ran counter to what they were attempting to achieve.

Nay, it was about trust. Gain a horse's trust—and honor that trust—and he would walk through fire for his master.

Gemma led Hannibal into the paddock and immediately saw they weren't alone. On the far end were Lady Artemis and her filly, Dido. The close bond those two shared was apparent for anyone to see. Dido was a sweet goer, that was for sure. A reflection of her owner, too, though Gemma had only seen Lady Artemis around the stables from a distance. A high-born lady wouldn't have noticed a lowly stable lad like Gem.

Gemma always thought well of an owner with a sweet-natured horse.

And the opposite of an owner when the opposite was true.

Which put her in two minds about Rakesley. The duke ran an indisputably good stable. Yet...he seemed single-mindedly intent on getting what he wanted out of Hannibal.

Which Gemma didn't like.

Hannibal had boundaries that needed to be respected and addressed before he could be the racehorse he'd been bred to be.

"Are you the lad called Gem?" Lady Artemis called out.

Gemma glanced up from beneath the warped brim of her slouch hat and found the lady watching her expectantly. She couldn't very well ignore the question, but, oh, how she wanted to. No good could come from "Gem" conversing with the duke's sister.

"Aye," she mumbled, gaze returned to the tips of her brown boots.

When the silence held for a few heartbeats longer than strictly necessary, Gemma risked another glance at Lady Artemis, who was now walking over with Dido. "Does my brother know you've been taking Hannibal out in the early mornings?"

"Can't say," was all Gemma mumbled. She'd been keeping her speech short and to the point since her blow-up at Rakesley a week ago. If she was found out as a woman, she was done for.

And she wasn't ready to be done for. She hadn't yet earned her fifty pounds.

There was also Hannibal to consider.

He needed her.

A smile entered Lady Artemis's deep brown eyes. Eyes so similar to her brother's. But where his were hard and unfathomable, hers were soft and kind. "Your secret is safe with me, Gem. You've done wonders for Hannibal already. You have a rare gift if you can achieve harmony with that beast," she finished on a laugh.

Though Lady Artemis had spoken the words with humor rather than cruelty, Gemma's hackles couldn't help rising—and she couldn't help speaking a bit of her mind. "That's where we think wrongly about horses. When they suffer a malady of the body, we do all we can to mend it. But when it's a malady of the mind, we call the horses *beasts* and dismiss them as worthless."

Lady Artemis canted her head to the side as she listened, her gaze narrowed not on Hannibal but on...*Gem*.

Oh, why had she opened her mouth?

"And you see all that?" asked Lady Artemis, slowly, an impressed smile spreading across her face. "You have the patience and the ability to heal such a malady, don't you, Gem?"

Gemma's gaze returned to her feet, a blush surely heating her cheeks. She'd never known what to do with compliments. "I wouldn't want to overstate my abilities."

"Whyever not?" laughed Lady Artemis. *"Don't hide your candle under a bushel.* Isn't that how it goes?" She wasn't finished. "Is that your mission, Gem? To help horses who are damaged in the mind?"

"Aye," muttered Gemma. Lady Artemis was quite the inquisitive lady.

Too inquisitive for Gemma's comfort.

Lady Artemis's eyes suddenly lit up. "Oh, I know," she exclaimed. "You could create a horse sanctuary."

Gemma almost snorted. *Nobs.* So wrapped up in their own little worlds.

Did none of them know the cost of anything?

"I don't have the blunt for that," she said mildly. "But I'd like to travel around someday. From stable to stable, where I'm needed."

"That's wonderful, Gem." Lady Artemis beamed with sincerity. Though the lady was a nob, she was a very nice nob. "When you're ready to embark upon such an enterprise, please call on me. I've a bit of blunt lying around, and I'd love to contribute to the rehabilitation of animals."

Gemma nodded her thanks, humbly, as a lowly stable lad would to his betters, and tightened her hold on Hannibal's reins. She could sense him growing restive from proximity to Dido and inactivity, and she needed him to be calm when she attempted to mount him.

Lady Artemis gave a parting nod and cooed to Dido as they walked away. "You're my perfect girl, aren't you?"

Alone with Hannibal, Gemma allowed the air to calm around them so the only sound and movement were his breath and hers. She ran a hand over his withers and allowed it to rest on the pommel of the saddle. She sensed no tense flexion of his muscles, so she slipped her boot into the stirrup.

Still, no tension.

The thing was that Hannibal wasn't an unbroken horse. He'd been mounted and ridden before, that was apparent. But those who had done so had used force and cruelty. What Gemma wanted was for him to accept a rider with readiness. To know and trust that when he was mounted, he would feel the wind in his mane and experience joy—that taking on a rider was freedom, not imprisonment.

She took a quick sip of air and, in one familiar, swift motion, dug her boot into the stirrup and pushed off the ground as she heaved herself onto this towering sixteen-hands horse. The next moment, she found herself astride, and it was all she could do not to let out an exuberant whoop. It felt like the sweetest gift—to have gained Hannibal's trust.

She leaned forward and stroked his mane. "Ah, we truly are friends, aren't we?"

She straightened and caught a glimpse of Lady Artemis watching from the other side of the paddock, a broad smile on her face.

But Gemma wasn't here to impress. She was here for Hannibal. Toward that end, she began to test him, to see what cues he took. She gave a light squeeze of her knees, and he began to walk. He had a smooth, easy action, she could already tell. Excitement that she hadn't yet allowed herself to feel stole through her. This fellow would be a goer. It wasn't only obvious from his size and pedigree, but from the way he walked.

"You have so much within you, don't you, my friend?" she cooed into his ear.

He'd been wanting this too. A connection with someone who understood him.

And he wanted to run. She could feel it as she reined him in and resisted urging him into a trot.

He'd trusted her thus far; he would still have to trust her.

"Oh, we will run, my friend, but not yet. Let's get to understand one another today," she said with rising anticipation of that future moment.

They'd circled the paddock a few times when Hannibal's ears flicked forward, and sudden tension entered his body. He'd seen something. She shushed him and stroked his mane, even as her gaze cast about.

Then she saw it beyond the paddock gate.

A figure, quiet and unmoving.

Rakesley.

She knew it with a certainty she didn't understand.

He stepped into light growing brighter in slow dawn increments, his dark, intense gaze upon her.

He'd been watching all this time.

She could be dismissed for insubordination.

A shiver curled up her spine.

But something else—something *more*—slid in alongside that shiver.

The something *more* his dark intensity provoked within her.

The something *more* she didn't want to understand…

But did.

It was a *something more* that could lead to trouble far beyond simple dismissal.

* * *

RAKE HAD ASKED his valet to wake him an hour earlier than usual this morning.

As he'd been doing for the last four days.

Earlier in the week, Wilson had informed him that the stable lad Gem had been walking Hannibal out to the south paddock before everyone waked. Rake had instructed Wilson to do nothing and allow him to continue. Clearly, lad and horse had an affinity for one another, and Rake was an experienced enough horseman to know not to interfere. Those bonds were useful, particularly with an ill-tempered horse.

The next morning, Rake had felt compelled to see lad and horse with his own eyes, and it had been as Wilson described—Gem leading Hannibal around the paddock a few times, then back into the stable.

Rake had begun looking forward to waking every morning to see what new progress Gem had made. A few days ago, Gem had even managed to get a saddle onto the beast's back. Then, today, the lad had done it—he'd convinced Hannibal to allow him to mount.

Though he'd naught to do with it, a genuine sense of accomplishment had soared through Rake.

At last.

Now he could start getting somewhere with an animal he was still irked about having been tricked into buying. It wasn't every day someone succeeded in getting one over on the Duke of Rakesley.

Now, Rake stepped closer, refusing to release the lad's gaze that wanted to skitter away. A long moment stretched between them.

What was it about this lad, anyway?

Something intangible pulsed between them.

Something that made Rake slightly uncomfortable.

"Brother," came a feminine voice.

Reluctantly, Rake flicked a glance toward Artemis, who was walking over with Dido.

"Can you believe it?" she asked, bursting with excitement, as they watched Gem circle the paddock with Hannibal.

"Hardly."

"He might not be a lost cause, after all," Artemis called out to Gem.

"No horse is a lost cause," he returned.

A mouthy lad, to be sure.

"*Milady*," he added in that low, raspy voice of his, as if only just realizing whom he was addressing.

Artemis wouldn't notice—or care, if she did—that a stable lad was speaking to her out of turn. All were equals on the turf, he'd heard her say more than once.

"Gem," began Artemis, her head canted slightly, gaze glinting with assessment.

Rake's hackles rose. Best to watch out when that particular look entered his sister's eye.

"Have you ever considered being a jockey?" she asked.

And the plain fact walloped Rake over the head. How hadn't he seen it before?

Gem...

A jockey.

Well, Artemis had seen it and was now attempting to poach the lad.

For his part, Gem looked utterly flummoxed. "I have, but—"

"*But?*" Artemis prompted. "*What?*"

Rake found that he, too, wanted to know *but...what.*

Gem's gaze slid to the ground. "The opportunity has never presented itself."

Artemis smiled like the cat who got the cream. "Well, you have the opportunity now."

Gem's head snapped up, his eyes wide as victory plates. "How's that?" he asked, wary.

"It's simple," said Artemis, only too happy to explain. "You could ride Dido in the Two Thousand Guineas. You should rub along together like two peas in a pod."

No, shouted every cell in Rake's body.

With Gem in the saddle, it was Hannibal who would not only win the Two Thousand Guineas, but also the Race of the Century.

And here was Rake on the verge of losing Gem to one of his biggest rivals—his sister.

That wasn't about to happen.

"I'm afraid that won't be possible, Artemis."

Two pairs of surprised and questioning eyes swung toward him.

"And why is that, brother?" asked Artemis, suspicious.

She'd never been able to abide not getting her way.

"Because Gem will be riding *Hannibal* in the Two Thousand Guineas."

Artemis's jaw clenched and released. Her eyes told him she hadn't yet ceded Gem. "Don't you think the lad gets a say in the matter?"

Gem squirmed uncomfortably in the saddle. He didn't want a say in the matter, that was apparent.

The lad cleared his throat and swiped his tongue across his plump bottom lip. Rake found himself following the motion, and again that uncomfortable feeling slithered through him.

Gem glanced between brother and sister a few times before his gaze landed…

On Rake.

"I'll ride Hannibal," said the lad.

Rake couldn't help directing a smirk at Artemis, who threw her hands into the air. "You don't have to ride for him, you know," she said. "I'll pay you double."

From his perch on Hannibal's back, Gem gave Artemis a smile of apology. "Hannibal needs me."

And that was the matter settled.

Artemis exhaled a gusty sigh of irritation and led Dido away without another word, leaving Rake and Gem alone.

Now that the sun had fully breached the horizon, Rake noticed something about Gem. His eyes, namely. Green with flecks of gold, framed by long lashes that shone strawberry in the dawn light.

Something else struck Rake.

Never in his life had he once noticed the subtleties of a stable lad's eye color.

Rake also noticed the smudges of grime on Gem's cheeks. "Don't you ever wash?" he found himself asking.

Gem shrugged, unbothered by the question.

Right.

"We have one thing to sort," mumbled Gem.

"What's that?"

A canny glint entered the lad's eye. "My pay."

Rake should've seen this coming. He couldn't very well pay a jockey a stable lad's wages.

"And," continued Gem, "what's my cut when Hannibal wins?"

Bold. That was certainly one word for this newly minted jockey.

Rake could appreciate it. Hannibal wouldn't beat a talented field of Thoroughbreds with a mouse for a jockey.

He didn't hesitate. "Ten percent of the purse if you take it."

Gem's eyes went wide. "Two hundred pounds?" His head cocked, suspicion in the angle. "Why would you do that?"

"The Two Thousand Guineas is a steppingstone. We're going to take the season." Rake let that settle into the air. "And the ten thousand pound purse in the Race of the Century."

Gem nodded, thoughtful. "I reckon you wouldn't let me have ten percent of that purse?"

A beat later, Rake realized the dour Gem had made a joke and found a chuckle escaping him. "I'm certain we can negotiate fair compensation when the time comes."

But Gem didn't respond with humor or agreement. He nodded noncommittally.

Curious, that.

"About Hannibal," said Rake, getting to the heart of the matter. "Do you think he'll be ready for the Two Thousand Guineas?"

"When is it?"

"Three and a half weeks."

Gem shifted his weight and dismounted in a smooth, efficient motion. The lad was well-accustomed to horses the size of Hannibal. He ran a hand across the horse's withers and along his back to his flank and rump, catching every detail by sight and feel, as if he didn't already know everything about the animal.

"Conditioning will be the key," he said, assessing. "Fortunately, he's in good fettle. I think he can get there."

The lad met Rake's gaze, and again Rake found himself noticing a pair of eyes that would be deemed pretty on a woman.

"Hannibal wants to run," continued Gem.

Rake snapped to. "You haven't yet had him on the track. How can you know that?"

"I could feel it just now. He's a goer, no doubt about it. And if he's not ready for the Two Thousand Guineas, he will be for the Derby."

And Rake caught a glimmer within Gem's gold-flecked, green eyes. A little bit wild…a little bit reckless…

A large bit confident and competitive.

Gem was a goer too.

The certainty solidified inside Rake that he'd made the correct decision. "When can we get him on the track?" No sense in beating about the bush.

"We give it another few days," returned the lad, promptly, as if he'd been expecting the question. "I'll feed and groom him now, then take him out again this afternoon for an amble around the estate. I'll do that tomorrow as well. Then the next day, I'll walk him around the practice course and give him his head a bit to see what happens. He'll know what to do on a course, so we'll have to see if he wants to do it."

With that, Gem nodded and led Hannibal away. Rake, slightly flummoxed, watched the pair go. Didn't Gem know he was supposed to wait to be dismissed by a duke?

But that wasn't all that was bothering Rake. It was that his gaze had slipped down and lingered for a beat too long on the back of Gem. All loose-fitting and dirt-encrusted, the lad practically swam in his clothes from hat to coat to riding breeches. But Rake had picked up a movement beneath those dingy, loose clothes. A subtle sway...

Of the hips.

Rake's brow furrowed into a painful crease.

This noticing of a stable lad's eyes and the sway of his hips was...*new*.

And...*unexpected*.

CHAPTER FIVE

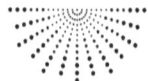

THREE DAYS LATER

emma took a deep inhalation of early morning air—air brisk enough to give the blood a little edge and ready it for the coming day.

It was her favorite sort of air.

Hannibal nudged her with his muzzle as she checked that bit and bridle were fastened correctly. He'd sensed the tetchy energy coming off her and knew today was different.

And, indeed, it was.

She stroked his nose. "You're going to run free today, my friend."

He whickered as she ran a palm across his withers before checking the saddle to make certain all straps were properly attached and tightened sufficiently. This saddle would be tested today.

Actually, they would all be tested today—saddle... Hannibal...*her*.

Today wasn't only a test of horse, but also of rider.

The notion had her palms slicked with sweat, and her heart thudding in her chest.

Reins in hand, she led Hannibal out of his box and then down the red-bricked center aisle, the hollow *clip-clop* of his hooves inviting the other Thoroughbreds to poke their heads out of their boxes in bleary-eyed morning greeting.

Cal stepped into view at the end of the aisle, a big smile spread across his face. "Yer gonna run that beast today, eh?"

Gemma nodded.

She wasn't the only one bursting with anticipation.

"Me and the other lads, we'll be out there on the rails, givin' ye a cheer. Never seen a lad jump up from muckin' stalls to jockey so fast." His head tipped to the side, a baffled expression crossing his features. "Or at all, come to think on it."

Gemma grunted, as was usual for "Gem," but she couldn't suppress the smile lifting about the corners of her mouth. Indeed, Cal had never seen a lad like her—if he only knew the half of it.

"I bet yer likin' yer new quarters." A thread of envy twined through Cal's words.

Gemma gave a shrug, as if indifferent, when she was anything but.

The instant she'd become Hannibal's jockey, her status at Somerton had risen. A man supremely aware of such matters, Wilson had provided a room for her sole use just off the hayloft. She would've been content to sleep on a cot in Hannibal's box, and she'd voiced as much, but Wilson wasn't having it.

And anyway, she hadn't put much passion into the protest, for she'd secured a luxury far beyond that of occupying a space with herself alone—the exquisite extravagance of unbinding her breasts every night before bed.

A luxury she would never again take for granted.

She and Hannibal stepped into the courtyard. The air wasn't clear, but rather gray with mist that would burn off in the next hour. She placed a foot in the stirrup before hauling herself up and into the saddle.

With a light squeeze of her knees, they began moving, passing beneath the wide arch of the gate and its impressive clock tower to make their way toward Somerton's practice track. The rising sun glowed hazy and golden through the trees, imbuing the cool mist lifting off the ground with a dreamlike radiance. The ride gave Gemma a few minutes to gather herself within—to call upon nerve that had never before been tested. She drew another steadying breath.

The track came into view, and she felt Hannibal ever so subtly tug at the bit. He was a three-year-old Thoroughbred entering his prime, and he wanted to run.

She wanted him to run too.

She wanted him to prove himself—to prove his worth to Rakesley.

And for that to happen, she needed to be at her best.

Toward that end, she'd snuck off to visit Liam last night at The Drunken Piebald. As usual, her brother had made the best of a bad circumstance, beginning with having wrapped one of the inn's scullery maids around his little finger, using the charm inherited from their Irish mother.

Charm that Gemma envied, for she possessed not a bit of it. Generally, people met her eye and saw not a twinkle but a resolute seriousness. They usually glanced away immediately.

"Talk me through tomorrow's ride," she'd said to Liam as the door clicked shut behind her.

"And a good evening to you, sister," he returned lightly.

She pulled the room's only chair close to the bed, perched on its edge, and waited.

Liam's smile fell away, and he considered her. "You've seen me do it hundreds of times on the courses, Gemma," he said. "You know what to do."

The doubts she'd been suppressing came tumbling out. "I

know how to ride, aye, but I've never done it like this." What she knew about riding and racing could comprise a large entry in the encyclopedia, but she'd never put the racing part into practice. "Not like what will be expected of me tomorrow."

"You'll be a natural out there." He grew serious. "You won't be using a crop?"

Gemma shook her head. "Of course not. You know they're not necessary when a horse wants to run."

Liam nodded, slowly. "Aye, but some owners want to see them for the show. The spectacle of it. You know that."

"No crop," she repeated. "I won't be riding the set-to with crop and spur. Hannibal wants to run."

"You'll be riding the Chifney style?"

"As you do," she reminded him.

"And you're comfortable with a simple snaffle and slack rein?" Liam canted his head. "You trust Hannibal?"

Gemma swallowed any lingering doubt. "I'm confident in him."

"And the rush at the end?"

The rush was the key to the Chifney riding style. To play a waiting game until the last furlong, then let the horse have his head at the finish. It was called the Chifney Rush, and it required patience and strategy.

"Hannibal is big and strong," she said. "I think he'll have it in him to be a goer at the end."

Liam went as somber as Gemma ever saw him. "But you're small, sister. It's one thing to win a race from the lead, but a whole other thing to spend the race in the pack and make a break at the end. It's not only patience and strategy. It requires strength and a large dollop of meanness. You'll spend most of the race muscling for your place."

Gemma understood that, but she couldn't see any other way to ride and do right by Hannibal. She had to try. "Well, tomorrow isn't the race."

"Start him slow," said Liam. "Allow him to work his way into the run. This will show him to his best advantage. Tell Rakesley you won't be testing starts but getting a feel for Hannibal's action."

Gemma's eyebrows shot toward the ceiling, incredulous. "Me telling the Duke of Rakesley what to do?" She snorted. *Not bloody likely.*

Liam cocked his head. "That's how jockeys talk to owners. Most of them need to be told, because they don't rightly know one end of a horse from the other."

"Not this owner."

Liam didn't blink. "You must establish it from the start, Gemma."

She'd nodded her acceptance of the advice, while a part of her stood back in skepticism.

Even now as she made her way toward the track with Hannibal, she still felt that trace of apprehension, familiar nerves skittering through her.

In truth, she'd done all she could to avoid Rakesley these last three days. Every time he entered the stables, she made herself scarce—slipping unnoticed into the tack room or finding a stall to muck out in the carriage wing.

It wasn't simply that she was spying on his operation and didn't want to draw attention to herself. Something else had her avoiding him.

Something that happened when their gazes met.

Something that she intuitively understood she needed to stay clear of.

Yet there was more.

Rakesley was no fool. Her disguise wouldn't hold up beneath the close scrutiny of that man's fathomless gaze. Particularly not when she kept inserting her opinions into every conversation.

She gave her head a clearing shake. She was only here to report the goings-on of the Somerton stable to Deverill. That was her actual job. The one that would be paying her life-changing money upon completion.

But Deverill's wasn't the only life-changing money recently offered to her.

Three days ago, on the spot, she'd had the brass to ask the duke about recompense.

But why not?

When Liam rode, he received a base pay for riding—*and* he got a cut of the purse for winning. One grateful, sauced-to-the-gills lord had even given him an entire purse, for he'd only been in it for the bragging rights.

Just like Rakesley, presumably. But...

Two hundred pounds.

She couldn't imagine having so much blunt that two hundred pounds would be as nothing to her.

Her mind couldn't quite grasp it.

But with opportunity came higher stakes.

More life-changing money on the line.

Life-changing money was being thrown at her from every direction.

All she had to do was steady herself and catch it.

And the powerful horse below her played a large role, for somehow, improbably, she'd become his jockey.

It wasn't worth denying that part of her relished it, but another part of her—the sensible part—understood how easily all could end in disaster. For now, instead of avoiding Rakesley's scrutiny, she was firmly...*decidedly*...in the center of it.

But what choice had she in that moment three days ago? Refuse both Lady Artemis and Rakesley? Tt hadn't seemed like an option. What reason would lowly Gem have for refusing? She still couldn't think of a single solitary one.

And the choice between Lady Artemis and Rakesley?

It hadn't been much of one.

While she would rather ride for Lady Artemis, she was here to collect information on Rakesley's racing operation. She couldn't lose sight of that.

Hannibal stepped onto the practice course, and tension shivered through him. Not to flee, but to arrive there faster. This tension wasn't about distress, but rather readiness.

For all her nerves, Gemma couldn't wait to test Hannibal out on the turf. Green and loamy, it was firm, but held a spring. They'd done a few laps yesterday, and Hannibal had shown he knew exactly what to do. He'd wanted his head. But she'd held the reins tight and hadn't given it to him, allowing him to go no faster than a trot.

That was yet another part of his training. Would he accept instructions he didn't like?

The answer had been *yes*—and what a relief.

A hive of activity, focused in the morning quiet, bustled about the course. Local women who had been hired to groom the turf filled pocks and holes. So, too, were there lads and grooms hanging about in small clusters, trying to appear busy, but really here to see Hannibal run. The black colt held a charisma that made eyes want to watch him.

But could he give them a proper show? That was top of everyone's mind.

Today they would know the answer.

Gemma's gaze caught on the pair of still figures inside the track's interior white fence—one tossing orders this way and that; the other propped against the rail, patiently taking it all in. To the uninitiated, Rakesley could appear relaxed, laconic even, so at ease was the man in his body. But beneath that insouciant exterior ran a focused intensity that it would be a mistake to underestimate.

For an instant, she wondered if she should pass that information along to Deverill.

No, was her instinctive response.

She was to report on the running of Somerton, not about its

owner. For some reason, that information felt like a step too far…like a betrayal.

Rakesley's gaze cut left and landed on her and Hannibal. A frisson sparked through her—of what she couldn't be sure. *Fear? Excitement? Anticipation?*

All of it.

But also something more.

The *something more* that ever sparked through her when his gaze landed on her.

"Gem," came Wilson's matter-of-fact voice. "Take Hannibal around the track and ease him into a trot halfway around."

Gemma nodded, complying only because she agreed with the command.

Anticipatory energy lit the air alive as everyone watched Hannibal. But Gemma only felt one pair of eyes—*Rakesley's.*

Taking everything in…missing nothing…drawing conclusions.

This duke was a thinker. But not in a dispassionate way. Rather she sensed a fire inside him that affected all he put his mind to. She couldn't help but like that about him—even if it struck cold fear through her.

Heaven help her if he ever set his mind to puzzling her out.

Hannibal gave his head a shake, pulling her from unhelpful thoughts and back into the moment. "Impatient to show them what you can do, my friend?"

He gave another shake of the head as if in answer.

With a chuckle, she eased up on the reins by a slight increment to test his sensitivity.

Immediately, he quickened into a trot.

Oh, he was a ready goer, all right.

Today would be fun.

After they'd completed the lap, they pulled up before Wilson and Rakesley. Gemma only realized she was smiling from ear to ear when she met the serious gazes of the two men. The smile fell, and she slid from Hannibal's back.

Again, it was Wilson who spoke and Rakesley who observed. "No starts today."

Gemma nodded, relieved. "You'll be wanting to get a handle on Hannibal's action."

Wilson nodded, a glint of respect in his eyes. "Aye."

Rakesley cocked his head. "You seem to know a great deal about horseracing, considering you were a stable lad only three days ago."

Gemma's gaze found her feet, and she lifted a shoulder indifferently. "You hear things around," she mumbled.

"Ah."

That *ah* didn't exactly resound with belief.

Wilson pointed toward the track. "You'll have noticed the course is marked in furlongs."

Gemma nodded. "Twelve of them." A beat. "Like Epsom."

In fact, that was exactly the information Deverill was paying her for. She would include the detail when she wrote him.

A twinge of discomfort niggled at her, which she instantly tamped down. In truth, the act of spying didn't rest easy inside her.

"Another interesting bit of knowledge there," said Rakesley, his eyes darkly opaque, as ever.

Gemma shifted on her feet and was saved from having to acknowledge the observation by Wilson. "But Newmarket is a mile and eight furlongs. So, you'll take Hannibal another lap at a trot, then ease into a canter. Four furlongs into the second lap you'll go full tilt into a gallop. Really stretch him out so we can see where he hits his stride."

Gemma liked the plan's simplicity and precision. Even though it was Wilson giving the instructions, it was obvious they came from the duke whose gaze hadn't once strayed from her.

"Is that why the racecourse was originally marked in

sections?" she found herself asking, instinctively meeting Rakesley's gaze.

A beat of time ticked past, and she wasn't sure he would deign to answer. After all, he was a duke very much aware of his place —and hers.

"Every horse is different," he said at last. "Each has different preferences, different ways of racing, different action. Some are fast starters, others slow. But none of those differences necessarily indicate weakness or fault. In fact, they can prove the opposite by telling us precisely where a horse's strength lies. But it's down to us to find it. Today, that's what we'll do with Hannibal. He's a strapping beast with both the physicality for racing and the lineage. What we don't yet know is what makes him different and what makes him special on a racecourse."

For the first time, Gemma felt good about this venture.

Better than good.

She felt *right* about it.

Further, she felt a deepening respect for Rakesley. The way he approached horses and racing wasn't entirely about winning, though she intuited the man liked to win. Perhaps it was even a compulsion, like so many caught in the orbit of horses and racing.

But it wasn't *only* about winning. He wanted to get the best out of his horses. There was rigor in the process—as was necessary—but there was patience as well.

He held out his hand toward her, and the breath froze in Gemma's lungs. She took a wobbly step backward.

The step had been instinctive, and the bemused smile that lit within the blasted man's eyes said he was curious why. He didn't withdraw. "Your coat."

Shock blazed through Gemma. "My coat?"

Over my dead body perched on the tip of her tongue.

Her coat wasn't simply her coat. It was a large part of what made Gem *Gem*.

Without the scratchy, filth-encrusted garment, she would be a little less Gem.

Which, flipped around, meant one thing:

Without it, she would be a little *more* Gemma.

She planted her will in place and continued to resist the pull toward the inevitable.

That Rakesley would win.

That was what his fathomless eyes were telling her.

The man didn't lose.

CHAPTER SIX

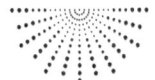

*W*hat had begun as a request borne of good sense had, in a snap, transformed into a war of wills altogether unexpected and befuddling.

From the hunted look in Gem's eyes, one would think he was being forced to strip down and run around the racecourse naked.

"*Why* do you need my coat?" asked the lad, eyes slitted with distrust.

Perhaps a duke had once made off with a moth-riddled, flea-bitten coat of his?

"It's too loose," said Rake, entirely logical.

He was only right.

"*Too loose?*" Gem's left eyebrow lifted in skepticism. He wasn't having it.

"On race day," Rake began as if he had all the patience in the world, "your clothes will be more fitted."

The color drained from the lad's face. "More *fitted?*"

"When you're wearing my livery." A thought occurred to him, and Rake turned toward Wilson. "Procure more suitable clothing for the lad. I can hardly have my jockey looking like a ragamuffin."

Wilson nodded with approval. "Aye, Your Grace."

Gem ground his back teeth, eyes dark with mutiny.

While Rake was at it... "And a wash-up wouldn't do you any harm either."

Few possessed the temerity to deny the Duke of Rakesley what he wanted. But, Rake suspected, this lad might've been one of those few as several beats of time ticked past, and Gem stood unmoving.

Then came a fractional movement of one shoulder, followed by the other, and the coat was sliding down the lad's arms and off. He shoved the garment toward Rake, who didn't feel as much satisfaction in the victory as he'd thought he would.

Instead, it was surprise that traced through him. He'd taken the lad to be slight of form, but now he could see the coat had comprised nearly half the mass of his person.

The lad slid a sure foot into a stirrup and mounted Hannibal in a few sure, experienced movements. Even though he hadn't won their silent war of wills regarding the coat, the lad appeared entirely too satisfied to be looking down upon Rake from a lofty perch.

Wilson gave Hannibal's hooves a quick inspection for small stones and loose rocks. Satisfied, he squinted up at Gem, for the sun had decided to make an appearance. "You got your instructions?"

"A lap at a trot, then a canter for four furlongs, then a proper gallop for eight," said the lad, repeating his orders back to Wilson.

"Then ease him back down to canter and trot."

Gem nodded, and, again, the question struck Rake—*How?*

How had a stable lad from The Drunken Piebald come into possession of horseracing knowledge?

A mystery circled this lad, and Rake couldn't help wanting to solve it.

He tossed Gem's coat over the fence rail and held out his hand. "And your hat."

He was testing Gem, but he wanted to see how far he could push the lad.

"My hat will be staying on my head," he retorted, firm.

"With Hannibal at full gallop?" Rake snorted. "Doubtful."

Still, he shrugged and let the matter drop. A surely louse-laden hat was hardly worth arguing over.

Gem looked to Wilson. "If that will be all?"

Wilson looked to Rake, who nodded. Wilson then gave his answer. "Aye."

His head groom understood the proper pecking order, even if Gem chose to ignore it. Jockeys were the known divas of the racing world, and Gem was proving no exception.

With that, the lad gave his knees a light squeeze, and he and Hannibal set off. Wilson at his side, Rake strode across close-clipped, spring-green grass to the small platform that offered a view of the entire course.

Energy snapped through the air as the grooms and stable lads gathered around the fence along with a few of the village women, imbuing the atmosphere with festivity.

How would Hannibal respond to the attention? Rake harbored doubts, viewing it as another test of the colt. Truly, the only person who believed in Hannibal whole-heartedly was Gem.

And yet... It was Gem's complete faith that had Rake joining in.

Strange, that.

Over the years, he'd seen plenty of horses like Hannibal. Horses gifted with the bloodline. Horses gifted with the physicality.

But horses not gifted with the extra something that made them a winner.

Horses he'd had to give up on.

Horses that had ripped his heart in two.

Gem urged Hannibal into a canter. The crowd gathered around the fence had doubled in the last five minutes. Word must've been spreading around Somerton, and all wanted to see how Hannibal went. It might amount to nothing. Or...

It could be something.

It could be the beginning of a championship season.

And Hannibal... A nervy energy radiated off him.

He wanted to run.

Gem had been correct on that score.

And Gem... Rake didn't know what the lad was saying to the horse, but he hadn't stopped talking to him the entire ride so far.

"His action is looking free," observed Wilson, a tinge of excitement in his voice.

This was what they needed to know about Hannibal in order to proceed with his training. If his action was cramped or round or extravagant, the colt would be better put to stud than on a racecourse, because he wouldn't be winning any races.

Except that didn't appear to be the case with Hannibal. He had a good length of stride at walk, trot, and canter, which boded well for his gallop.

"Alright, here we go," said Wilson, crossing his arms over his chest, his gaze intensely focused on Hannibal.

As Gem and the colt entered the fourth furlong of the second lap, the lad angled forward and lifted slightly, making himself lighter in the saddle, and anticipation took wing inside Rake, soaring through him as his jaw tightened and his hands clenched into fists at his sides.

They crossed the line into the fifth furlong, and they were off. Beside Rake, Wilson kept a running commentary on Hannibal— his smooth, easy action; his low, swinging stride; the powerful thrust of his hind quarters; the free, forward lift of his shoulders. Rake heard all this and nodded in agreement.

Hannibal was a right goer. With him, they would be winning the Two Thousand Guineas in a few weeks, and more races too. Rake felt it down to his marrow.

He found himself watching Gem. The way he rode Hannibal

without crop or spur, but with utter skill and joy. *Abandon.* Gem possessed the ability to let go and fly. Grit and determination showed in the firm set of the lad's mouth, as did the shadow of a smile. One couldn't help but be infected by the exhilaration coming off the lad as he stretched Hannibal out and urged the best out of the colt.

The action was there.

The power and speed were there.

Yet...something about Gem worried at Rake. The lad rode like a demon. Entirely without fear. So...how was it the lad hadn't already started making a name for himself at Newmarket or Epsom?

Well, he would in a few weeks' time. That was certain. The Ring wouldn't know what hit it when Hannibal and Gem took the turf, and every owner in England would try to poach the lad. And yet...

He was such an unlikely lad—possessed of hardly any physical substance. How such a slight lad could control the likes of Hannibal was beyond Rake. But he knew this—that was exactly what a talented jockey could do—and Rake was the sort of owner who knew not to question it. It was part of their magic.

And that was what Gem had with horses. More than any other jockey Rake had ever happened across.

Magic.

Just as they reached the eleventh furlong—Hannibal's speed only increasing as they neared the end of the ride—Gem's ever-present slouch hat flew off his head, as Rake had predicted.

On impulse, Rake ran to retrieve the hat. From the middle of the course, he watched Gem finish the run on the final stretch, hat slapping against his thigh.

Gem spared a rushed glance behind him, a halo of sun-streaked hair flying about his head. Rake held up the ragged hat.

Before this moment, he'd only caught glimpses of reddish tips of hair that curled at the ends peeking out from beneath Gem's slouch hat. But, now, exposed and free... A crowning glory, that head of hair.

Again, the idea that Gem was an unlikely lad poked at Rake. He could've easily handed the hat off to Wilson, but he was holding on to it. He wasn't sure why, but he suspected it originated in the desire to make the lad come to him. Make those gold-flecked, green eyes meet his. Gem had been avoiding him these last three days. Rake hadn't been particularly irked. His calendar kept him busy every waking hour of the day.

But he'd noticed the evasion.

A thought slid in before he could catch it as he watched Gem begin to slow Hannibal into a canter.

Fetching.

His jockey had a fetching, round little backside.

He'd never once in all his life caught himself admiring a jockey's backside. He simply wasn't that sort of man. He knew a few who were, but not him.

Perhaps that was why he needed to meet the lad's gaze.

He needed to understand why he kept noticing characteristics about the lad that, hitherto, he'd only ever noticed about women —the gold flecks within his green eyes...the light streaks of hair that glinted strawberry in the sun...his fetching backside...

Wilson joined Rake at the fence, his eyes bright with exhilaration. Nothing like a prime bit of horseflesh pounding the turf to get the blood flowing in one's veins. "Who woulda known that foul-tempered Hannibal would be a sweet goer." He laughed and shook his head. "Did you notice how he didn't need but a light command or two?"

"Aye," agreed Rake.

"You saw what no one else did when you matched that horse and rider."

"No one could've predicted it would work," Rake deflected.

The fact was he had, indeed, known it would.

He'd felt it deep in his gut.

"There's the magic of racing, innit?"

"Indeed," said Rake. "But..." How to say this... "Do you think there's something different about the lad?"

He had to ask.

Wilson chuckled. "Aye, he's an odd one, that Gem. But he's the one to get the best out of that horse."

"And we don't argue with that."

Wilson cut Rake a sharp glance. "Nay, Your Grace." A beat. "We don't."

And that was Rake told—in the only way anyone would ever dare tell a duke anything.

Around the track, horse and rider circled. Gem settled back into the saddle, patiently slowing furlong by furlong, as was right. The cooling down of a horse couldn't be rushed.

Yet more knowledge the unlikely Gem possessed.

But then everyone knew that, even coaching inn lads.

At last, Gem gently pulled the reins so Hannibal stopped. He slid from the horse's back and walked him around the final bend, coming within a few yards of Rake and Wilson. Gem's eyes shone bright, his cheeks stained red from exertion. Sweat glistened on horse and rider alike, the pair only just recovering their breath. The joy that Rake had detected during the ride yet echoed about the lad.

There was no doubting he'd just done what he loved most in the world.

Rake experienced admiration—and a dollop of envy.

And more worry.

In his experience, loving too much or too freely only invited trouble—even disaster.

Wilson called out a hearty *well done* and immediately set about inspecting Hannibal from all angles, asking questions like, "How was his wind?" and "Did you feel him favoring a leg?"

All the while, Rake watched and listened as Gem answered each question, clearly and equably. Rake slapped the slouch hat against his thigh, drawing Gem's attention. The lad had already retrieved his coat from the fence rail and shrugged it onto his bony shoulders. All he was missing was his hat.

The one Rake yet held.

The lad extended his hand. "If you wouldn't mind." A beat. "Your Grace."

Viewing Gem up close without the hat, Rake could see why the lad wore it. Sun-streaked red-gold curls rioted untamed about his head, just touching his shoulders, hardly kept in check by the queue at the nape of his neck. The auburn of his hair pulled the gold flecks from his green eyes.

There, again, went one of those observations he'd never had about a jockey.

Rake released the hat, which was immediately snatched away and affixed onto Gem's head, covering his wild glory of hair.

"If that will be all, Your Grace?" said Wilson, clearly satisfied with his inspection of Hannibal. "I'll be gettin' the lads back to it. They seem to think it's Boxing Day."

The stable lads and grooms did give off a holiday air as they continued to lag about and make jolly with each other. Rake nodded, and Wilson pivoted, already barking orders to the cluster of lads unlucky enough to be nearest.

Gem must've taken it as his dismissal, too, for he began leading Hannibal down the track for his cool-down.

"Not you, Gem," said Rake, falling into step beside the lad. Though he had a busy day and hadn't the time to spare, he had a few questions for his jockey. Best start with the one that had been at the top of his mind all morning. "How did you come to know horses the way you do?"

Gem shrugged. "Bouncing between stables here, there, and everywhere," he mumbled.

Rake shook his head. "You don't get to know horseflesh the way you do like that. Try again."

Rake could see that every admission—every syllable—would have to be pulled from the lad bit by reluctant bit.

"I spent much of my life in a lord's stables."

Each syllable sounded bitten off with great difficulty.

"Like Grimalkin the stable cat?"

This got a barely-there exhalation that might've been a laugh.

"How did you come to be in a lord's stables?" Rake's patience was beginning to wear thin.

Gem swiped the sweat off the back of his neck. "My Mam was the lord's cook."

Ah.

That made a modicum of sense.

But the information only provoked another question. "Which lord?"

"I'd rather not say."

I won't say, the lad might just as well have said.

Rake's question had been little more than an idle one—one not intended to lead anywhere. It wasn't as if he would be checking into Gem's story. But Gem's response turned the idle question into something altogether different.

No longer was Gem a lad of few words, but a lad who chose his words—*carefully*.

A lad who was hiding something.

And there was something else about Gem that Rake hadn't been able to lay a finger on, that now struck him.

The lad's grammar.

The words that he did choose were of a social class that, in the general course of events, stable lads didn't rise to.

He didn't say *me* Mam, but rather *my* Mam.

A subtle but important distinction.

Rake cut a glance toward the lad's profile—cheeks streaked with dirt, gaze set firmly ahead, mouth pressed into a straight line. Rake would be getting no further admissions from Gem, his demeanor all but said. Fair enough. He had a day to get on with, anyway. "Gem," he said in farewell and peeled away at the next gate.

Rake could feel the lad's relieved gaze on his back as he exited the course and made for the house, ready to sit down with his secretary and talk new roofs for the local village. Yet…

Now he had a puzzle to solve.

And he knew his mind wouldn't let up until he had all the pieces in place.

One and one didn't make two with Gem.

It was both an obvious fact and a feeling deep in his gut.

He should leave it.

The lad was his jockey, and the best one he'd ever come across, at that.

Leave it.

But even as he knew he should leave it, he knew he wouldn't.

CHAPTER SEVEN

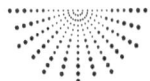

*I*t was the end of the day, the evening meal finished, and Rake found himself with a rare night at loose ends. Artemis had accepted an invitation to attend a local assembly—one he'd sent his apologies to.

In truth, when he was away from Town and residing at his Suffolk estate, he rather liked the quiet evenings. The days started early here, and the nights tended to end early too. Quite unlike the life he led in London.

Even if one might mistake him sitting in his study beside the evening fire for a man in his dotage.

The day had been long and productive in the specific way of a duke's day. After Hannibal's successful morning ride, he'd met with his secretary and gone over the needs of Somerton and several other estates besides. The new roofs were to start construction within the fortnight so as to be completed before first frost. Then there had been Mother to consider and her monthly allowance, which could meet the needs of the king himself—but never hers. Of course, Rake had approved the two hundred additional pounds she'd asked for—some might say *demanded*—and let the matter go.

To argue with Mother was as fruitless as arguing with a thunderstorm. One quickly located the nearest shelter and took cover. What one didn't do was quarrel with it—or one was likely to be struck by lightning.

Mother's bolts were not to be trifled with.

He snorted and settled back into his comfortable chair and considered the letter he'd been putting off reading. Nothing notable stood out about his name and address emblazoned on the front. Rather, it was the pink wax seal on the back that sparked his interest.

This letter was from the Duchess of Acaster.

He'd begun to accept that he'd been mistaken about her. Perhaps she was the sort of widow who had no interest in shackling herself to another husband. And he wouldn't blame her one bit. From what he'd observed over the years, wives got the mucky end of the stick when it came to marriage.

He took his penknife and sliced the missive open, giving its contents a cursory scan before going over them again, more thoroughly. A satisfied smile curved the corners of his mouth. She was giving due consideration to selling him Silky Sadie, but she wasn't ready to make a commitment as she hadn't yet decided on the price.

That last bit provoked the smile. Perhaps her price might not be in coin.

The Duchess of Acaster was flirting with him.

Which Rake took as a very good sign.

Perhaps she was encouraging him to pursue that other matter with her—*marriage.*

He set the letter aside. It would keep until tomorrow.

For now, the brandy cart beckoned. A nightcap while he read the latest adventure by the Scotsman Sir Walter Scott would be his evening done.

What was that about his dotage?

Behind him, he heard a terrace door terrace creak open. He

didn't need to turn to know who would dare enter his study through an exterior door. Without looking, he asked, "Would you like me to pour you one, Julian?"

"Sure," came his friend's response.

Rake's head cocked. A note sounded decidedly *off* in Julian's voice. A slur in the single syllable that only someone who knew him well would detect. Rake half pivoted and gave his friend a once-over—typically impeccable blond hair mussed...cravat loose and askew...jaw stubbled golden, as if it hadn't seen the sharp side of a straightedge in days.

It wasn't merely that something was off.

Julian was soaked to the gills.

Rake stoppered the brandy snifter. "From the sauced look of you, you likely don't need one."

Julian snorted, but there was no humor in it. He crossed the room and reached for an empty crystal tumbler, holding it out expectantly. "But I'll take one anyway."

Rake had no choice but to pour. His friend was determined to get foxed tonight, and who was Rake to stop him?

Julian obviously had a weight on his chest that he needed to unload. *Kenilworth* could wait until tomorrow.

Tonight, Rake had a friend in need.

He resumed his seat before the fire and indicated the chair opposite. Julian sprawled ungracefully into the proffered seat and pointed at the letter on the side table. "Anything important?"

Rake shrugged a mostly indifferent shoulder. The letter had been forgotten the instant he'd set it down. "From the Duchess of Acaster."

Julian nodded with slow exaggeration. "About the mare? What was her name?"

"Silky Sadie."

Julian held up his half-full tumbler as if toasting the horse, then tossed the entire contents back.

Something was wrong.

Very wrong.

Julian wasn't given to strong drink—or any vices to think of. Even in the world of horseracing, he didn't partake in betting or gaming. In fact, he was set against those activities, even as he accepted them as part of the atmosphere. Like Rake, his love for horses and the competition of racing was simple.

Julian sank deeper into plush cushions. "You're a good friend, you know that?"

"And you're drunk."

Julian wagged a finger, as if chastening Rake. "Not a lot of people know that about you."

"Thank you?"

"But you're selective. You choose who you love." Julian tapped his temple. "*Smart.* But someday, old chap, you're going to find yourself loving someone you didn't choose."

Rake tapped the duchess's letter. "Not if I have any say over the matter."

Julian gave a loud bark of a laugh, not a hint of jollity in it.

"Is there something you wish to discuss?" asked Rake, deciding it best to get to it.

Julian's semblance of a smile fell away. "Today—" He squinted up toward the coffered ceiling. "What is today, anyway?"

"The seventeenth of March," said Rake.

"Yesterday, then." Julian gave a befuddled shake of the head. "Yesterday was the anniversary."

Rake didn't need to ask which anniversary. Only one anniversary held the power to plunge Julian into the depths of despair Rake was presently witnessing.

The anniversary of his adored older sister Clarissa's death when he'd been but aged seven...

And the anniversary of the death of his father, who had taken his own life exactly twenty years later to the day...

The three-year anniversary of Lord Julian Batchelor becoming the Marquess of Ormonde.

Yesterday.

Julian looked as if he'd taken his first drink before he'd rolled out of bed yesterday and hadn't stopped since.

"Would you like to talk about it?"

Julian stared into the fire and gave his head a shake. "No."

Rake wasn't offended in the least.

So, he began talking. Starting with which horses would be contenders for the racing season, then on to the Jockey Club and the disarray it had fallen into since the death of Sir Charles Bunbury last year. No one possessed the Perpetual President's—as he'd come to be known—authority or moral rectitude in matters of the turf. Soon, it would be the blacklegs and touts running the racing meetings with impunity.

Julian swatted the idea away. "Pish and rot. *You* should become president of the Jockey Club."

Rake snorted. "Not bloody likely."

That got a good, long laugh from Julian. "By the by," he said, his mood considerably lighter than when he'd entered the room an hour ago, "how's your new jockey working out for you? Word has it that Hannibal ran today."

"Do you have touts spying at Somerton?"

The spies sent by the Ring to scout the horses were relentless. Wilson had uncovered and routed two this year already.

Rake despised spies.

Julian shrugged a shoulder. "Servants like to talk, and our estates are only five miles apart."

Rake believed his friend. "Aye, Hannibal ran."

"He's a goer?"

"Better than expected," said Rake, tightly.

Julian was a friend off the racecourse, but the competition on it. Rake wouldn't be volunteering any useful information.

Julian smiled and shook his head. "That new jockey of yours… What's his name?"

"Gem." Rake didn't want to talk about Gem, either. Yet... "What do you make of the lad?"

"I only met him the once at The Drunken Piebald, but..." Ormonde swirled the last dregs of brandy in his tumbler.

"*But?*" Rake tensed. Whatever insights Julian could offer, Rake wanted to hear.

"The lad seemed to know what he was about is all. And he must've because you're letting him ride Hannibal."

There was that.

"Really, it was a bit of luck happening across that lad in a coaching inn," continued Julian.

While Rake agreed, he hadn't precisely considered it in that light. "How so?"

"It's clear he was raised around quality stables," Julian mused as only a man in his cups could. "There's a story there."

And there it was.

Rake's thought precisely, spoken aloud.

There *was* a story there—and the fact that a man three sheets to the wind could see it meant it possessed a kernel of truth.

Out of the mouths of babes—and drunkards.

That was how Milton should've put it.

And Julian wasn't finished. "Sometimes with a person, we only see what we expect to see, and not what's really there."

Julian's smile fell away, and his clear blue eyes darkened, regaining the hollowed-out quality he'd entered the room with. He was no longer speaking of Gem.

"Take my father, for example," he continued, almost conversationally. "I spent years thinking he was nothing more than a drunken sot determined to plunge the family into bankruptcy and land us all in debtor's prison."

"He was that," said Rake. It was the truth, and it needed to be said.

"Ah, but there you're only halfway right." Julian wagged a

finger at Rake. "It was really only a symptom of the problem." His false levity fell away. "What he *was*, was a drowning man."

Rake held his silence. Julian had more to say—and needed to say it.

"He was a man being dragged under by the weight of his daughter's death."

And there it was—the thing on his friend's mind. The thing that had him imbibing spirits for two days straight. The thing that needed to be said.

But Rake had something to say, too. "Your father had a choice."

Julian cocked his head. "Do you have a choice when you're drowning?"

Rake held his friend's eye. "You learn how to swim—or you accept someone's hand."

Julian sat forward, his eyes a blaze of anguish. "But what if those closest to you take you for a lost cause and don't bother extending one?" The pain and guilt in those words were evident.

Rake had no ready answer, but he did have something to say to his friend. "Your father's death is not your fault. It was of his own making."

The statement hung in the air between the two men, an obstacle to further conversation. Rake wished his friend would allow the words—and the truth they held—to sink into him and find purchase. Perhaps, in time, they would.

Julian pushed heavily to his feet and listed slightly to the left.

"Somerton has twenty guest rooms. Stay the night." Rake wasn't asking.

Julian shook his head. "Nay, old Petunia girl knows her way home blindfolded."

"Even when you're blind drunk?"

Julian shambled toward the door he'd entered through an hour ago. "I'll see you in a day or two," he tossed over his shoulder.

"It might take more than that to sleep this one off," Rake returned, lightly, hoping to get a chuckle.

Julian snorted and waved the words away. "I'll be right as rain tomorrow."

Relief traced through Rake. It was the assurance he needed to hear to let his friend go into the night.

He stood at the door and watched Julian clumsily mount the ever-patient Petunia and then find the back path that connected their two estates at the west boundary. His friend faded into the night, leaving Rake alone with the words he'd left behind.

Sometimes with a person, we only see what we expect to see, and not what's really there.

The words now struck Rake sideways. What was he not seeing with Gem?

He sensed whatever it was, it had been before his eyes all this time.

All he needed to do now was actually see it.

CHAPTER EIGHT

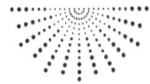

NEXT MORNING

The sky grew bright with dawn too quickly for Gemma's liking as she rushed across Somerton's wide drive, its gravel road flanked by sweet chestnut trees green with budding spring. She'd stayed overlong catching up with Liam at The Drunken Piebald. She could only hope her absence hadn't yet been noted by Wilson.

Liam had demanded a full accounting of yesterday's ride from beginning to end. Gemma left nothing out, from the moment she'd led Hannibal from his box to the moment she'd returned him.

"How was Hannibal's action?" asked Liam. "He isn't a daisy-cutter, is he?"

Like the Arab horses from which they were bred, Thoroughbreds could run too close to the ground. The risk was a stumble, and there went horse and rider, tip over tail. She'd assured her brother that Hannibal hadn't any such tendency.

"He's perfect, Liam."

Those had been her exact words.

Liam's gaze went narrow and sharp. "There is no perfect horse, sister. You would do well to remember that. It's the perfect horses that will break your heart."

Gemma moved on to the day. Dreamy mist burning off the track with the morning sun. All the grooms and lads—maids, cooks, and footmen too—gathered around the course, shouting their heads off when Hannibal got up to speed and showed the stuff he was made of. The crisp air cutting harsh against her face, through her hair. The sweet sweat of exertion coating every inch of her skin. The ride had been everything she'd dreamt it would be—pure freedom and joy.

Liam's familiar easy smile returned. "Aye, it can be like that." Wistfulness traced through the words.

"Liam, you'll be riding again," she said, grabbing his hand as he turned to stare out the window. "*Soon.*"

He nodded, but doubt was writ clear upon his face. A leg broken above the knee was no minor injury. That was the fact they left unspoken. Some people never fully recovered. Some walked with a limp for the rest of their days. And a man with a limp would no longer be hired as a jockey. They left that unsaid too.

Not one for a morose state of mind, Liam's gaze cut toward her. "And Wilson? Was he satisfied?"

"Aye." Even as Gemma spoke the word, tension entered her body. She braced herself, knowing what question would follow.

"And Rakesley?" asked Liam.

A simple *aye* would've sufficed. But she had to be careful how the *aye* emerged from her mouth. Liam would be able to hear or sense a *tone*.

That was the tricky thing about a twin. They heard and sensed all about each other.

Fortunately, just as that dreaded *aye* was emerging from her mouth, a knock sounded at the door. A light two taps, but enough to distract Liam from the squeak that had surely sounded in her voice.

He pulled himself straighter against the headboard and ran his fingers through his hair in a futile attempt to subdue his short red-gold curls. They were untamable, as Gemma knew from experience. "You may enter," he called out.

The inn's scullery maid entered the room with a charmed smile on her face and a serving tray bearing tea, toast, ham, and eggs. "A good morning to you, Master Li—" Her bright gaze landed on Gemma. "Oh, yer brother is just payin' a visit. I'll just set this on the table and leave ye two to yer—"

Liam met Gemma's gaze and subtly jutted his chin toward the door. She took the hint and shot to her feet. "No need for that," said Liam. "Gem's just leaving."

Gemma's gaze fell to the tops of her mud-encrusted boots, and she gave a surly grunt of farewell. As she made her hasty way out of The Drunken Piebald, she only just remembered to post a letter for Deverill with the innkeeper, whose dour visage wasn't improved by daylight.

She tamped down the pesky trace of guilt that had begun nipping at her. Truly, the information she'd shared wouldn't cost Rakesley anything.

Wasn't life simply a game for a duke?

That was all horse racing was, really—a game.

And the duke could stand to lose every once in a while.

She'd provided information about the track itself—the marked-out furlongs, the maintenance of it—but she'd left out information about Hannibal and the ride. It felt oddly personal, and she wanted to keep it for herself—though she would soon have to reveal that Hannibal was now rideable.

And that *she* was riding him.

That particular truth could wait for the next letter.

And Rakesley? Liam's question echoed in her mind.

A strange relief pulsed through her. She hadn't yet had to

discuss Rakesley. The duke was easy enough to omit from her letters to Deverill, but it would present more difficulty with Liam. She would open her mouth and surely stumble on her words, and Liam would know.

Not *know* know, but hear enough hesitation and know something was amiss.

But…was there anything to *know*? Was anything really amiss?

She wrestled with the question.

The short answer was *no*. She was solidly embedded in the Somerton stables, both groom and jockey for Hannibal—the only person who could handle him, in fact—and she would be riding him in the Two Thousand Guineas.

The simple fact was things were better than *not* amiss.

And yet… Something was setting her nerves ajangle.

Something in the way Rakesley looked at her…

Nay, not looked at her.

Observed her, more like, as if watching her from a distance and taking measure—like one would with a dodgy piece of horseflesh.

And he kept those observations to himself.

Still, she'd caught a tell in his dark, inscrutable eyes. A glimmer of light…the light of interest.

Did he somehow…*know*?

Could he know she was not a Gem…

But a Gemma?

Impossible.

He would've dismissed her on the spot.

She needed to hold on to her nerve. Only a few weeks remained until the Two Thousand Guineas, and then she and Liam would have enough blunt to stop running and begin again with a new life.

Gemma's boots crunched across the gravel at a light jog as she passed beneath the clock tower that hadn't yet struck seven. The stable yard was empty of grooms and lads, and a blessed feeling of relief soared through her. Her absence hadn't been discovered.

"Gem," sounded an authoritative voice at her back.

Startled, she whipped around, her heart banging out a hard *thud* against her ribs. Wilson strode toward her, his mouth compressed in its usual down-to-business line, a question in his eyes. He was wondering where she'd been this early in the morning. Gemma braced herself for the question.

"His Grace wants a word with you," he said, instead, leaving the question unasked.

But that didn't mean he hadn't stored it away for the future.

Gemma's stomach flipped over and dread stole in. She gave a tight nod and made for Hannibal's box, braced for the inevitable —Rakesley was about to call her out for the woman she was and give her the sack.

Frustration traced alongside the dread.

She'd been so very, very close.

"Gem," she heard at her back.

She cut an impatient glance over her shoulder. "Aye?" She'd rather get this over with before the grooms and lads with their curious ears began milling about.

"Not there," said Wilson.

Gemma's brow furrowed, and her feet stopped. "At the practice course?"

"In his rooms."

Her eyebrows released and arched toward the sky.

"He's in a right rush to get to London," continued Wilson, "and he has a few questions for you."

Questions. More questions. Did the man never stop asking them?

And the answers to those questions...

He wouldn't like them.

Gemma somehow managed to nod.

"Enter the house through the kitchen, and a footman will lead you to His Grace. Now get on with you." Wilson's eyes narrowed. "And wash your face first."

That was precisely what she wouldn't be doing.

In fact, she might smudge on a little more dirt for good measure.

Still, she managed to say, "Aye."

The now-familiar sequence of emotions marched through her. *Fear...excitement...dread...*

But mostly fear.

The duke held her future in his hands—and he hadn't the faintest idea.

* * *

RAKE HAD NEVER BEEN MUCH for waiting.

Which was what had him summoning Gem to his rooms at the break of dawn.

Sometimes with a person, we only see what we expect to see, and not what's really there.

Julian's words had followed Rake to bed last night and greeted him upon waking this morning.

Whatever it was he wasn't seeing, he needed to see it.

Sooner, not later.

His ear picked up the creak of his dressing room door opening and closing. He listened for further sounds and heard none, but he sensed a presence.

The lad was waiting.

Rake glanced down at his half-clad state, towel cinched about his waist, straightedge in one hand, washcloth in the other. His valet had taken ill with influenza these last three days, and Rake had been fending for himself with mixed results, if the two nicks beading red on the indent of his chin were any indicator.

"Enter," he called out and swished the blade around the wash-basin before he made another go at his black-stubbled jaw.

Behind him, the door opened, and the shuffle of hesitant feet crossed the threshold. Before he could get in a word of greeting, a gasp sounded.

Startled, Rake nicked himself, *again*. He pivoted and found Gem, mouth slightly agape, eyes wide as saucers. The lad's source of alarm was clear.

"That shocking to find a duke shaving himself?"

The lad's brow furrowed. "Like a common man," he mumbled in his voice that sounded entirely composed of muddy gravel. "Except..." The lad seemed to be thinking better of continuing. He hadn't blinked once since entering the bathing room.

"*Except?*"

Rake wanted to know what wasn't common about him. He'd been told as much, but mostly in bedrooms—from women who'd discovered as much with hands and mouths...other parts too.

He stopped the sequence of thoughts there.

Before he gave himself a cockstand.

Gem shrugged, as if indifferent. It was apparent he was anything but. "There isn't much common about you, I suppose," he muttered.

What a strange footing this conversation had started upon. Still, Rake relented. "One man is much the same as another."

What was that crimson flush shoving through the grime on the lad's cheeks?

Was Gem...*blushing*?

"And," began Gem. His gaze didn't seem to know where to land, as it ranged from Rake's bare chest to bare feet, just skimming across the towel in the middle, which only provoked them upward to a point just above Rake's head.

"You're not a man. You're a duke."

Rake snorted. "Perhaps we can meet in the middle and agree that I'm both?"

He returned to his present task—the sorry job of shaving his own face.

Gem's throat cleared behind him.

"Yes?" asked Rake without moving his jaw.

"Is this usual for you?"

"What is that?" With studied concentration, Rake scraped the blade down his cheek, feeling no small amount of triumph that he'd managed to do so without drawing blood.

"Summoning jockeys to your dressing room?"

Rake shrugged. "On occasion."

He didn't owe this lad an accounting of himself. Who worked for whom, anyway?

"And then invite them into your bathing room?" Gem pressed.

Rake's hand stopped mid-neck, and his gaze found the lad in the mirror. He shimmered with nerves and...*indignation*—which only provoked a baffled laugh from Rake.

Which only increased Gem's indignation, judging by the thunderous expression darkening the lad's visage.

Still, Gem seemed to be possessed of enough sense not to give voice to that indignation as his lips—the bottom one decidedly pouty—pressed into a firm line.

Right.

"I summoned you here to ask a question that I didn't think to ask yesterday," said Rake, slowly. "How was the saddle during Hannibal's ride? Did you feel it impede his shoulders in any way?"

"Nay."

"Notice any chafing when you groomed him?"

"None."

Gem had retreated to his monosyllabic answers.

"And you?"

A few ticks of time beat by as Gem made his peace with the fact that a one-syllable response wouldn't suffice. "What about me?"

"Is the saddle properly fitted to you? To your—" Rake stopped himself right there.

Bottom.

That was the word he'd bitten back and the horrified look on Gem's face said he knew it.

Fetching.

That was the adjective his mind had supplied yesterday in regard to Gem's bottom.

He didn't want to discuss Gem's bottom, but here they were.

He'd only brought this on himself.

"My, *erm*," Gem struggled out. "Well, *erm*, all was satisfactory."

"Right," said Rake, relieved, and he resumed hacking the stubble off his face. "Anyway, I think a lighter saddle would be the thing."

Not ten seconds passed before Gem said, "Is that all?"

"One moment." Rake took one final swipe with the straightedge, set it down, and wiped the steamy washcloth across cheeks, chin, and neck. That was as good as it was going to get.

He turned to find Gem edging toward the open doorway.

It wasn't all, in fact.

They hadn't yet broached the topic Rake wanted to discuss.

"You say you grew up on a lord's estate?" he asked without preamble. He wanted to gauge Gem's reaction directly. Questions about his past had the effect of throwing the lad off balance.

And this question was no different, for his hands clenched into fists at his sides as he gave a tight nod.

Good.

Rake pressed on. "What I can't understand is why you would leave your place at a lord's estate to seek work at The Drunken Piebald."

Gem opened his mouth, surely to defend himself, but no sound emerged.

Rake sensed he was on the correct track. "The lord surely would've been keen to keep a lad such as yourself in his stables. With your knowledge and the genuine care you show horses, you would've made head groom within the decade." He cocked his head. "Were you sacked?"

A curt shake of the head was his only answer.

"And yet…"

He made Gem wait for his next words. The lad's nerves hadn't eased one bit, his gaze still unable to settle, stealing up and down Rake's person—mostly his bare chest. With the five or so pounds of dirt encrusting every visible inch of him, perhaps Gem had never seen clean flesh. Perhaps it was cleanliness itself that made Gem anxious.

"You walked away," finished Rake.

Emotion flashed behind Gem's gold-flecked, green eyes, and his mouth twitched.

There. Rake had located the loose thread of Gem's story—but how to gain purchase and fully unravel it?

"And your mam was cook for this lord?"

Gem nodded.

"Other family?"

Another nod.

"Brother? Sister?"

"Brother."

"Your last name is Cassidy. Irish?"

An uneasy nod, as the lad stared at his boots, which had surely tracked muck through the house.

"And an education?" asked Rake, taking another tack. "You received one at the lord's estate?"

The lad's gaze startled up, golden eyebrows crinkling together. *At last.* "Whyever would my education be of importance to you?"

A few facts struck Rake at once. *It* had made its reappearance —Gem's correct grammar. His manner of stringing words together in a way that stable lads generally didn't.

Further, the lad wasn't mumbling or muttering or grunting or grumbling. He was speaking in a clear voice—his true voice.

A voice Rake had heard hinted at, but not fully expressed.

Rake's brow furrowed.

That voice… It sounded like it belonged to a—

Rake noticed it.

The bead of sweat.

Before—*before* this conversation…*before* the voice—it would've gone unnoticed.

After all, the air was warm and sticky with humidity that slicked the gray marble floor and wall tiles. A bit of perspiration was only natural in the atmosphere of a bathing room. In fact, he was perspiring himself.

In fact, the lad's gaze appeared to be following one such bead of sweat down the center of his chest at this very moment, even as Rake tracked Gem's bead of sweat trickling down his smooth cheek…over his pert chin…down the elegant, ivory column of his neck…to dip into the delicate indent at the base of his throat in a glistening, little pool…

Sometimes with a person, we only see what we expect to see, and not what's really there.

And Rake saw…

He *knew*.

He'd been seeing Gem all wrong.

As a lad.

But the person standing before him wasn't a lad at all…

But a lass.

The realization felt…confusing. And…

Right.

This was what he'd been sensing and refusing to see.

Gem was no lad.

Rake's body had certainly known it, even if his mind hadn't.

A blade of anger cut through him. This was nothing of short outright deception.

He'd been made a fool of. If anyone had found out, he would've been made the laughingstock of London.

Again.

"So, tell me, *Gem*," he began. "Have you yet begun shaving?"

Gem opened her mouth to reply, but when Rake stepped forward, the lass's words froze in her mouth. The room felt suddenly sapped of air, neither of them able to draw breath.

Gem gave a terse shake of the head.

"Not the easiest task, I've found since my valet took ill."

Rake advanced another step.

Gem swallowed.

"So, I'm doing for myself."

He'd closed half the distance between them, so near he could reach out and touch this lass, if he chose.

Gem cleared her throat and swallowed. "I didn't know dukes could do for themselves."

A humorless laugh escaped Rake. Ah, there was Gem's fire returned. A smart mouth on this lass.

Again, he marveled at his capacity for self-deception. No lad —or lord, for that matter—would ever dare speak to him that way.

Only a woman.

This woman.

He followed where instinct led and stroked her downy soft cheek with the back of his hand. Awareness stole into the moment as their gazes held.

Another realization struck Rake. Not only was Gem a *she*, but she was a beauty.

Tawny freckles scattered across her straight nose and fine cheekbones. Bow lips that formed into a pretty mouth perched above a pert chin that spoke of determination and no nonsense taken.

But it was those gold-flecked, green eyes fringed by golden lashes that had first drawn him in and now held him rapt. Replacing the edge of anger was an altogether different feeling...

Attraction.

Attraction that had been shadowing the margins of their interactions but now freely felt.

And a point beyond attraction...

Desire.

Desire that wanted to move closer...to reach for the nape of her neck and draw her forward...to feel the press of his mouth against hers as her head tipped back to maintain the contact of their gazes...

Her eyes...

What did he see in there?

Uncertainty...

But possibly a *yes* too.

And he knew.

He wouldn't.

Not now...

Possibly not ever.

So, he took the most difficult step of his life—and stepped backward.

She blinked, as if released from a spell.

And now he was only more curious about this lad turned lass.

As Julian had said, there was a story there.

And Rake understood—if he revealed that he knew her for a woman and demanded her story, he would never get an answer.

She would flee—and he would never see her again.

So, he spoke the only sensible words he possibly could in this impossible moment. "You may go."

A befuddled second ticked past before she pivoted on her heel and fled without another word. Rake watched her and her fetching bottom disappear around a corner.

He snorted, though there was nothing funny about it.

The *why* question marched into the void she'd left behind.

Why was she masquerading as a lad?

What was her story?

What if the answer were as simple as she was playing the lad so she could be employed at a stable? That could be all there was to it. She simply loved horses and wanted to work with them, and women weren't allowed such an occupation. So, she'd disguised herself as a lad to get what she wanted.

He could admire the gumption, if not the deception.

Rake readied himself for his ride to London and found himself wanting to believe this scenario. *But...*

The world of horseracing was a competitive one, and other scenarios wasted no time in presenting themselves as possibilities—one a strong contender.

She could be a tout for the Ring.

In other words, a spy.

And he despised spies.

With these possibilities in play, he knew he'd done right in keeping his newfound knowledge to himself.

Until he discovered her game.

That was the logical approach.

Yet a feeling that had naught to do with logic presented a potential difficulty.

Desire.

He was attracted to her...

He *desired* her.

Really, he should've called her out and let her run and been done with the entire mess.

But something inside him wouldn't allow it.

Something that likely wouldn't be good for him.

Not that he'd ever given much credence to such ideas, but it felt like a fated path.

One he must follow to the end.

Like a story.

For like it or not, whatever story Gem held within her, it had become part of his.

CHAPTER NINE

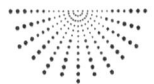

*N*ight Gemma crossed the threshold to her bedroom, let the door snap shut behind her, and sagged against it, grateful for privacy—*at last.*

What a day.

Anxiety still jangled through her veins from the early morning meeting with Rakesley.

Meeting.

That couldn't be the correct word for what had occurred between her and the duke in his bathing room. All day, she hadn't been able to safely blink without risking a vision of his bare, black-fuzzed chest, the hair inviting her gaze to explore the muscles beneath, leading her gaze lower...to his taut, ridged stomach...*lower...*

Her cheeks blazed even now.

She supposed she should've been grateful for the towel.

And she was.

Truly.

Even if her imagination wanted to fill in the thick, heavy bulge she'd detected beneath.

She didn't dare close her eyes to sleep tonight for fear of the dreams…

But…what had actually occurred?

Her mind had run at it from every direction all day.

Rakesley had summoned her to ask about Hannibal's saddle—surely not an unusual query when it came to jockeys and race-horses. And he'd asked where she'd come from. It didn't mean she had to reveal anything. But she had—a little. Information that wouldn't be of much use to him.

Then he'd asked if she'd begun shaving.

She reckoned men asked such questions of lads in their teen years. Surely something to do with virility, or some other such male nonsense.

But that wasn't what had the blood rioting through her veins.

He'd touched her—a barely-there brush of the back of his hand against her cheek—and lightning had sparked through her, enlivening every cell, leaving no part of her untouched. She'd stood there and allowed it, the breath refusing to leave or enter her lungs.

And his dark, fathomless eyes… They'd captured hers and refused to let go. This wasn't mere surface curiosity, but some-thing deeper…more intense—a determination to know…

Everything.

About her.

But…

Why?

Why would Gem, the filth-encrusted stable-lad-turned-jockey, elicit even a speck of curiosity within the vaunted Duke of Rakesley?

Yet something else had sparked in his eyes.

A spark that sent a current of sensation tracing through her.

A spark that had made her want to sway into his capable, masculine hand and know its feel on other parts of her.

Then, like that, his hand dropped, and he broke the contact—the moment gone.

Except the moment wasn't gone.

It had stayed with her all day.

Now that she was alone, safely inside the refuge of her private room, she could release the breath she'd been holding for hours. The room was spare, but clean, with a small fireplace on one wall and a bed on the other. A table and chair. A stand topped by washbasin and water jug. *Serviceable*, that was this room.

She'd just unlaced and kicked off her boots when a single light knock sounded at the door. That was her evening meal tray delivered.

When he'd appointed the room for her, Wilson had also given her the option of taking her meals here—and she'd accepted the offer. Jockeys were in a class of their own and preferred their own company to that of the lads and grooms. She'd seen the type strutting about London stables.

Gemma waited until the soft tap of the maid's footsteps faded entirely before she opened the door and picked up her meal tray. She set the salver onto the table and got on with the part of her day she'd come to look forward to the most—the removal of the clothing that turned her into Gem.

A few shrugs of the shoulders and the coat five sizes too large was sliding down her arms. Trousers were quick to follow. Then her shirt was over her head and one last article of clothing remained. "Clothing"—a rather generous interpretation of the long swath of linen tightly wrapped around her chest. She untucked the end and shimmied her shoulders, encouraging the cloth to loosen and fall to the floor.

The next breath she drew was always her favorite of the day, her body—and particularly her breasts—finally free from restriction. She wasn't possessed of a particularly generous bosom, but what she did have was decidedly grateful for a few hours of respite every night.

Though Gem appeared to have never bathed in his life, the same couldn't be said for Gemma. Clad in naught but a pair of woolen socks, she stepped to the washbasin and gave herself an invigorating scrub. It was enough that Gem appeared filthy. She didn't actually have to *be* filthy.

Finally clean, she threw on a fresh shirt she'd borrowed from Liam, then gave the shirt she'd worn today a quick wash and hung it before the fire to dry.

Evening routine complete, she lifted her meal tray and then settled onto the middle of the bed with it. It was a strange little luxury she'd discovered—eating in bed. This must be how nobs felt every morning when their servants appeared at their bedsides with trays bearing tea and toast.

If it weren't for the stress of being Gem all day, every day, she could see herself rather taking to the indulged life of a jockey.

But that wasn't to be—not for any longer than a few weeks... and only if her luck held.

She bit into a chunk of stewed mutton and couldn't help idly wondering if Rakesley took meals in his bed.

The blasted man's eyes rose in her mind.

This morning, in his bathing room, there had been a moment...a moment where she would've sworn he'd known she wasn't who she said she was. But...

If that had been the case, wouldn't he have cast her out of Somerton and sent for the local magistrate for good measure?

But he hadn't.

Instead, he'd taken himself off to London to procure a new saddle for Hannibal and visit his clubs and whatever else dukes did with their time. A visit to Tattersall's. A visit to a mistress.

Yet she was still here for one very simple reason:

He didn't know.

And though the temptation had been strong to leg it to The Drunken Piebald, collect Liam, and flee Suffolk before he *did* know, she'd remained in the duke's employ.

She had too much at stake.

Her future and Liam's, in fact.

She couldn't walk away from all the blunt on the line.

Her nerve must hold.

She had no choice.

Rakesley didn't—*couldn't*—know.

And he wouldn't.

She would be doubly vigilant in her disguise as Gem—double the dirt, double the incomprehensibility of her mumbles, avoidance of all eye contact, hat slouched lower on her forehead.

And at the end of the next few weeks, she would be collecting £250.

A knock sounded on the door, startling Gemma so forcefully she nearly dumped her stew all over the bed. This was no discreet, muted tap that heralded the arrival of her meals. This was an insistent haranguing of oak.

"Gem," shouted an impatient voice, adding to the cacophony.

Gemma scrambled off the bed, calling out, "One minute," in as gruff a voice as she could muster at volume, grabbing trousers, boots, and coat, only remembering to jam her slouch hat onto her head just before she jerked open the door. "Is it Hannibal?" she demanded, heart racing, gut churning.

Cal shook his head. "The duke's favorite hunter, Flicka, is foalin' early, and the mite is comin' out all funny. Flicka is a right mess—all wild-eyed and scared, and ye've got yer way with horses and all…"

Gemma's brow gathered. Something wasn't adding up. "Did Wilson send for me?"

"He's in Newmarket for the night."

"And the animal surgeon?"

"He's been sent for."

Thank goodness for small blessings. "And the duke?"

"*Erm…*" Cal shuffled on his feet.

Gemma knew evasion when she saw it. "The duke's favorite

hunter is foaling. He needs to be notified, or it'll be you getting the sack."

Cal glanced up at Gemma—a little resentful, a little awed. "Ye've really taken to yer new place in the world, haven't ye, Gem?"

Gemma only just didn't snort. No doubt she'd just been called uppity.

"Notify the duke, and I'll see to Flicka," she said, brushing past Cal and taking the stairs two at a time. "And don't dawdle," she called over her shoulder.

"Aye," said Cal as he descended the stairs behind her. Gemma detected a distinct lack of appetite for the task.

No one wanted to deliver bad news to a duke.

But it wasn't Rakesley who concerned her. A mare and her foal were in trouble. She wasn't sure what she could do for them —she wasn't an animal surgeon, after all—but she could provide comfort and support.

There was no place she would rather be.

She suspected Rakesley would feel exactly the same.

She wasn't certain how she knew this about him.

She simply did.

* * *

RAKE STAMPED his wax seal on the final letter of correspondence for the day and sat back in his capacious leather chair.

The subject that had been hovering at the edges of his mind all day as he'd traveled up to London and back immediately swooped in and filled the void as it had been waiting to do.

Gem.

What was he going to do about Gem?

He snorted.

Gem wouldn't even be her real name, as it was a man's name.

For the sake of expediency, Gem would do, for now. But the question remained.

What the blazes was he going to do about Gem?

The possibilities for her deception had only multiplied over the course of the day, plunging him into a foul mood that no amount of new saddlery or drinks at Brooks's with friends could soothe.

Most of those possibilities cast Gem in the light of a scoundrel.

Again, he snorted. There he went again thinking of Gem as a lad—and Gem was no lad, but a lass.

And not merely a lass, but a woman.

As a lad, Gem looked to be of sixteen or seventeen years. But as a woman, Rake would put her in her twenties…

A woman.

A woman who was lying to him.

But here was the crucial thing—he didn't want to sack her. She was the most talented jockey he'd ever seen.

With Gem riding Hannibal, they were going to win the Two Thousand Guineas—and then on to the Race of the Century. However…

If London society discovered Gem to be a woman, it would be Rake's reputation in tatters.

And he would become a laughingstock.

The idea had his hands wanting to clench into fists.

Nay, not *idea*…

Memory.

The fact was he'd once been made the laughingstock of London by a woman.

Felicity.

Julian had spoken of Rake's single-mindedness in choosing who he loved, and Felicity was the reason. With her, he'd chosen wrongly and very publicly—and had become the butt of

London's favorite joke for a week or two until society moved on to some other unfortunate wretch.

But the experience had stayed with Rake, and he was none too keen to repeat it.

So...

Gem had to go.

That certainty was the true source of his foul mood—for deep in his gut, he'd known all day.

She was a woman.

But that wasn't the main thing.

She was a liar.

And that couldn't be tolerated.

Sudden anger flashed through him, and he pounded a frustrated fist against the checkered mahogany of his escritoire. The fact was he wouldn't be able to run Hannibal if Gem didn't ride the foul-tempered beast. It was too late to try someone else.

Blast.

Very rarely did things not go his way, and he found it intolerable when they didn't. He'd always—*always*—been able to squeeze a gain out of a loss.

Not always, a little voice reminded him. *Not with Felicity.*

He expelled a blustery sigh. *"Women."*

"Well, hello to you, too, brother," laughed a feminine voice.

Rake pulled himself from thoughts that could surely reach no satisfactory end and found Artemis already halfway across the room.

"You're too deep in thought," she said, propping a hip against a chaise longue and crossing her arms over her chest. A light smile played about her mouth. "That's never a good thing."

A dry laugh erupted from Rake. That was Artemis—ever in good spirits and ever honest, which could lead to interesting consequences. Like her telling an unfortunate truth with a smile on her lips. She had a way of brightening any situation.

"Come," she said, pushing off the sofa, "let me trounce you at billiards."

Rake snorted and followed his sister into the gaming room adjacent to his study. With the efficiency of experience, they each chose their preferred cue and set the two white balls and one red ball onto green felt.

Artemis propped a shoulder against the wall. "You can go first," she said with a smirk. "You look as if you need the leg up."

Rake didn't bother rising to her jibe. Instead, he leaned over the table, cue in hand. With a single precise strike, he sent her cue ball to one corner and the red ball to the other, potting both. "That'll be five points," he said.

It wasn't his early lead in the game that put a smile on his face, but rather, the quick explosion of controlled violence. It proved to be the release he needed.

But Artemis was no dull hand at billiards, and after a few rounds, she had them tied in points. She struck her cue and pocketed his before meeting his gaze across the wide expanse of the table. "What's troubling you, brother?"

He'd known the question wouldn't be long coming. "I have to get rid of Gem."

It only took an instant for Artemis's face to go from light and playful to dark and thunderous. "What's this?" she demanded. "First, you don't let me have him. Then you go and decide to sack him?"

"I'm not exactly happy about it," he groused. As a duke, his sister was the only person in the world to whom he could vent.

She nodded slowly. "Let me have him."

Rake shook his head. On this point, he was adamant. "He has to go. He can no longer be employed in our stables."

Artemis leaned over the table and struck a ball with more force than necessary, sending a ball flying.

"It wasn't your turn," Rake pointed out.

Artemis blew a gusty raspberry and pointed her cue directly

at the center of his chest, possibly considering running him through. "You are a damned frustrating man, brother. Why can't I have him for Dido?"

"Because he isn't who he says he is."

Artemis leaned over and struck her cue ball again. She'd clearly lost all care for the game. Now, she was the one who needed the release of controlled violence.

Of a sudden, she went stone still. Her brow furrowed, and when she straightened, a little smile played about her mouth. "Ah," she said. "I understand now."

"Understand what?" he asked slowly. He wasn't sure he wanted Artemis's understanding.

"You mean because Gem's a woman."

Rake caught his mouth before it gaped open. "You knew?"

Artemis shrugged. "Of course. Anyone with eyes could see."

"I didn't."

Artemis bit her bottom lip, as if on the verge of laughter. "I prefer not to comment." Her careful diplomacy was worse than outright laughter.

"And you never said anything?" Rake demanded. Couldn't she see this was serious business?

Again, Artemis shrugged, and Rake's teeth ground together. "Then you understand why he...*she*...must go."

"I understand no such thing."

His sister was fiddling on his last nerve. "She's a liar, therefore, she's untrustworthy."

Surely, Artemis would see the necessity of the situation.

But judging from the expression on her face, she saw no such thing. In fact, she was looking at him with such incredulity he began to wonder if he'd suddenly turned a noxious shade of mustard.

"How easy it is for you, Rake," she said with an uncharacteristic burn of intensity. "Sometimes I forget that."

"What are you on about, Artemis?"

He wasn't wrong about Gem, that much he knew.

"*You* are a duke with all the freedoms the title entails."

"And responsibilities," he pointed out. Responsibilities he'd never once shirked.

"You can do anything you please, any time it pleases you." She hadn't blinked once. "*Anything*, Rake."

"And you can't?"

"No, I can't. For the simple reason that I'm a woman."

"Artemis, what on earth have I ever denied you?"

"That's just it, brother. It's in your power to deny me. The life I live isn't mine for the taking, but rather, mine because you're a permissive brother who allows me to have it. Surely, you can see the difference."

And he did.

He didn't like it, but he did.

Artemis cocked a hip onto the billiards table. "I figure Gem has a good reason for disguising herself as a man. It's not easy in the world of horses for a woman whose interests and talents range in that direction. Haven't you considered as much?"

In fact, he had—therein lay the problem.

He wanted that to be the reason for Gem's deception—too much.

But a feeling wouldn't stop nagging at him. There was more to Gem.

And it was neither simple nor straightforward.

A light tap sounded on the door. "Expecting anyone?" asked Artemis.

Rake shook his head and called out, "You may enter."

The door opened a crack, and a stable lad sidled through, his hat in hand, his gaze on the dusty tips of his boots. Cal, he believed was the lad's name. "Flicka's foal is comin', and she's in trouble," said the lad in a rush.

Rake's billiards cue clattered to the table, alarm surging through him. "Did Wilson send you?"

The lad shook his head. "He's in—"

"Newmarket," supplied Artemis, who suddenly looked as anxious as Rake felt.

Rake's feet were already on the move. "Who sent you?"

"*Erm*, Gem, Your Grace."

Of course. Rake had become so fixated on what he didn't know about Gem that he'd lost sight of what he did. Like the fact she had nerve and audacity. She *would* send a stable lad to summon a duke.

"Good night, Artemis," he tossed over his shoulder as he strode out of the room.

Rake's mind racing as fast as his feet, it was a quick journey to the stables, which buzzed with an energy both tetchy and muted. Without Wilson around to send them packing, the lads and grooms loitered in the aisle outside the foaling box and spilled into the courtyard beyond. One saw Rake coming and nudged his neighbor, who elbowed his neighbor. Within a few seconds, they'd scattered to the four winds.

His presence tended to have that effect.

Silently, Rake stepped into the opening of the foaling box and found only three occupants inside—Flicka, Somerton's animal surgeon, Foley, and...

Gem.

Of course.

Sleeves rolled above his elbows, the sweat of exertion dripping down the sides of his face, Foley crouched at one end of the mare, trying his best to turn the foal, while Gem maintained a calm presence at Flicka's head. She'd folded her body so her legs were beneath the mare's neck, while she kept a firm hand on Flicka's shoulder. Her other hand stroked Flicka's head, as all the while she whispered into the distressed mare's ear.

Gem's gold-flecked, green eyes startled up and met his. As ever, a frisson of connection passed between them. She jutted her chin, and it took Rake a moment to understand the import of the gesture. She was beckoning him over to help soothe Flicka. She intuited he would need to make himself useful.

Strange, that... That she understood something so fundamental and true about him.

He closed the few feet between them, directing a nod toward Foley, and lowered beside Gem at Flicka's head. He began stroking the mare's velvety nose and making a shushing sound between his teeth, instinct guiding him. He sensed Gem's approval and couldn't understand why it would matter to him—but it did.

Foley shot them a quick glance across the length of Flicka's outstretched body. "The foal is in good position now. On the next contraction, let's get him delivered. *Now steady on.*"

Serious and calm, Gem nodded. She was ready beside Rake.

Time went still as they waited, then raced ahead as Flicka delivered her foal like it were an everyday occurrence. "Well done, old girl," said Rake, relief rushing through him with such force he felt nearly giddy with it.

Foley stood and washed his hands in a nearby bucket, toweling them off as he offered a proper greeting to Rake. Though he wasn't sure he wanted to, Rake gave Flicka's nose a parting stroke and came to his feet, leaving the mare in the capable hands of Gem.

While he conversed with Foley, Rake kept half an eye on Gem as she settled back onto her haunches and watched Flicka tend her foal. She accepted he was no longer needed by the pair, who were now bonding. But her work wasn't finished. She grabbed a pitchfork and began mucking out the box.

Gem hadn't an idle bone in her lissome body, had she?

Lissome...fetching...a beauty...

That was no productive way to be thinking about his jockey.

Foley finished scrubbing and packing the implements of his trade into a capacious, leather satchel. "Flicka had a hard time of it. You'll want a lad in here with them for the night."

Gem didn't hesitate. "I'll see them through."

Rake wouldn't have expected any other response.

Yet one more fact he knew about the mysterious Gem.

The Gem he was planning to sack.

He supposed the sacking could wait until tomorrow.

Satchel in hand, Foley thanked Gem and spoke his farewells. Then the animal surgeon was gone—and Rake was left alone with his jockey.

He felt no small bit useless in the face of Gem's efficient industry while he stood idle. "You're a jockey now," he said. "You don't have to muck out boxes anymore. There are more than thirty lads at Somerton who can do that."

She shrugged and didn't stop pitching hay. "I don't want a lad coming in and unsettling Flicka," she mumbled. "Besides, I prefer the work."

"Can I help?" he found himself asking.

Was he truly offering to help muck out? What was his world coming to?

Gem appeared not to think anything of it. "I'm nearly finished. Can you fetch a few clean blankets from the saddle room?"

Rake moved to fulfill the request that sounded more like a command. How was it that this woman, disguised as a man, was so comfortable ordering a duke around?

When he returned with the blankets, he found the occupants of the foaling box busy and contented each in their own way—Flicka tending her new foal, the foal happily nursing, and Gem packing the last of the fresh hay against the box walls to prevent a draft.

At last, she straightened and swiped the sweat off her brow with the back of her hand, eyes closed with exhaustion and relief. Rake opened his mouth to ask where she wanted the blankets when a small movement of her shoulder froze him in place, and all he could do was watch.

A single, feminine shrug, followed by a subtle arcing of her back. A working out of the kinks in her muscles. Then another shrug, and a roll of her head. Unguarded, her voluminous, worn-to-threads coat fell open at the front, revealing a man's shirt, laces loose, so a V opened down the center of her chest, giving a hint of what lay beneath, and Rake's mouth went dry.

A *hint*?

He would say more than a hint. Twin peaks of nipples puckered beneath the fabric.

Given her red-gold hair and ivory freckled skin, her nipples would be rose-hued.

He was halfway to a cockstand just thinking about those nipples.

Unbound.

She must've been interrupted in the process of preparing for bed and had neglected to bind her breasts before coming to the foaling box.

She'd have rushed without thinking. The hour was late—gone past midnight—and she'd been distracted. Too distracted to pretend to be the lad she wasn't and, instead, *be*...herself.

What else could explain what he was witnessing—and all but gawking at like a green youth catching a stolen first glimpse of female flesh?

Right.

He cleared his throat. "The blankets."

Gem visibly gathered herself before opening her eyes and stepping forward to take the blankets from his outstretched arms, leaving him one. "Thank you." A beat ticked past before she remembered to add, "Your Grace."

When Rake didn't move, she shifted on her feet and muttered, "I'm sure you have somewhere else to be."

She was trying to get rid of him.

"As it happens," he began, all aristocratic arrogance, "I don't."

Her mouth twitched with annoyance. She couldn't very well tell a duke to leave his own stables.

"I'll help," he said, stepping around her and shaking open his blanket.

In unison and without conversation, they spread blankets over mare and foal, a strange sense of comradery stealing in as they completed the task.

"I'll be sleeping here tonight," she said, tossing her sole remaining blanket onto the hay.

Rake almost said he would, too, but stopped before he made a fool of himself.

He was the duke. He didn't sleep in foaling boxes to see horses through the night. He paid people to do that.

Like the person before him.

The person he would be giving the sack tomorrow.

The person staring at him with a curious expression in her eyes.

Right.

He spoke a gruff farewell and turned on his heel, vacating the foaling box and stable without further ado. As his boots crunched against crushed gravel, he realized that, in the course of this night, a certainty had crept in. More than one certainty, in fact.

He admired Gem.

He might respect her too.

And yet another certainty followed.

He wouldn't be giving her the sack tomorrow.

Or any other day.

True, she had her secrets—but didn't they all?

The fact was, she was born to work with horses. It was her talent and passion, and who was he to deny her?

Deny himself, in fact.

It wasn't that he wouldn't let her go.

He *couldn't* let her go.

So, he would let her keep her secret.

And yet...could matters simply carry on as they had been?

The fact was, he felt a powerful, unexpected pull toward this woman he both knew and didn't know at all.

This pull was about more than her talent and skill.

It was a pull toward the physical.

He desired her—*wanted* her—in a way that felt new.

This wasn't the familiar desire for beautiful flesh—though that was part of it.

It also had to do with that talent and skill of hers—her capability.

And possibly the character he detected within her.

The simple answer was he would stay away from her.

Gem had a job, and all Rake had to do was leave her to it.

A vow that sounded simple in his mind.

And doubtful in practice.

Could he know her for a woman and not want her as a woman?

That was the question.

And the answer was—possibly for the first time in his life—he wasn't sure.

CHAPTER TEN

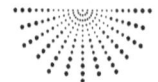

*G*emma gave Hannibal's lustrous black mane one final stroke of the brush and, without thinking, leaned over to set the tool on the half wall separating his box from the next.

A stab of pain shot through her, eliciting a wince and a grunt, her hand immediately reaching for her lower back and applying firm pressure.

It had been a long, bruising day.

A long, bruising week, in fact.

Wilson had returned from Newmarket with a trainer—one Mr. Blankenship. The man had taken over Hannibal's training schedule. Gemma had been wary at first and had complained to Liam. But, as usual, her brother had talked her around. "Hannibal could win one race with natural ability, but not an entire season. A horse has to be tested to become the best. People aren't much different when you think about it. And don't forget that. They're also testing you."

Gemma supposed Liam was right.

But that didn't mean she had to like Blankenship, with his rigid bearing and cold, calculating stare. And it certainly didn't mean she had to accept all his methods. The exercise and feed schedule, she'd come to agree with, even if she did slip Hannibal a few slices of apple or turnip here and there.

The sweating of Hannibal, she was less sure about. It was the prevailing practice of all racing stables to sweat a horse to dissipate excessive heat and prevent illness. Many trainers took it too far by piling layer upon layer of blankets onto a horse's back to achieve the desired sweating. While Gemma didn't speak openly against the practice, she didn't sweat Hannibal half as often as Blankenship instructed.

However, Gemma had put her foot firmly down on one front —the use of crop and spur.

She wouldn't.

That was the end of it.

Blankenship must've been quite accustomed to always having his way, for he'd turned a livid shade of crimson at her refusal. She could've given him the show—as Liam had suggested—and donned spurs and carried a crop without using them, but she'd chosen not to.

Instead, she'd made a different choice—to stand her ground. The practice of whipping and spurring horses would never change if more people didn't openly repudiate the practice. Chifney had shown such implements were unnecessary when he'd won race after race without them, proving that methods of force were the lazy—and cruel—way to pressure a horse into doing one's bidding. Less physically aggressive methods got the best out of a horse, but most trainers and jockeys refused to listen.

But, with Hannibal, Gemma held a trump card.

She was the only jockey he would allow on his back, so she'd won the battle.

No crop and spur.

A mean, little thrill of triumph sparked through her at the memory of Blankenship's thin lips pressed into a straight line. He hadn't wanted to yield but had to.

Now, however, as Gemma bent to grab a bucket and dump its contents into the alley, it occurred to her that Blankenship may have had the last laugh. The training this week had been a step beyond bruising.

It had been punishing.

And every muscle in her body felt it—from the tension in her neck and shoulders all the way down her legs. Somehow, even her calves were sore. It wasn't only Hannibal who was being trained into fine racing form, but her as well. Liam had been correct on that score.

This week she'd discovered muscles she hadn't known existed. Rather than rising from bed, she'd taken to rolling over, then scooching and scuttling out from beneath the covers. When she began to move, the muscles loosened, increment by stiff increment, but if she remained still for the any length of time, her muscles took the opportunity to tighten up again.

Wilson had noticed and asked if she was fit to ride. She'd brushed off the question. As for Blankenship, a little, knowing smile had curled at the corners of his stingy mouth. He knew what he was doing, that man.

Now, she held her breath and straightened, slowly, carefully. It was only when she was fully upright that she released a slow, measured exhalation. A slight movement caught the corner of her eye, and she gave a mild start when she saw it was a footman.

Nerves shimmered through her. Footmen ever made her tetchy. They were so tall and handsome and so very aware of both. But it wasn't for that reason *this* footman made her nervous. Only when one was being summoned by the duke, did *this* footman appear.

"His Grace has requested your presence in his study."

"Has he?" she asked, the question a reflex, a little rebellion.

The footman blinked. "Indeed."

Oh, but this duke's footman was a haughty creature.

As was the duke who issued his orders.

She exhaled a rather self-pitying, long-suffering sigh and finished her routine of settling Hannibal for the night. Only then, she muttered a grumbly, "After you."

As Gemma entered the house through the kitchen, the memory came to her of the only other time she'd been inside the house proper.

The day she'd watched a duke shave.

A sliver of heat curled through her.

A *half-clad* duke.

Which was only another way of saying a *half-naked* duke.

She squeezed her eyes shut for an instant, willing the image away, and concentrated on the footman's back.

Though she'd spent the first nineteen years of her life in an earl's household, its splendor hadn't sufficiently prepared her for the opulence of a duke's household. Every room, from chairs to sofas to the walls themselves, was done in bright silks—one room floor-to-ceiling peacock blue, the next tranquil rose and cream, and the next cheery sunshine yellow. A color for every mood.

After they'd traversed no fewer than eight corridors, the footman finally stopped at a closed door and gave a light knock.

A muted, "Enter," sounded through solid oak.

She'd been expecting the study to hold a single occupant—Rakesley—but as Gemma moved deeper into the room all done in rich mahogany and walnut woods, she registered three occupants bent over a large, rectangular table—Rakesley, his sister Lady Artemis, and the Marquess of Ormonde.

At Gemma's hesitant approach, all eyes swung her direction. My, but they were a handsome, imposing trio. One couldn't help but be impressed and a little awed by their combined aristocratic glory.

Gemma didn't often regret her disguise, but there were times she wished she hadn't made herself quite so filthy and repulsive. For instance, when she was in a duke's study with three sets of noble eyes assessing her from moth-eaten hat to muck-encrusted boot.

"Ah, Gem," said Lady Artemis, her ever-present smile beaming. "Just the person we wanted to see."

Lady Artemis contained a bit of sunshine inside her. One couldn't help but feel warmed by it. The Marquess of Ormonde gave a nod of greeting. He seemed nice. If Lady Artemis contained sunshine, then Lord Ormonde looked like sunshine personified with his longish blond hair, bright blue eyes, and easy smile.

Gemma returned their greetings with a short, sufficient nod, but her gaze couldn't help being drawn toward Rakesley.

Dark...unfathomable...magnificent.

Almost too handsome to behold directly.

And when she—inevitably—met his eyes, she found she'd been wrong in her assessment. They were no longer inscrutable to her. She read connection there—and something else.

Awareness.

A slow shiver purled up her spine. Within his gaze lay depths unexplored.

Depths unexplored places inside her wanted to know...

Desired to know.

Oh.

Rakesley gave two sharp taps of forefinger onto tabletop. Gemma startled and blinked, pulled from thoughts that were creating uncomfortable sensations in her body.

"We asked you here to settle a matter," he said, beckoning her closer with a jerk of his chin.

Gemma stepped forward and winced. It was always the first step that was the worst.

Rakesley's brow furrowed. "Are you injured?" The question held the timbre of a demand.

She shook her head. "Merely sore."

"You didn't take a fall from Hannibal?" He looked slightly...*thunderous.*

Again, she shook her head. "Nay." But Rakesley's unappeased gaze told her she would have to explain. "Hannibal's new training regimen has entered a, *erm*, vigorous phase."

Rakesley's gaze searched hers until, at last, he nodded, mollified.

Strange, that.

That he'd needed to be mollified.

And that she'd known it.

She shuffled to a spot at the large table on the end the farthest away from Rakesley. Splayed across its vast surface were four large rectangles of paper, each containing meticulous racecourse drawings—the Rowley and Ditch Miles at Newmarket and the courses at Epsom Downs and Doncaster. These were the racecourses where the five main races of the season took place. Scribbled in the margins were notes—dips and divots on the turf, wet-to-dry conditions, the angle of the sun at every hour of the day... No detail was too minute to be marked down.

"Blimey!" Gemma exclaimed, her reaction eliciting chuckles from the gathered. Even Rakesley smiled.

"You only thought Rake was serious about his racing," said Lord Ormonde. "Now you know."

"No half measures for my brother," said Lady Artemis.

Rakesley accepted the ribbing with good humor, which spoke well of the man and his relationship with his sister and friend.

Gemma saw him—necessarily—as someone to be avoided at best, and an adversary, at worst. After all, she was spying on his racing operation. They weren't friends, no matter the connection that pulled between them when their gazes met.

Her body's reaction to that connection suggested it had naught to do with friendship.

But rather that other word...

Desire.

She wasn't a virgin. She knew this feeling.

Except...

She'd never felt it like this.

Like the merest meeting of their gazes sparked a blaze inside her capable of turning her into a pool of molten lava.

She gave her head a little shake, hoping to clear it of ideas that could only get her into a parcel of trouble. "You summoned me to show me the courses?" she asked, reaching for a topic.

"I summoned you here to ask for your assessment of the turf at Somerton," said the duke. "How is Hannibal handling it?"

"It's the best turf I've ever encountered," said Gemma, truthfully.

"Would my brother have any other sort of turf?" inserted Lady Artemis.

"But," continued Gemma, a not-insignificant fact occurring to her.

"*But...what?*" prodded Rakesley. There seemed to be something he wished her to speak aloud.

"The Two Thousand Guineas is run on the Rowley Mile, which is dry and hard." In fact, it was the most severely testing of all the racecourses in England.

"See?" said Rakesley, now looking at his sister as if he'd just won a bet. "I keep telling you to enter Dido in the One Thousand Guineas. The Ditch Mile would suit her better."

"You know what I think, brother?" asked Lady Artemis.

"What is that?" Rakesley asked, leery.

"I think you're afraid of my Dido besting your Hannibal."

From what Gemma had observed on Somerton's practice course this last week, Lady Artemis made a valid point. Simply put, Dido's speed was blistering. She could very well beat

Hannibal on a straight, which the Rowley Mile was. But for all Dido's sweetness and speed, she possessed an unsettled spirit and needed to be handled delicately. "You need to race her from the lead," said Gemma without thinking.

It was only when all three sets of eyes landed on her that she realized no one had asked for her opinion. "That's how Dido will win races," she continued for some reason. "You'll have to work on her starts."

When Lady Artemis opened her mouth to surely ask Gemma to elucidate further, Rakesley held up a staying hand. "Artemis, Gem is my jockey, not yours. You'll be wanting to consult with Deeds about your race day strategy."

Lady Artemis caught Gemma's gaze. "Thank you, Gem. I shall pass along your suggestions."

Deeds was Dido's jockey. He'd arrived with Blankenship from Newmarket and possessed a distrustful, ferrety demeanor. Gemma intuited that if the man ever took the time to really look at her, he would see through her disguise in three seconds flat. She gave him a wide berth.

Lady Artemis's eyebrows crinkled together. "Gem, are you quite alright?"

Gemma only just realized she'd begun rubbing her lower back. Nothing got past Lady Artemis.

"I'm, *erm*," began Gemma, trying to think of anything that would deflect the group's attention. "Stiff muscles," she settled for muttering.

She shifted and propped an elbow on the table, hoping to appear relaxed. Everyone's creased brows suggested she appeared the opposite. She'd likely winced.

Lady Artemis's face went bright, like a wondrous idea had occurred to her this very instant.

Gemma tensed further.

"I know precisely what you need."

Gemma only just didn't groan. Lady Artemis would mean well, but...

"A long soak in a hot bath."

Gemma felt her mouth gape open and barely thought to close it. When Rakesley began to nod in agreement, her jaw dropped again.

"Would you mind if I asked you a personal question?" he asked, the query directed square at Gemma.

Personal.

Which meant pertaining to her person.

Every cell in her person screamed *no, no, no,* even as she gave a curt nod of assent.

"Have you ever taken a bath?"

Indignation flared through her. "Of course, I have."

The cheek!

His dark gaze narrowed. "Not a washing up, but a bath. A proper bath in a proper tub."

"I've washed in a tub." In second, and sometimes third-hand water, but he didn't need to know that.

He gave a slow, measured nod. He seemed to know it, anyway. "That's what I thought."

Annoyance bolstered by a large dose of recklessness flared through Gemma. "What do you care if I've had a bath?"

"You're Hannibal's jockey, and since I plan on him taking the entire season—"

"Hey," piped up Lady Artemis and Lord Ormonde in unison. But their protest was only half-hearted with a good amount of humor.

"—I need you to be in your best form," he finished.

Lady Artemis shook her head and chuckled. "Oh, brother, you can be such a duke sometimes."

"And who doesn't know it," Gemma mumbled, provoking another hearty round of laughter.

Rakesley, as ever, remained undeterred. "As the Duke of

Rakesley, I cannot have my jockey walking around like an old man and, for that matter, *smelling* like an East End beggar."

Oh, that last part was low.

But not entirely unearned, Gemma could concede.

"Now," he continued. The blasted man seemed...*triumphant.* "You'll have a bath."

While Lady Artemis and Lord Ormonde looked at her with sympathy in their eyes, she could see they agreed whole-heartedly with Rakesley on both points—and perhaps the latter in particular. It hadn't only been Hannibal sweating buckets today. She had too. A particular musky scent wafted about whenever she lifted an arm.

And that settled the matter.

Not half an hour later, Gemma found herself gingerly lowering her aching, unclothed body into the Duke of Rakesley's deep bathing tub, lavender-infused steam rising from the surface.

Her eyes drifted shut, and a long exhale poured from her lungs. It was quite possibly the best her body had felt in a week— possibly *ever*—as she sank so low her chin dipped below the piping-hot surface. Like magic, the tension in her muscles began releasing, increment by slow increment.

She would have to find a way to thank Lady Artemis for this.

She might even consider thanking Rakesley.

Then she drifted away on a sea of lavender, her parting thought *maybe.*

CHAPTER ELEVEN

*R*ake was unable to settle.

That was all there was to it.

One moment he was seated before the fire that ever burned low in his bedroom's fireplace—even in summer, for Somerton was a drafty old pile—and the next he was striding across the room and staring sightlessly out the window that was black with night.

Yet, again, he was on the move, this time finding the brandy cart where he filled a crystal tumbler half full.

One sip later, he was at loose ends again.

Of course, how could he possibly settle?

Gem was only two doors away, in his bathing room...soaking in his bathing tub...her fetching bottom sliding against slick enamel...her pert nipples breaching the water's surface...

Naked.

Every so often his ear picked up the muted splash of water.

Which didn't invite calm into his body.

Quite the opposite, in fact.

She hadn't needed to bathe in his tub.

That was the truth.

He could've instructed the maid to lead her to any number of the many guest bathing rooms scattered throughout the house. He calculated at least ten of them.

But, no, he'd had Gem led to *his* private bathing tub.

He hadn't planned it.

That was his defense.

In fact, if he'd given the matter a moment's forethought, he surely would've had her placed in one of those ten other bathing tubs.

Surely.

Wouldn't he?

Because he'd vowed to stay away from Gem, and he'd succeeded this last week.

Inviting her to bathe in his rooms was the very opposite of keeping away from Gem and letting her do her job.

Of course, he could leave. He could easily walk out of this room and go to his study and leave her to bathe in peace…

But he couldn't.

Not with her bathing—*naked*—thirty feet away, no matter how many closed doors stood between them.

Flimsy…cheap… Those were the adjectives someone might use to describe his excuses.

But he thought he could live with them.

He grabbed a tight cylinder of paper and strode to the table at the opposite end of the room. He set the tumbler of brandy down and then unrolled the paper until it lay flat, placing weights on the four corners to prevent the edges from curling. While he had Gem up here, they might as well discuss Epsom in further detail.

A faint sound drew Rake upright, ear cocked.

A voice…a woman's voice…soft, raspy, direct…

Her voice.

Through the closed doors of dressing and bathing rooms came a muted, *"Hello?"*

Every muscle in Rake's body tensed.

He should send for the maid… He should send for the maid… *He should send for the maid.*

A few weighty beats of time ticked past. "Your Grace?"

He heard it plain in her voice. *Confusion.*

Well, he was confused too.

At himself.

A few more seconds of silence ticked by.

And he knew why.

He waited for the inevitable.

"*Erm*, Your Grace?" she called out, louder, firmer.

"Yes?" He knew precisely what her next words would be.

He crossed the room and opened the dressing room door. So he could hear her better, he told himself.

Flimsy…cheap…

"My clothes seem to have vanished."

And here they were—the words he'd been waiting for.

"The scullery grabbed them while you were napping and took them for a wash."

"A…a…a *wash*?" No mistaking the panic in that voice.

"I believe you're now acquainted with the concept."

No mistaking the indignant, feminine gasp that flew through the door. If Rake hadn't known Gem for a woman before, he would've certainly had it confirmed now.

"They'll be returned to you on the morrow."

The words were met with weighty silence. That wouldn't have gone over well. Mostly due to the length of linen he'd pulled from the clothing pile as the scullery had passed him in the corridor.

That flimsy length of linen was Gem's most vital secret to being *Gem*.

"*Tomorrow?*" A cacophonous riot of splashing sounded as if it would flood the entire upper story. "Is this a kidnapping?" she demanded.

He snorted. "Hardly. I believe you're here of your own volition."

"I'm beginning to wonder," she shouted.

"There's clothing beside the door that will do for the present."

As wet footsteps slapped against marble tile, he anticipated precisely what she would find.

A man's shirt.

And only a man's shirt.

His shirt, in fact.

Flimsy...cheap...

"I have a change of clothes in my room," she called out. "I must insist you send for them."

A reasonable insistence, to be sure.

One he wouldn't be honoring in a hurry.

"Are you planning to stay in my bathing room until your clothes arrive?"

That got another ten seconds of silence by way of response.

"Perhaps you'll find my shirt will do for now," he said. "It's only us lads."

Now that was a fair bit of audacity on his part.

Audacious... Yet another adjective.

What had gotten into him?

Was he that desperate?

He didn't much like the immediate answer provided by his gut.

But, really, the true question was—how audacious was Gem? How far was she willing to take her ruse?

"Meet me at the table on the opposite end of the room once you've dressed," he said. "I've more race strategy I wish to discuss with you."

A long sigh of resignation just carried to him. The ball was well and truly in her court now.

No denying he'd gone about matters flimsily, cheaply, and audaciously, but she held all the power in reality. She could step out of the bathing room, claim her womanhood, and put an end to the charade in a few quick seconds.

The door to the bathing room creaked open, and tension filled Rake's body.

Soft footsteps padded across dense Aubusson carpet, then she appeared in the doorway connecting dressing room to bedroom, and Rake's mouth went dry.

His white muslin shirt reaching her knees, she hesitated at the threshold, shoulders hunched forward so as to give no indication of the feminine form beneath, gaze warily searching the room for him.

Relief streaked through Rake. She'd made the choice to continue the ruse...

To continue the game.

He wasn't ready for this person to march out of his life. He didn't yet know nearly enough about her.

Another feeling stole in alongside the relief.

Desire.

While she was thoroughly, if inappropriately, covered, her feet were yet bare...her slender ankles and calves too. She held the V of the shirt tightly clutched before her, which only...*well*... which only drew his gaze toward taut nipples shadowy within white muslin. He detected a hint of color. *Rose.*

In truth, her nipples were making a minor spectacle of themselves. His cock noticed and wanted to join the show.

He tore his attention from her nipples and gave his throat a loud clearing, pulling her gaze toward him. What shone within those gold-flecked, green depths was vulnerable and feminine and lasted for only the split of a second, but long enough for him to register it—and store it away.

Her jaw clenched. Annoyance and determination swept away uncertainty and provided a shield for the true Gem to hide behind.

It struck Rake how exhausting her disguise must've been.

Was any woman that desperate to muck out horse stalls?

"I take it you've sent for my change of clothes?" were the first words out of her mouth.

Rake gave a noncommittal *mmm* and beckoned her closer. "Come and see this."

Footsteps hesitant, she picked her way across the room. He caught a hint of lavender and couldn't help breathing it in.

She walked to the opposite side of the table and scanned the drawing lit by a single candlestick. Her gaze lifted, and she cocked a curious eyebrow. "Do you eat, sleep, and breathe horses?"

"Like you?" he returned.

A laugh escaped her before she could tamp it down.

But he'd caught it.

Was that the first time he'd made her laugh?

He rather liked her laughter. It suited her.

He wanted to make her laugh again, but the look in her eyes made it clear it wouldn't be easy. She was still entirely annoyed with him.

He couldn't say he blamed her.

"What course is this?" she asked.

"Epsom."

"Where the Derby and the Oaks are run."

"It also happens to be where the Race of the Century will take place."

Humor shone within her eyes. "Are you, perhaps, getting a little ahead of yourself?"

It was he who was all seriousness when he tapped the paper. "Hannibal will be there."

With you on his back, he caught himself before saying. She'd only just stopped being openly hostile to him. He shouldn't push his luck.

She moved to the side of the table adjacent to his, knuckles showing white as her grip on the shirt relented not one whit.

Closer.

That was all his body comprehended.

She was closer.

"Though I was hoping for Goodwood."

"Goodwood?" Her head canted with curiosity. "I'm not familiar with that course."

"It's the best racecourse in the country," said Rake, matter-of-fact. "One description I've heard is there's an elasticity in the air which communicates itself to the turf."

Another laugh from Gem.

"More concretely," he continued, "is it's located on the Duke of Richmond's land, and he runs his course like a tight ship. Horses are saddled in public view. Starts are punctual. That sort of thing."

"Then why aren't more major races run there?"

Rake waved a dismissive hand. "The usual reasons. Tradition. Politics. Petty personal grievances. The racing world runs rife with all three."

Gem nodded. "Isn't that what makes the racing world go round?"

"A fair point."

Drawn by curiosity, she moved to his side of the table. With her free hand, she reached across him to point out this or that particularity about Epsom. Rake hardly registered her questions or the answers he gave. He was too busy inhaling and picking up the scent of lavender from her hair—her clean and slightly damp red-gold hair. She'd pulled it back into the familiar queue, but a few errant curls had escaped. He only caught himself before reaching out and tucking one behind her ear.

He needed to get a hold of himself.

Yes, Gem was a woman.

But she was his jockey.

That was all.

And now his jockey was regarding him with a quizzical

expression on her face. She'd asked a question—and expected an answer.

"Or is that impertinent of me to ask?"

She'd not only asked a question, but an impertinent one.

Blast.

"Possibly," he ventured. It seemed a safe response.

"I don't understand it. Not many owners invite their competition to tea to discuss track qualities. They tend to want to keep that information for themselves."

Ah. She was wondering about Artemis and Julian.

Truly, it was impertinent of her.

But, strangely, he never minded her impertinences.

"Artemis and Julian are my biggest competition, but they're also my sister and best friend, respectively. They're family." He let that settle into the air before continuing. "While I eat, sleep, and breathe horses—as you so aptly put it—I won't sacrifice my relationship with my family for a win."

Understanding entered Gem's eyes. And something else. Something he hadn't known until this very moment that he'd wanted from her.

Respect.

"That's a rare thing," she said, nodding as if arriving at a conclusion. "So, that's why."

"*Why* what?"

"Why you've been pushing Lady Artemis to run Dido in the One Thousand Guineas instead of the Two Thousand."

He confirmed it for her. "I want Hannibal and Dido to meet head-to-head for the first time at the Race of the Century."

"But surely they'll meet at the Derby when colts and fillies race together again after the Oaks."

Rake shook his head. "Julian's Filthy Habit will take the Derby."

"How can you—" Her eyes went wide with realization. "*Oh.*"

Her eyebrows drew together at a thunderous angle. "If Hannibal wins the Two Thousand Guineas—"

"*When* Hannibal wins the Two Thousand Guineas," he inserted.

"—you're not racing him again until the Race of the Century."

She was quick—and correct. "I've decided not to risk him. A win at the Two Thousand will assure him his place."

Gem wasn't giving up. "But Hannibal could take the Triple Crown this season."

Rake shrugged. "I don't care about the Triple Crown."

She blinked, and her brow released. "You care about your sister and friend more."

"Don't get my intentions twisted around," said Rake. "Come September, Hannibal will beat Dido and Filthy Habit by three lengths."

"You're ensuring all three horses will be there."

"If Fate decrees."

"*Fate?*" scoffed Gem, incredulous. "And since when has Fate been named the Duke of Rakesley?"

Rake remained serious. "They still have to win their races." Something more needed to be said. "And I won't cheat to get them there, if that's what you're thinking."

Gem shook her head—and another red-gold tendril loose. "Not at all." But she was clearly thinking something. "You have doubts about Dido."

"Aye." A beat. "As do you."

"She's fast."

"Her speed is blistering."

"But…"

"You were right about the correct way to race her," he said. "From the lead."

"The start will be the key."

"If the blacklegs catch wind of Dido, we'll have twenty false starts on race day."

Gem nodded, pensive. "To rattle her."

"Indeed."

Rake found that, in the course of the discussion, many happenings had occurred. Gem's grip on the shirt had, first, loosened, then fallen away entirely, leaving the V unguarded and open, exposing creamy flesh...the subtle curve of her breasts beneath.

Further, her speaking voice had altered. Nay, not changed, but she'd begun speaking in a voice entirely her own, and he noticed subtleties within it. The raspy quality no longer gruff but possessed of a warmth and sensual femininity.

She'd forgotten who she was pretending to be and was simply being herself.

He noticed something else.

The look in her eyes when she glanced up at him. Within lay a suggestion that she'd taken note of a few things about him too.

Yet it was more than mere observation.

Awareness.

That was what he saw in her eyes.

Awareness of herself.

As a woman.

Awareness of him.

As a man.

Awareness of *them*.

As something that could be.

Of its own accord, his hand reached for a loose tendril and tucked it behind her ear.

And she let him.

His hand didn't return to his side. Instead, light fingertips traced the whorl of her ear...touched the ivory column of her neck...slid around...wove through silky hair the color of an autumn sunset...unloosing the leather tie, so her curls now fell free...

And her direct, gold-flecked green eyes didn't flinch or shift.

In fact, as his head instinctively angled down, she might've lifted onto the tips of her toes, so her parted mouth was but a hairsbreadth from his...the soft susurration of her breath a light whisper of air across his lips...

Which left him with but one choice...

CHAPTER TWELVE

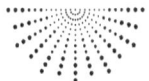

*P*ulled along by utter and complete, impatient and irresistible—*absolute*—want, Gemma strained upward. Her breath caught in her throat...until...*at last*...her mouth touched his—lips firm, but yielding, against hers...

He tasted of brandy, delicious and intoxicating, as his tongue stroked her bottom lip. She groaned into his mouth, and her tongue met his and she fell headlong into his kiss.

Of a sudden, hands were everywhere. Hers tousling through his dark hair. One of his woven through her curls, the other at the small of her back, pulling her close...*closer*...so close her body now strained against him...the length of his manhood thick and *hard* against her stomach.

Another groan poured from her. This one borne of pure, impatient lust.

Her body had become a vessel of raw, needy ache. It *needed* the feel—the *fullness*—of *that* inside her *now*.

Yet...through the desire prickled another feeling...

Unease.

And it struck her.

She was Gem...

Rakesley—the man she was presently mad with desire for—thought her Gem.

Rakesley was kissing...*Gem*.

On a muffled yip of distress, she planted firm hands in the center of his chest and gave a determined push, breaking them apart.

Panting for breath, they stared at one another. She detected surprise in his eyes, but nothing near the shock and confusion currently rioting through her.

"You..." she gasped. She hadn't properly caught her breath. She might never catch it again. "You were kissing *Gem*."

His gaze went opaque. "Aren't *you* Gem?"

"I...I..."

Oh, how to answer such a question...

"I know."

She blinked. That *I know* caught her on the back foot. It didn't sound like agreement, but rather like acknowledgement.

Every part of her went still as stone—except her heart, which battered wildly against her ribs. "What do you know?" A question she found the nerve to ask...but not the nerve to complete. *That I'm a spy?*

"*I know.*"

The way he was looking at her with curiosity rather than anger...

She knew.

He *knew*.

Still, their combined knowledge refused to penetrate her mind. "You know," she said, seeking confirmation.

His hand lifted, as if he were about to touch her, and she took a step backward. Little good could come from him touching her again.

Her body, on the other hand, could think of a lot of good him touching her again could do...

Bodies could be incredibly frustrating vessels.

He cocked a hip against the table and crossed his arms over his chest. His silence was almost worse than his words.

Almost.

Her instinct told her to run.

But what good would running do?

Because the fact was Rakesley *knew.*

Which meant he'd *known.*

Past tense.

Which meant he'd known her for a woman...and hadn't sacked her.

Yet.

If she ran, however, he would have no choice.

And all would be lost—two hundred and fifty pounds...her and Liam's future.

No.

She couldn't let that happen.

Audacity had brought her this far.

Audacity would see her through.

Mirroring him, she crossed her arms over her chest, great folds of muslin gathering beneath her arms. She would ignore the fact his shirt smelled deliciously of him—sandalwood combined with *male.* "So, you know I'm a woman," she said with as much insouciance as she could muster. "What of it?"

Oh, that was certainly audacious.

Surprise flashed behind his eyes, and one corner of his mouth lifted. Was that a smile threatening?

Then the smile disappeared before it could fully reveal itself. "Why are you here?" he asked, low, serious.

Though a warning sounded in his tone, she didn't heed it. "You're the one who summoned me to your study, then insisted I take a bath. *Then* you stole..." The rest of her words fizzled away when he began shaking his head.

"Why are you *here* at Somerton?"

She sniffed and drew herself fully upright, which left her

several inches shy of his towering height. "I came to work in your stables," she tried.

"True. But...*why?*"

"I love horses."

Thus, she was able to adhere close to the truth, but a feeling nagged that it wouldn't hold.

He gave a slow nod. "That's apparent. And you're good at tending them. No, not *good*."

Gemma felt her brow furrowing.

"You're the best I've ever seen."

She tried not to warm to his praise—and failed.

The best.

But his praise sparked another feeling. One that had begun to gnaw at her these last few days.

Guilt.

"But that's not why you're at Somerton," he said, certain.

"It's not?"

Rakesley shook his head and spoke so low she found herself straining forward to hear him. "Is that why the lord sent you?"

The breath froze in her chest. "*The lord?*" she barely managed. "What lord?"

"The lord you're spying for, of course."

Gemma's stomach fell to her feet. Her voice wanted to desert her, but she couldn't let it. "I'm not spying for a lord."

Another truth. Deverill wasn't a lord.

The cant of Rakesley's head told her he wasn't finished with this line of inquiry. "You grew up on a lord's estate, no?"

Gemma's brow knitted with barely suppressed frustration—at herself. Here was solid proof of how the truth only got one in trouble.

Give a duke one truth and he would surely want another.

"I did," she muttered, surly like Gem.

"Is it Nestor?"

"Who?" She'd been so sure *Bolton* would be the name.

"Nestor's been trying to get one over on me for years."

"I've never heard of the man." What a relief to be able to keep speaking the truth.

"I'll surely regret this, but I don't think you're lying," said Rakesley. "Why did you come to Somerton, then?"

"For employment."

More truth… Close enough to it, anyway.

"And that's why you're disguised as a lad?"

Gemma nodded.

"Surely, there's easier employment to be found than mucking out horse stalls. You could've sought work in the house."

"Have you any notion of the work a scullery maid does in the course of a day?" she scoffed. "I'd rather muck out horse stalls."

Rakesley snorted.

He seemed somewhat mollified, but Gemma distrusted it. The ax would be falling and slicing through her neck any moment.

She'd never been one for waiting, so she would just hurry it along… "So, this is me sacked?"

Rakesley's head cocked. "Why would you make that assumption?"

"Because women don't work in stables."

"I haven't decided what to do with you yet."

Of a sudden, Gemma felt like a cat whose fur had been rubbed in the wrong direction. "I have news for you, *duke*," she said, a fiery flush of anger heating her to the tips of her ears. "*I* am not *yours* to do anything with."

He remained unmoving, merely watched her as if observing a feral animal.

She didn't like that, either.

"Tell me to leave—or ask me to stay."

His eyebrows drew together in a straight, flummoxed line. "*Ask* you?"

Gemma's temper was now fully up, and she was feeling reckless. It wasn't only freeing, but a relief. "*Beg* me to stay, then."

He stared at her as if she'd gone quite mad. "I don't beg."

A beat of time ticked past. "Then find someone else to ride Hannibal."

A mean, little note of triumph sounded in her voice, even as she knew she was walking the sharp edge of a razor. She'd surely gone too far. The air was ripe with that knowledge. And yet...

She experienced the sudden, almost irresistible, inexplicable urge to rush forward and kiss him again. A willful energy flowed through her and demanded a very specific release.

His lips against hers...the rigid press of his body...

It was, to be sure, a very naughty energy.

Because if she started kissing him again, she wouldn't stop until she'd had him.

All of him.

A hot, liquid feeling melted through her at the remembered feel of the hard length of his manhood pressed against her.

She needed to leave.

Now.

As she turned, an object on the carpet caught her eye. The leather strip she used to tie her hair back. Without thinking, she bent to retrieve it. When she attempted to straighten, her back decided it wasn't having it as all the muscles seized, instantly locking her into place. A cry escaped her, as she froze, bent over like a two-hundred-year-old woman.

Spurred into action, Rakesley closed the distance between them, his feet appearing in her limited line of sight. "Are you hurt?"

"My back," she groaned. "It's done this every night this week. It'll pass. I just need to stay here for a minute or two."

Her words were met with silence—and feet that didn't budge.

A full minute passed. All she could hear was the sound of her own breath roaring in her ears—and the silence.

The man had a loud silence about him.

At last, he asked, "Any better?"

"Not exactly," she couldn't not admit. "When it passes, it goes all of a sudden, like it never happened."

"And it started this week?"

"Aye." She tried shifting her weight to one side...

"Since Blankenship arrived?"

She went still. She didn't want to answer that question. The truth was she didn't like Blankenship, but the man was helping to get the best out of Hannibal. She wouldn't speak a word against him. Besides, she was no grass.

Another minute passed. She tried shifting her weight the other direction... Another pained groan emerged from her.

"Right," she heard. Rakesley's feet moved out of view.

Next thing she knew, a warm palm was pressing against the small of her back. She gasped, shock streaking through her. Her instinct was to bolt upright—but that wasn't possible.

Which was rather the point of the hand—*Rakesley's hand*—on the small of her back.

A protest sputtered out of her as a matter of habit—and principle. "What are you—"

Then he began to apply more pressure and movement, and her protest died away. It felt so...*good. Ahh* poured from her parted lips.

"Does this hurt?"

"*Erm*, no."

He increased the pressure, now using both hands and really working the muscle. Gemma reached for the table to steady herself. His large, skilled hands were nothing short of amazing, and her mind couldn't help wondering... How would those hands feel on other parts of her body? Touching secret places...*digging in*... Places that were beginning to ache with curiosity and need...

Oh.

She felt her back arching and realized the muscles were no longer seized up. He would realize it at any moment—and then he would stop.

And she couldn't let that happen.

"Is it feeling better?"

"*Mmhmm.*" She couldn't lie.

His hands stilled but remained. How very aware she was of his warmth, his strength...the position of her body bent forward —of him standing behind her...

"Perhaps, I should..." he began, his voice low and gravelly.

Her body knew what it heard in his voice.

Desire.

Then she did it—committed the boldest, most audacious act of her life.

She reached back, placed her hand over his larger one, holding him firmly in place, and met his dark, intense gaze over her shoulder. Her fingers tightened around his. Even this felt like an intimacy—the connection of their hands...the humidity of skin against skin.

Only a scrap of thin white muslin stood between her body and his palm as she guided him around the curve of her waist... the flat of her stomach...beneath the hem of the shirt...to the V of her sex...her *mons pubis*...

Though his eyes were black as night, she could see the flare of his pupils had pushed the irises into thin rings. It was all she could do not to shift backward and press her bottom against the front of his trousers. She knew what she would meet there. His thick, hard manhood—*ready.*

"Touch me," she said.

He didn't move.

He didn't speak.

"*Please.*"

And there it was. The smile from a few minutes ago. The one that just tipped at the corners of his mouth.

And now she knew it for what it was.

A wicked smile.

A shiver of anticipation traced through her, purling up her

spine, tightening her nipples, swelling her sex with utter and absolute *need*.

He angled farther forward so his long body fully draped over her slighter one, and yet the only part of him that touched her were his long, masculine fingers pressed against the curls of her sex.

Oh, the fever of want and lust that licked through her.

His mouth met her ear. "Now who's the one gone begging?"

CHAPTER THIRTEEN

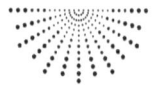

*R*ake didn't wait for her answer.

He knew it, anyway.

His mouth trailed to the curve of her neck, and his hand slid lower. The breath froze in her lungs, he could sense it in her stillness, the entirety of her being concentrated on the press of his fingertips as they made contact with her sweet, slick cunny.

Her bottom gave an impatient wiggle, and his cock beat out a hard throb, straining against the superfine of his trousers. If she kept at that, his control would slip.

His fingers slipped lower, until he found the sensitive nub she was hungering for him to touch. She gasped, her knuckles showing white as she gripped the table.

This wouldn't take long.

Unable to resist the impulse, his other hand lifted the hem of her shirt, exposing her bottom. Just as fetching and rounded as he'd imagined. And right now, it was arching back, leaving him no choice but to angle forward so his hard length pressed against her. He sucked in a sharp breath at the firm feel of her flesh, even as a layer of cloth stood between them.

His cock needed to know the feel of *her* around *him*.

It wasn't yet time for that. For now, however…

He made quick work of the falls of his trousers, and his throbbing length fell forward, a light slap against the downy skin of her bottom.

"Oh," she gasped, and lust-glazed eyes met his over her shoulder.

He could enter her now.

And though it took all his willpower, he didn't.

Not yet.

Not until she begged him for it.

He'd rather liked it when she'd done it the first time.

But, first, *this* release.

He pressed against her bottom and steadied her with one hand at the small of her back, even as the fingers of his other hand stroked her cunny—sliding against her nub with light, slick pressure, teasing all the nerve endings into life.

"What is…*oh*…what is happening to me," she exhaled.

"You've never been brought to climax?"

"No, I…*oh*…I don't think so."

He continued to stroke her. "You're almost there, my sweet."

She wasn't a shrinking virgin, but that didn't mean she'd ever achieved release. Most men didn't give two tosses for a woman's satisfaction.

Though his body wanted her—would likely combust if he didn't enter her soon—he wanted her to have this one…*here…now.*

"Your sweet cunny is so hot and wet and ready," he growled. "You want my big cock inside you?"

"Oh," she groaned, "*yes*," and ground her bottom against him.

"Not until you come for me," he breathed into her ear.

And that was the little push she needed, as her body went tense in that specific moment where release held one suspended in the grip of uncertainty—and promise. The next instant, a lever clicked open, and she gasped on a small cry, her quim pulsing in quick, tiny spasms against his fingers. Though he didn't experience the sensation with her, he felt no small satisfaction in having brought her this pleasure.

Slowly, deliberately, he eased the pressure of his fingertips, and she exhaled a wobbly breath.

Every cell in his body demanded he grab her hips with both hands and enter her in a single claiming stroke.

So, he took hold of the hem of his shirt and tugged it over her fetching bottom, leading himself away from temptation.

She hadn't yet asked for his cock.

Hadn't yet *begged* for it.

She glanced over her shoulder, annoyance in her glare. "What are you...why aren't you..." she sputtered.

She couldn't seem to finish a question. That was a start. A good climax could certainly tie one's tongue into knots.

He took her hips in hand, but not to guide himself into her as he wanted with a need that had begun to border on the desperate. Instead, he turned her to face him. How gorgeous she was— all tousled spark and fire, curls rioting about her shoulders, cheeks bright, eyes flashing with heat and desire and pique.

He was denying her what she wanted.

Him.

He wasn't the only desperate one.

He lifted her onto the table.

That should be about the right height.

He parted her legs and just stepped between creamy thighs but moved no farther.

Her head tipped back, and her gaze met his, the question within replaced by realization. "You want me to beg for it, don't you?"

A slow smile was the only answer he gave.

She laughed, even as intention deepened within her eyes. "My duke—"

"*Rake.*"

"My Rake—"

"Just Rake." Though he didn't mind very much being claimed as her Rake.

"*Rake*," she said. "I'll beg for it, but…"

"*But?*"

"Only after you remove your shirt."

On a chuckle, he grabbed the offending garment, lifted it over his head, and flung it away. "Better?"

Slowly—*thoroughly*—her gaze roved over him, leaving no detail unexamined. Her eyes went black with desire, pupils expanding until the green vanished. "Better than I remembered," she muttered, her voice gone to gravel.

Her tongue swiped across her pouty bottom lip, and he felt…

Desired.

And to be desired by this woman…

It meant something.

She shifted forward, and before he knew what she was about, she reached out and feathered her fingertips along the length of his manhood, lazily circling the crown, a teasing little smile twitching about her mouth.

Rake sucked in a sharp breath. How much of this was he was expected to take?

"*Rake*," she said, low and sultry. "I'm begging you to take this big, heavy, *hard* cock of yours and tup me silly with it."

The thing was she didn't seem very much like she was begging. In fact, her plea sounded more like a command.

And he understood something about himself in relation to this woman—she could order him around all she liked.

He took her heart-shaped face in his hands—how had he ever thought this goddess a lad?—and drew her so close their mouths nearly touched. "Say please."

Her smile fell away, and all that was left in its place was true, earnest need. "*Please.*"

He reached for her hips, sliding her to the edge of the table…

and onto his big, heavy, *hard* cock. Entering her, inch by inch, he gave her sweet cunny time to adjust around him, flesh slick against flesh. Her arms wound around his neck, and her head tipped back, as small sounds of pleasure escaped her. His tongue found her throat and stroked up the ivory column until, at last, his lips found hers. She exhaled a long groan into his mouth as he began to move, slowly, measuredly.

He grabbed the shirt and lifted it over her head, her ivory body made golden by flickering candlelight. And her nipples...

As he'd imagined them. *Rosy.*

He couldn't resist a lick and a suckle, and a little nip too.

How well she'd hidden her true self away, he couldn't help marveling. For this woman was nothing less than a beauty without flaw.

How had he not seen her?

Sometimes with a person, we only see what we expect to see, and not what's really there...

And he was tupping this beauty on a table.

Which was no way to conduct himself the first time.

First time?

That implied a *next* time...

He was getting ahead of himself.

There was only now—*this* time.

He would make it count.

Perhaps, then, she would beg him for a second time.

Or, suggested a small voice, would it be *him* begging *her?*

He wasn't sure he was above it.

His mouth met her ear. "Hold on tight."

Her long legs tightened around his waist and her arms twined about his neck, bringing him deeper into her, her nipples tight buds against his chest. He lifted her off the table—but not off *him* —as he carried her to the bed, laying her onto the ivory silk coverlet, her red-gold curls tossed about her. Lust-glazed eyes stared into his as he planted one hand to the side of her head and hovered just above her. She gave a little thrust of her hips, then another, taking him in and out of her. His mouth found her neck and his hand cupped her breast as he thrust and joined the rhythm.

"You feel so—*oh*—so good," she groaned, her head arched back as she spread her legs wider to receive more of him.

If she wanted more, he could give it.

His strokes became more focused—*demanding*. "That other climax was only prelude," he promised as he pushed into her —*hard*—her hips meeting his stroke for stroke in a give and take.

Her moans and groans turned into sharp, little cries, bodies, hot and sweaty, focused on the receiving of pleasure—and the giving of it. Her gaze began to turn inward, and she strained against him, mindless. She was close—and getting closer—her cunny begging him to deliver on his promise, as she bucked wildly beneath him. He took a hip in hand and slowed her rhythm, stroking in and out of her with measured deliberation.

She wanted release—and he wanted to give it to her.

But this was no cold, calculated tup, and his body had ideas of its own—like its release, which had begun to build. He'd wanted her, but somehow the abstract wanting hadn't accounted for the reality of her. He'd had his share of women, but none had prepared him for *this* woman. The sight of her...the feel of her... the way her sighs of pleasure compelled him to give her more— to give her everything he had.

And so, he did—driving into her with a lack of restraint that her abandon demanded. Then she was on the precipice, and he met her there, gazes locked, poised on the edge until, together, they broke as one and tumbled headlong into that promised oblivion, her quim pulsing around his length. She cried out into his neck, and he shouted into her hair, the scent of lavender mingling with the musk of bodies coupling.

Explosive—that was one word for it.

Exquisite—that was another.

Unexpected—that was the best word for it.

The satiety flowing through his veins, he'd expected that.

But another feeling raced beside it—one that tapped deeper than satiated flesh.

A feeling that had him burying his face in her hair and inhaling and wrapping his arms around her and bringing her with him as he lay flat on his back, her head nestled into the crook of his shoulder.

A feeling that made him never want to let her go.

He wasn't sure he liked this feeling.

In fact, he knew he didn't.

In no way did this feeling align with his vision of an ordered universe.

Bodies and feelings were better left separate.

She placed her palm on his chest, and for a moment, he thought she would feather her fingertips across his skin. Instead, the palm firmed and planted itself as she made to push away. Instinctively, he wrapped fingers around her wrist so she hovered just above him. "I have a question for you," he said in a lazy drawl that belied the urgency he felt to make her stay.

Curiosity shone in her gold-flecked eyes and held her in place.

"What's your name?"

He'd made love to this woman without knowing her name.

A smile played about her mouth. "Perhaps I shouldn't tell you."

"Oh, I very much disagree."

This felt dangerously like...*flirting*.

The moment held, then she relented. "Gemma."

"*Ah.*" *Gemma...* He liked that name for her. "Clever of you to choose Gem."

She gave a one-shouldered shrug. "Is that all?"

"One more question," he said. "More of an observation."

Her head canted. She truly had the prettiest eyes. "Yes?"

It was an observation he had no right to make, and yet, still... "You weren't a virgin."

"Does that matter to you?"

"No." And it didn't—*mostly*. Unless... "Unless it wasn't your choice."

He wasn't sure why he'd spoken such words. It was as if a murderous part of him wanted to know, so he could do violence to any such man.

"A bit of youthful curiosity." She shrugged again. "A few times."

He searched her eyes for the truth and found it. The tension left his body.

"I wondered what all the fuss was about."

Now, this line of questioning was one he definitely wanted to pursue. "And all the fuss?" he asked. "Was it worth it?"

Her laugh reached all the way to her pretty eyes. "I wasn't sure until tonight."

"And now?" Rake found he couldn't draw breath, his heart a hard thump in his chest.

Her smile slipped into one more thoughtful, and a light blush stained her cheeks. "I'd say it is."

Though her words were few, Rake wasn't sure he'd ever been paid a higher compliment.

"Now, I have a question for you." Her lightness fell away. Rake braced himself. "Am I sacked?"

"Pardon?"

"Am...I...sacked?"

"For...what?" Rake was utterly flummoxed. "For what we just did?"

If she thought she was getting the sack for *that*, she could rest assured that wouldn't be the case.

"For being a woman," she said. "And for lying about it."

Ah. At least one of them was thinking straight. "Are you going to keep being Gem?"

"Aye."

"Then I see no reason to sack you."

As Gemma, she would have to go, because, as Gemma, she would cause quite a stir amongst the lads and grooms. But as Gem, she could stay.

She gave a slow nod, and it struck him that while her eyes were bright, they weren't particularly easy to read. In fact, he hadn't the faintest idea of what was happening within those gold-flecked, green depths.

And he didn't like it.

It felt like an imbalance.

For here was the thing—he suspected he was all too easy to read in this moment.

And he didn't like that, either.

But he wasn't sure he could do anything about it, for all he wanted was for her to relent and shift her weight over him and straddle him and…

They could go from there.

Instead, she reclaimed her hand and bolted from the bed. With a sigh of resignation, he settled a few pillows behind him and relaxed back against the headboard. Sheet at his waist, torso bare, he watched as she began stalking about the room, clearly on the hunt.

"If you're searching for your clothes," he said. "You'll find a stack folded neatly in my dressing room."

She whipped around, annoyance blazing about her. "Were they there all this time?"

He shrugged, letting the lie remain unsaid, but not unknown.

She rushed from the room and returned with the folded stack. "These aren't the clothes I arrived in."

"I've had others made. As my jockey, you represent me, of course. I couldn't continue to allow you to walk around as a bundle of filth. Now"—he patted the coverlet beside him—"set those clothes down and come back to bed. Morning is yet many hours away."

Gemma didn't budge. In fact, she looked as if she had something she very much wanted to say. "Women like me don't wake up in the beds of dukes."

Reckless words were flowing from his mouth before he could stay them. "They do when they're his mistress."

Had he actually said that?

The lift of her eyebrows told him he had.

And he had no inclination to take it back.

Yet, she stood, unyielding. She didn't look offended, but entirely obstinate. "I'm not exactly mistress material."

"Why not?"

In fact, he thought her perfect mistress material.

"Because I can't center my entire existence around pleasing a man."

"What if it's your very being itself that pleases the man."

Though they were only bantering, Rake felt the pull of truth in the words. This bold, unyielding woman pleased him very much.

"That doesn't sound like a mistress," she said. "It sounds like a—"

Her mouth snapped shut, leaving the unfinished sentence hanging in the air between them.

It sounds like a...

Wife.

That was the word left unsaid.

Better it stayed that way.

Silently, she began dressing, and, silently, Rake watched.

Once finished, she met his gaze. Again, it struck him that he was unable to read her gaze. Too many emotions conflicted within. But he might recognize one...

Guilt.

Without a parting word, she was slipping out the door, and he was left wondering—what did those pretty eyes have to feel guilty about?

What they'd just done?

No.

She didn't feel guilt over that.

Her ruse as Gem?

He didn't think that was it, either.

It was something else.

Something more to her story that he didn't yet know. He sensed it down to his bones.

And it was located somewhere in her adamancy not to become his mistress.

He'd meant the offer half in jest—though it was what he truly wanted when he thought about it.

But her reaction had him curious…

What was Gemma's story?

His attraction for her tended to distract him from the fact that he still didn't know anything of substance about her life.

He still didn't know the *why*.

And he would have it.

CHAPTER FOURTEEN

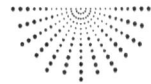

THREE DAYS LATER

"*A* cheat, you say?"

Rake wasn't sure which he despised more, spies or cheats, and everyone in his orbit knew it.

His secretary, Mr. Nesbitt, looked him square in the eye over his coin-shaped spectacles. "Aye."

This was no small accusation that Nesbitt was making, and they both understood it.

"And I suppose you've the proof to back this up?"

Mr. Nesbitt looked slightly offended at the suggestion he wouldn't. But an estate manager bilking a duke out of a hundred pounds a year was no small thing. A man's future was at stake, so there had to be certainty before the man was confronted with his crime.

Rake had never liked this part of being a duke. Though the estate was on the other side of England, he knew that particular estate manager had a wife and three small children. Many futures hung in the balance, not only that of one man, who might or might not be guilty.

A distant throat cleared. A footman stood across the study, awaiting Rake's attention. He could leave the lad standing there for the next three or so hours, his message poised on the tip of his tongue, yet to be delivered, until the whim struck Rake to allow him to speak. Such was the prerogative of a duke, not only within his own household, but in any household in the land. But Rake wasn't that sort of duke. "Yes?" he asked.

"A visitor has arrived, Your Grace."

"Lord Ormonde?" It was no rare occurrence for Julian to drop by unannounced. The servants knew they need never announce him. "Show him in."

Rake returned his attention to the invoices spread across the table, each adding up to tell the story of a crooked estate manager, who was looking more guilty by the minute.

Again, the footman's throat cleared. Again, Rake glanced up. The servant hadn't budged an inch. "Yes?" asked Rake, impatience fraying the edges of the question.

"A *lady* visitor, Your Grace."

"The dowager?" asked Rake. This interaction grew more tiresome with every word that remained unspoken. "Show her in, then."

Though her visits were rare, Mother was known to extricate herself from London on the odd occasion and take herself to the wilds of Suffolk to visit her son and daughter.

The footman shook his head.

"Does this lady have a name?"

"The Duchess of Acaster, Your Grace."

The Duchess of Acaster...

Rake's brow furrowed.

At Somerton?

Had he missed a letter?

He turned to Nesbitt. "This will keep until later."

He had no appetite for it, anyway. The destruction of a man's life was no happy thing, even if the man was a cheat.

Rake stood. "Where have you left the duchess?"

"In the stables, Your Grace."

"You left a duchess waiting in the stables?"

"She insisted."

Rake almost laughed as he strode through the house and outside toward the stables. This duchess certainly wasn't a woman of subtlety. If she was, indeed, trying to instigate a courtship with him, she was going about it the correct way.

Bold.

He didn't mind a bold woman—within limits.

Some women took it to extremes.

Like the woman who hadn't been too far from his mind these last three days.

Just before he passed beneath the clock tower leading into the stable yard, his gaze caught upon three riders—a lead pair followed by the groom Cal—trotting across a not-too-distant field. Of the pair, one was Artemis on her gray hunter, Helen of Troy. His sister had a penchant for naming her horses after the tragic heroines of antiquity. But it was the other rider that his gaze narrowed upon.

Gemma.

He would know her anywhere, from any distance.

In fact, such was his body's visceral response to the sight of her that one would think it knew her before his mind did.

Unable to resist, he watched her ride astride with utter freedom—the only way she knew how to ride.

It was the first time he'd caught sight of her in three days. He'd let her avoid him, and, well, he'd been avoiding her, too, the temptation to ravish her again too great.

His body wasn't finished with hers yet.

In fact, if it had its way, it had only just begun.

His gaze, inevitably, slipped lower. Her bottom had been haunting his dreams these last three nights.

He had but a single regret regarding their encounter.

That he hadn't placed his mouth on that fetching bottom and tested its firmness with his teeth.

That was a regret.

And his body wanted nothing more than to rectify it.

This very moment, going by the half-aroused state of his cock.

He attempted to push the image of Gemma's bottom from his mind. It wouldn't do to greet the Duchess of Acaster with a raging cockstand.

It might send the wrong message.

Artemis and Gemma topped a far-off hill and disappeared down the other side. Artemis was leading Gemma to the folly. While part of him wanted to saddle up a horse and follow, his sensible side prevailed and convinced his feet to start moving again—toward the duchess.

The stable yard was a hive of activity as lads and grooms tended to the duchess's newly arrived coach-and-four with well-practiced efficiency, Wilson ensuring all proceeded smoothly with his usual calm and command. Rake scanned the cobbles until his gaze lit upon two still figures, standing off to the side—a fifteen-hands chestnut Thoroughbred and a lady. Reins in one hand, she stroked the horse's velvety white snip with the other.

Silky Sadie was the horse.

And the lady in the coral wool and velvet traveling habit was the Duchess of Acaster.

The duchess was much as Rake remembered her from over a decade ago—and yet *more*. She'd fulfilled the promise of her youthful loveliness to become a true beauty. Statuesque and curvaceous, she had the sort of body that could keep a man occupied for a good long while. More than one young buck had commented on it all those years ago. Luminous brown eyes. Not nearly black, like those of Rake and Artemis, but amber, as if lit from behind. Her thick sable hair was knotted in a neat chignon at the nape of her neck and topped by a stylish hat adorned with a jaunty white ostrich feather.

If the Platonic ideal of an English duchess existed, she would be the Duchess of Acaster.

And Rake felt not the slightest jolt of desire for her.

She was perfect, yet…

Too perfect.

She looked as if she smelled of the most expensive perfume.

Unlike the woman he'd just watched ride across the fields. That woman likely smelled of horse and perspiration at this very moment.

She wouldn't smell like perfection, and yet…

What he would give to inhale her.

Across the cobbles, the duchess registered his arrival—and smiled.

Her smile caused a small alarm bell to clang inside him.

The duchess smiled as if she had to remind herself to smile.

And the smile he returned might not have been all that different.

"What a—" His mouth hung up on the next word.

Pleasant. That was the word supposed to follow.

Her smile faltered for a fraught instant, and he continued. "What a *pleasant* surprise, Your Grace."

A flash of relief passed behind her eyes. The vulnerable expression was replaced by aristocratic hauteur so quickly he could almost convince himself he'd imagined it. "Your Grace," she said on a curtsy that ceded none of her ground as his equal.

He couldn't very well ask what this woman he'd only met once on a single formal occasion years ago and with whom he'd exchanged a few letters was doing by arriving unannounced on his doorstep.

But that didn't mean he wasn't wondering it.

What the blazes was the Duchess of Acaster doing at Somerton, anyway?

A small voice couldn't help reminding him that only a week ago he might've been a little less skeptical and a lot more welcoming.

But that was *before*.

Before Gemma.

He gave himself a mental shake. He couldn't think about Gemma.

"A fine day for traveling," he said, for lack of anything else to say that met the standards of courtesy.

"Please, call me Celia," she said with a gracious smile.

He nodded.

And waited.

She gave her throat a little, feminine clearing. "With the races at Newmarket just around the corner, we've begun walking Light Skirt, the filly I'm entering in the One Thousand Guineas."

Racehorses weren't ridden to racecourses, but walked, so as to save their strength and energy for race day.

"And with all our back and forth about Silky Sadie," she continued, "I had a whim to bring her along and show her to you in person." She gave a little shrug and breathy laugh that would charm most of London. "So, here we are."

Rake's head cocked. "Surely, there are more direct routes from Ashcote Hall to Newmarket."

Another little laugh escaped her. He detected nerves in this laugh. Further, she looked slightly nonplussed. She wasn't accustomed to men offering up much resistance to anything that came out of her mouth.

For some reason, Rake found he couldn't leave the matter be. "It would've taken you a good four—"

"Five."

"*Five* days to walk her here from Ashcote Hall."

Again, the duchess's charming little smile appeared.

Again, Rake wasn't all that charmed.

"Whim was a bit of an understatement. But I thought there was no time like the present."

Rake didn't know the duchess—*Celia*—well enough to gauge the veracity of her words, but he sensed a certain falseness within them.

He shifted his attention toward Silky Sadie. The mare was a fine piece of horseflesh, her chestnut coat shiny, her black mane lustrous, and her demeanor settled.

He walked around and inspected her from all angles. "She's without flaw."

"Of course, she is," said the duchess—*Celia*, he kept having to remind himself.

A pleased smile played about Celia's mouth, as if he'd paid her the compliment. Of course, how many times had this flawless woman been paid that compliment in her life?

Countless, no doubt.

He nodded. "She would be a fine addition to my breeding stock."

Something flickered behind Celia's eyes.

If he wasn't very mistaken, it was very akin to distaste.

Perhaps she'd been described in such terms. Most prospective duchesses were.

But this duchess didn't like it.

He couldn't say he would, either.

Then the moment vanished, and, dutifully, she gave a light laugh. "I believe it might be possible that you and I already agree on her price."

In an instant, the price struck him.

Marriage...

Theirs.

Here was his opportunity. He could propose marriage to this woman right here and now, and he would've secured both mare and duchess.

And yet...he couldn't.

Not yet, anyway.

And he couldn't understand why not.

Standing before him was the duchess he wanted—possessed of flawless beauty and the sort of body that could breed more than a few heirs and spares.

Sure, he was thinking of her in horse breeding terms, but he couldn't help thinking she was presenting herself to him in those terms.

She hadn't simply wandered the fifty miles from Ashcote Hall to offer him her horse—but to offer him herself too.

Her approach to the state of wedded bliss might rival his for clear-eyed cynicism.

Instead, however, he found himself asking a different question, lest he propose marriage to a duchess on the cobbles of a stable yard. "Would like you like to go for a ride?"

She blinked. Perhaps she had been expecting that marriage proposal. Most men would've done, if presented opportunity and encouragement. "*A ride?*"

"I could have a couple of hunters saddled within ten minutes."

The more Rake considered the idea, the more he liked it. It would give them something to do other than stand here, not agreeing to marry one another. He suspected that proposal of marriage might very well slip out for want of anything else to say.

"I thought you might appreciate a ride after four—"

"*Five.*"

"Five days in a carriage, no matter how well-sprung."

Like most women would—with the exception of one woman —Celia glanced down at her attire, her traveling habit no doubt in the first stare of fashion. "I suppose this will do for riding," she said. No mistaking her lack of conviction.

But Rake was in no mood for it. "Somerton has a folly with a dead spectacular view of the next valley over."

"Then, let's," she said, tightly, as if each word had been extracted from her with pliers.

They should've ridden in the opposite direction of the folly, Rake thought fifteen minutes later as he and the duchess made straight for it.

For, in the deepest, darkest corner of his heart, he knew—he was riding toward Gemma. Here was the opportunity to be near her, and he was seizing it. Three days had been long enough.

Flimsy...cheap...

No.

He was being a good host to the Duchess of Acaster.

No better time to start than the present. "I was sorry to hear about the loss of your husband. The Duke of Acaster was..." He wasn't quite sure how to finish that sentence. The truth was the Duke of Acaster was a miserable lech the world was well rid of.

But he couldn't go saying that to the man's widow.

Celia shot him a surprised glance. "Oh?" She was an accomplished horsewoman, even riding sidesaddle as was expected of ladies. "You were *truly* sorry to hear of his death?"

The question put Rake on the back foot. He'd merely expressed the platitude that people expressed on such occasions.

"Well," she continued, saving him from having to tell a lie, "*I* wasn't."

Rake had heard the phrase "Merry Widow," but here he was seeing it in action. "Not a love match, then."

Of course, he and all the *ton* knew it hadn't been.

A flinty laugh escaped her. "Hardly. My father is a wealthy baron who had a hankering for a duke as a son-in-law. Acaster had a hankering for food on his table, with a little left over."

Rake nodded. "For horses."

Acaster had built quite the formidable racing stable over the last decade.

Again, came the duchess's flinty laugh. "Edwin's tastes ran to fillies of the two-legged variety."

Rake's brow lifted. "At his age?"

"Men," was all she said.

All she needed to say.

Men, indeed. Rake supposed certain parts of men were indefatigable until the moment they drew their last breath.

"Anyway," continued Celia, "the horses were my idea."

"Is that so?"

Perhaps this duchess was even more well suited to him than he'd supposed.

She nodded tightly, looking decidedly disinclined to carry on with the subject.

There was no need, for they'd topped the hill and the folly came into view. She pointed. "Is that where we're going?"

"Aye."

"What a splendid view," she said, urging her mount into a canter.

"Aye," he repeated.

Rake wasn't referring to the land spread below them or the blue sky dotted white with lazy cotton puffs of clouds. But rather the distant figure ahead wearing trousers, red-gold hair tied at her nape, and slouch hat pulled low over her forehead.

Gemma.

From her place on the folly's steps, Artemis gave a shout of greeting and an enthusiastic wave, which Celia returned mildly.

Gemma's gaze, though, slid past the approaching duchess and landed square on Rake.

Time had a way of slipping out of its usual rhythm when his gaze met hers.

Within her eyes, he saw everything and nothing. He knew this woman—*knew* her...*intimately*—and yet he didn't.

These last three days had done nothing to suppress his appetite for her. Instead, he understood, in this timeless moment, it had only whetted it.

And now he was to make civil conversation with her in front

of others—including the woman who would likely become his wife.

Right.

He was making a bad decision.

A very bad decision.

It was objectively true.

And yet…

He was powerless against it.

This very bad decision held a momentum of its own.

And like any man with a sliver of remaining good sense, all he could do was hold on.

CHAPTER FIFTEEN

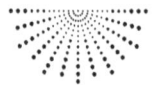

*T*hrough a series of events Gemma hadn't heeded closely enough, she somehow found herself riding across the Somerton estate alongside Lady Artemis, with Cal trailing at a distance.

She suspected that was how most things went with Lady Artemis. Behind the lady's good humor and generally sunny disposition hid a will of iron. If she wanted something, she had it.

And for some reason, she wanted to go for a ride with the taciturn stable lad Gem.

Not that Gemma minded. Hannibal was resting in his box after a morning's hard training, and the warm sun was presently soaking through her clothes and into her skin.

It was a good day to be out.

"We should've brought Hannibal and Dido," said Lady Artemis, face pointed up to the sun, eyes closed, a relaxed smile about her mouth.

"They've earned their afternoon rest," said Gemma, diplomatically. But, really, aristocrats could lack sense of the common variety.

Lady Artemis slitted one eye open and directed it at Gemma.

"How did you come to be so wise, Gem? What are you? Fifteen? Sixteen years of age?"

"*Erm...*" Gemma searched her mind for Gem's age. "Seventeen?"

"Don't you know your own age?" asked Lady Artemis.

The full brunt of her gaze was directed at Gemma now, and a twinkle shone in her dark eyes. Though those depths were as dark as her brother's, they held an easy-to-read openness. If Gemma was reading them correctly now, they were toying with her.

A swift change of subject was in order. "Have you considered giving Dido another year?" asked Gemma in what was likely the clunkiest change of subject since grammar had been invented.

Lady Artemis rolled her eyes skyward. "Not this again."

Fair enough.

"Dido is a goer. I know it. You know it. Anyone with eyes knows it," continued the lady, exasperated. "It's settled."

"But," said Gemma, "why does the Two Thousand Guineas have to be her first race?" And it hit her. "You want to best your brother."

Lady Artemis smiled as if the stable lad Gem was a bit thick. "Of course."

"But you could best him at the Race of the Century."

Lady Artemis laughed. "I prefer to put him out of his misery sooner than later."

The lady's confidence in Dido was clear, but an uneasy feeling snaked through Gemma's gut. She couldn't let up just yet. "Have you considered entering her in a small racing meeting? Maybe take her to a less crowded course to gain some turf experience, then on to Newmarket?"

Lords and ladies didn't like to be told what to do, so Gemma knew to approach the subject with an abundance of caution.

"No one will know what hit them when Dido takes to the

turf," said Lady Artemis, blithely brushing off Gemma's suggestion. "You've seen her. Her speed sets the track on fire."

"Aye," was all Gemma could respond. Making an owner see the truth about a beloved horse could be nigh on impossible. She'd sooner get agreement from a wall.

They topped the rise of a hill, and the valley spread below them, green with summer. A canal glinted silver in the sun as it lazily wove through and divided lands into townships, farms, and estates. From east to west, Gemma counted three church steeples, in three different villages.

Lady Artemis pointed across Gemma. "We're going there."

A few hundred yards away, on a slightly higher hill, stood a ramshackle structure that looked to have been built a few thousand years ago. "Are you sure?"

This amused Lady Artemis, for she laughed at length. "It's actually quite structurally sound." Gemma's doubts must've shown on her face, for the lady continued, "It was constructed to look that way. Although there is still a portion of original Roman wall on its west side."

Only aristocrats would purposefully build a structure to look as if it were about to collapse into rubble at any moment. Such things amused them, and aristocrats were nothing if not dedicated to their own amusement.

After they'd dismounted and then settled the horses with Cal, Gemma began exploring, finding the old portion of Roman wall. Tentatively, she laid her palm on those two-thousand-year-old stones. Warm from the sun, their stored heat seeped into her. They'd survived all this time, without a hint of mortar, for her to arrive at this moment and touch them.

"Gem?"

Gemma found Lady Artemis propped against an archway, observing her with curiosity. Gemma was instantly on edge. "Yes?"

Lady Artemis pushed off the support and clasped her hands

tightly before her. She was nervous. "I'm going to say something," she said. "And I hope you won't take offense."

"Mmm," was all Gemma responded.

Lady Artemis held a look in her eyes both determined and unpredictable. Gemma knew enough about the aristocracy to give a wide berth to determined and unpredictable sisters of dukes.

"My brother knows."

"Knows what?" Gemma asked, even as her heart beat a hard, wobbly *thud* against her ribs.

She knew *what*.

Lady Artemis lifted a single, disbelieving eyebrow. "That you're a woman, of course."

Suddenly, it became difficult for Gemma to draw breath. She may have even made a choking sound.

"Are you quite alright?" Lady Artemis asked in mild alarm.

Gemma swallowed. "*Erm*, yes."

That seemed to appease the lady. "Any man who thinks you a lad lacks fundamental powers of observation."

"Plenty of them around, I can assure you," said Gemma, only just recovering her ability to speak.

This got a breezy laugh from Lady Artemis. "I can assure you my brother isn't one of them, which is why I thought you should know."

If only Lady Artemis had thought to warn her three days ago, the night in Rakesley's bedroom could've been avoided. Except...

Certain parts of her had no interest in having avoided that night.

In fact, if those parts of her had their way, they would have another night just like it.

"Anyway," continued Lady Artemis, "you'll want to tell him that you know he knows and get it out of the way."

"Ah."

Two riders appeared in the distance. The lead rider was a

woman dressed in pale coral with a single feather in her cap that rippled in the breeze. Even from the distance of a hundred yards, Gemma could discern a few facts about the woman. She was a lady—and she was a beauty.

As for the other rider…

Gemma would know him anywhere.

Rakesley.

What a dashing figure he cut astride a horse. More than one lady in London must've swooned at the sight of this duke enjoying a morning's ride on Rotten Row. Black, wind-tossed hair. The hard angles of his face kissed by the sun.

All magnificent duke.

All devastating man.

Her gaze found his firm mouth.

That mouth had kissed her…suckled her breasts…whispered dirty little nothings into her ear…

And his hands with their long, capable fingers…

They'd touched her…every part of her…

Which was why she'd avoided him like the plague these last three days.

This man—this *duke*—held an undeniable power over her.

Lady Artemis held one hand to her mouth and gave an effusive shout of greeting as she waved broadly with her other arm. The distant lady offered a small, feminine wave, and Rakesley merely rode on. He wasn't the sort to give effusive shouts or waves of greeting.

A few seconds later, they'd drawn to a stop beside the other horses where Cal waited. Rakesley swung his leg over his saddle and then jumped to the ground, while the lady made no similar move. She was patiently waiting for assistance.

It only occurred to Gemma that Gem the lad should've rushed forward to assist the lady, but the lady looked too expensive to touch with her grimy hands.

Another observation struck Gemma as the lady's dainty feet

landed on the ground. This expensive-looking lady and the Duke of Rakesley perfectly complemented one another in both looks and aristocratic bearing.

The observation made Gemma a little sick to her stomach.

As she took in her surroundings, the lady's gaze swiped across Gemma as if she were a bland bit of scenery and landed on Lady Artemis. Rakesley—*Rake*, he'd asked her to call him only three days ago—introduced the lady as the Duchess of Acaster. *Celia*, the duchess insisted on being called amongst friends.

Gemma suspected *Celia* wouldn't like it one bit if she heard Gemma take the liberty of addressing Rakesley as *Rake*…amongst friends.

Though tempted, Gemma resisted and made to slip away to the horses. She was more comfortable with animals than with people, anyway.

"Gem?" intoned a deep voice at her back.

She froze mid step. Why wouldn't Rakesley just let her go?

Slowly, she turned, but kept her gaze fixed upon the mud-encrusted tips of her boots as, like a good, respectful lad, she waited for the duke to proceed.

"Hannibal's been out on the track today?"

The question irked her. As if he were questioning her sense of duty and devotion. "Took him out for his paces first thing," she said in Gem's surly voice—in *her* surly voice. "As usual," she added, then she kept talking. "I'm a firm believer in a set routine." And, oh, she just couldn't stop… "As you're well aware."

That last bit had been entirely unnecessary—but also impossible for her not to speak.

She risked a glance up. He knew it, too, judging by the clench of his jaw.

Her gaze shifted. The lifted brows of Lady Artemis and *Celia* said they knew it as well.

Splendid.

Now, everyone knew she'd gone too far with a duke.

In more ways than one, spoke a small, unhelpful voice.

The ladies couldn't possibly know that—unless...it was somehow obvious.

It certainly *felt* obvious.

Rake's gaze didn't relent. "And the saddle?" he asked, as if they were the only two people on this hill.

"The saddle?"

"The new one from London."

Ah. "It's lighter, and the leather is thick and pliable. Hannibal has taken no issue with it."

Rakesley nodded. "And you?"

"Me?"

"Do you take any issue with it?" he asked. "Is the cantle low enough for your—"

Now, it was Gemma's eyebrows lifting alongside those of Lady Artemis and the duchess.

If Gemma wasn't very mistaken, that sentence ended with...

Bottom.

The Duke of Rakesley was concerned about her...*bottom.*

Wouldn't be the first time, returned the small voice.

Heat crept up her throat, reaching the tips of her ears.

There was no such thing as a discreet blush for the red of hair.

Lady Artemis turned to the duchess. "Celia," she said brightly, as if suddenly struck by an idea. "I must meet Silky Sadie. Any filly who could go the distance in the St. Leger is a legend in my book."

The duchess blinked her luminous amber eyes at the awkward change of subject. "Oh, yes, she is certainly a fine mare."

"No time like the present." Lady Artemis stepped forward and took the duchess's hand.

As the two ladies made their way toward the horses, where Cal stood waiting to assist them, Lady Artemis tossed a wink over her shoulder at Gemma.

Lady Artemis...

About as subtle as a hammer.

And that was Lady Artemis, the Duchess of Acaster, and Cal gone back to Somerton…

And Gemma left alone with Rakesley.

He cocked a hip against the low Roman wall, crossed his arms over his chest, and stood observing her.

"That wall is older than England," she pointed out.

He shrugged an indifferent shoulder. "Then it'll hold."

She snorted.

Dukes.

"Your sister knows," she said, speaking what occupied her mind.

"I know."

Gemma moved to the other side of the wall. Better to have a barrier between them at all times. "You lot are big on being the ones in the know."

He shifted, keeping track of her movements. "A family failing, I'm afraid." He wasn't apologetic in the least.

A sudden chirrup of laughter burst from Gemma. Rakesley's mouth twitched, then smiled, and he was laughing alongside her.

Something happened in the air when it was only the two of them. It was if the elements changed their composition.

Or perhaps it was elements exposed.

Elements that pulsed between them when it was only them.

Elements given permission to collide.

"The Duchess of Acaster…" Gemma wasn't sure why she'd begun such a sentence or where she intended to go with it. Better to stop talking.

"She arrived an hour or so ago." A shadow of Rakesley's smile remained. "Unexpectedly."

"Do duchesses often land unexpected on your doorstep?" Gemma wasn't particularly proud of the pettish note that accompanied the question.

"It's been known to happen."

Of course, Gemma didn't say. More pettishness. But, honestly, after what he and she had done in his bedroom three nights ago, she could hardly blame all those duchesses. Her body had never been the recipient of so much pleasure in all her life.

She still tingled with it.

"She's walking her filly Light Skirt to Newmarket for the One Thousand Guineas."

"Ah."

Gemma doubted that was the sole reason for the duchess's sudden arrival.

"Hannibal will be ready to leave in a few days?"

"Aye," said Gemma, glancing up toward a darkening sky. In the course of a few minutes, the clouds had gone from harmless white to threatening gray. "We should probably be getting back. I think it's about to—"

Then she felt it—the first drop of rain on her nose, quickly followed by another and another.

"Follow me," Rakesley shouted over his shoulder as he disappeared inside the folly, around one corner, then another, the sudden summer shower breaking upon their heads. Though surprisingly labyrinthine, unsurprisingly, the folly lacked a roof.

Around yet another corner they went, and then Gemma had a roof over her head. To call the surrounding four walls a room would've been overstatement. It was closer to the size of a closet. But it held a glorious defining feature—a rectangular window so large she could've easily stood on its stone casement with inches to spare above her head.

And the view it offered of the mist-shrouded countryside below…

"Stunning," fell from her mouth.

Rakesley took a seat at one corner of the window, his back propped against stone, one leg stretched before him, the other propped in his hands. She sat at the opposite corner and tried to keep her attention on the valley. But it was the view before her that her gaze wanted to feast upon—Rakesley, wet and tousled.

Oh, but he was a stunning view.

In a strange way she felt nervous of him. She didn't know how to be around this man in this context.

Where she was herself—*Gemma*—and he was Rakesley…

Rake.

His gaze slid over to meet hers. "This was my favorite place as a child."

"Oh?" she asked, slightly breathless.

The openness in his gaze…

It was new.

"Besides the stables, of course."

She couldn't help smiling. "Of course." It went without saying —for both of them.

"I would escape out here whenever I wanted a few hours to myself."

"I can see why," said Gemma, appreciatively.

"Then my father died, and I became a duke and stopped coming as often."

"Surely, you were allowed to come here as the duke. Aren't dukes allowed to do anything? Isn't that rather the point of being a duke?"

"Yes and no," he said, his smile patient.

It occurred to Gemma that she very much wanted to kiss his lips again.

"Certain expectations are placed on a duke," he continued. "As a result, his movements are ever known."

"*Expectations?*"

"His education, duties, and responsibilities. I was shipped off to Eton, then to Cambridge. Even before I attained my majority, I'd taken the lands and tenancies under control."

"And marriage?" Gemma found herself asking.

Not that she had any right.

Wariness entered his eyes. "I've always been aware of my duties on that front as well."

A weighty beat of time passed. "And the Duchess of Acaster?"

"Yes?"

Gemma shouldn't ask the next question poised on her lips… "Are you going to marry her?"

Rake's jaw clenched and released. "Likely."

Gemma shook her head on a dry laugh. "Nobs."

He cocked his head. "What are you on about?"

"The way you approach marriage—like you're Thoroughbreds. It's all about the bloodlines, isn't it?"

"There's that," he conceded, but his voice held an unfinished note.

"There's more?" She was genuinely curious.

"It's simple. I prefer a union where my wife orders her own affairs, and I order mine, and we leave each other to it."

"And never the twain shall meet?"

"Something like that."

A note in Rakesley's voice sounded…*off*—and Gemma couldn't leave it. "You've always felt thusly about marriage?"

A war waged behind his eyes, as if she were asking him to speak aloud his most closely guarded secret, one he'd never shared with another living soul. "Not always," he said, at last. "I once made a love match—or thought I had."

Something yet remained between the words. "You're either in love, or you aren't."

"If only love were that simple. But you're forgetting one vital detail," he said, eyes dark with intensity. "It takes two to form a love match."

CHAPTER SIXTEEN

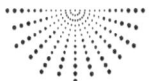

A man of forward momentum, Rake wasn't one to cast his gaze to the past.

But it was Gemma who asked, and for some reason he couldn't fathom, he wanted her to know.

Nay, not just know.

But understand...

Him.

"I was in my third year at Cambridge and enjoyed playing the young buck around Town. No different from the sort you see now."

Though Gemma remained serious and intent, a smile pulled at her mouth. "From a great distance."

Fair enough. Sometimes, he forgot they weren't of the same social standing—a fact that mattered less and less with each passing day.

"One evening, I was pulled into attending a ball at Almack's and I saw Felicity across the assembly room." He spread his hands wide. "And I was lost. It was that sudden."

"You were in love."

He snorted. "I certainly thought I was. I wrangled an introduction from the patronesses and danced with Miss Felicity Bamford twice, which was as many dances as were allowed with the same partner. I even managed to sneak a third at the very end of the night."

Gemma's brow lifted with irony. "Scandalous, to be sure."

"From that moment, all London knew that the Duke of Rakesley was utterly besotted with the daughter of Sir William Bamford. A proposal of marriage was expected by the end of the season."

"And was there?"

"I've never been one to wait for anything. I proposed in the middle of the season."

Gemma held a watchful reserve. She understood this story didn't end well.

"And neither was I one to do anything by half measures." Rake didn't like the bitter note that sounded in his voice. "I proposed at a ball...in the middle of the dancing floor...down on one knee...in front of the *ton*. All the ladies, some of the lords, too, found a few tears in their eyes. Felicity and I had just proven that true love existed."

"And?" asked Gemma, dread hanging about her.

"It was a lie."

"What happened?"

"Felicity ran off with her father's estate manager a week later." Rake spoke without emotion, simply relating facts.

"Oh my."

"It turned out that Felicity wasn't as keen on our courtship as her father. A duke is a great catch, in case you didn't know." The bitterness again. "Sir William had known of Felicity's affection for his estate manager and had wanted her married before she could make fools of her family."

"So, she made a fool of you."

And there it was.

The truth of the matter laid bare.

"I was the laughingstock of the *ton*, of course," he said, attempting levity. "Nothing the hazing at Eton hadn't prepared me for."

No responding lightness came from Gemma. "Somehow, I doubt that very much," she said. "So, you made a decision."

"Oh? And what is that?" He didn't necessarily mind Gemma telling him about himself. In fact, he found himself tensing with anticipation.

"You decided that in matters of marriage, your heart would never become entangled again."

She would see that.

"It will come as no surprise to you that I didn't take to being a laughingstock." He shrugged, hoping the dismissive gesture masked the seriousness behind those words. "I decided Mother had it right about marriage."

"*Your* mother?"

A sudden chortle erupted from him. "I didn't spring from a pod fully formed."

Gemma laughed, sheepish. "One could almost forget."

"What does that mean?"

"It means…" She gazed out across the cloud-cloaked, rain-soaked countryside and searched for the correct sequence of words. "You're so…" Again, words appeared to be failing her.

"*Magnificent?*" he asked with a single lifted eyebrow.

"You know that about yourself, do you?"

Never once had Rake conducted a conversation like this one. It put him on the wrong foot. The fact was he did know that was what people thought of him. Whether or not it was true was beside the point.

"I've been assured of my magnificence all my life," he found himself saying. "And believed it." A beat. "Until…"

"Felicity."

"Perhaps I was a little less magnificent than I'd supposed."

More words wanted to be spoken... "Perhaps a little more human."

Gemma nodded, slowly, absorbing his words...his confession. "What did your mother have right about marriage?"

"Love has no place in it," he said, able to quote Mother word for word. "Love within marriage is a concept better left to the lower classes."

Amazement flashed in Gemma's eyes.

"Does that shock you?"

"No," she said. "But to have it spoken so bluntly is...jarring. Aristocrats don't think much of the rest of us, do you?"

Rake flinched.

You.

He didn't like that *you*. It set him apart from her and lumped him in with the rest of *them*, and he didn't want that.

He'd rather form a *them* of two—with Gemma.

"And *your* view on marriage?" he tossed back at her.

Actually, he wanted to know.

Very much.

She shrugged. "No one would want to marry me."

"Oh?" He couldn't imagine that was the case.

"Just look at me."

"I am."

Those two words startled a blink from her.

"Why would no one want to marry you, Gemma?" he asked, determined to have the answer.

"No one wants to marry the by-blow of an earl."

The by-blow of an earl...

A lord...an *earl*.

Of course.

"Your mother was the cook for a lord—an *earl*," he said, slowly, making sure he'd puzzled it together correctly.

"She was." Gemma hesitated, unsure whether to reveal more. "And his mistress."

Very little shocked Rake, but this did. That was bold, even for an aristocrat. "And you were raised in the earl's household?"

Rake would keep asking questions as long as she kept answering them.

"Along with my twin brother, aye."

Ah. It explained so much. Her proper grammar... Her knowledge of fine horseflesh... But it didn't yet explain enough... "Which earl?" The question sounded more like a demand.

He needed to tread carefully.

Her gold-flecked, green eyes went suddenly murky, and her jaw clenched. "That is none of your concern."

Rake nearly told her it was very much his concern. But the truth was...

It wasn't.

He didn't like that.

He found he very much wanted it to be his concern.

But he couldn't force her.

He would get nowhere that way.

And *nowhere* wasn't an option.

He sensed she needed protection.

And he was the man to provide it.

* * *

GEMMA HAD REFUSED to answer a duke...*this* duke.

She couldn't imagine he was refused often, but he left her no other option.

Besides, it was only the truth. Her life was none of his concern, and he needed the reminder.

As did she.

A pivot was necessary. "Something has been bothering me," she said.

"Oh?"

"For a man called Rake, you aren't much of one, are you?"

He blinked.

Good.

"What is *your* name?"

"Rake."

She wasn't having it. "The name your mother gave you."

Gemma found herself being distracted by the smile now tipping about his mouth.

A rather rakish smile, actually.

"That's rather complicated."

Gemma canted her head, curious. "How is that possible?"

"It was my mother who gave me the nickname Rake."

Gemma nearly gasped. "That cannot be."

The laugh that escaped him didn't contain much amusement. "You haven't met my mother."

"I'm not sure I would want to." Since they were being—*mostly*—truthful. "She sounds…formidable."

"That's one way of putting it," he said. "My father named me Edward, if that's what you're asking."

"It *was*," she said, emphasizing the past tense. "But now, I'm more curious about the name Rake. I'd assumed it was, *erm, earned.*"

"After Father passed from a sudden fever when I was eight, and I inherited the title, Mother took to calling me Rake."

"Why on earth would your mother do such a thing?"

"Her rationale was—and still is—that a rake gets what he wants out of life."

"You're already a duke. Don't you get enough already?"

This earned another humorless laugh from him. "Mother has a specific way of viewing the world." A beat. "Too much is never enough."

"That would certainly explain your stables."

"The best in the land."

"And only the best for you?"

"*Only.*"

His head cocked, his dark, fathomless gaze locked onto her. A flush of heat pulsed through her, provoked by its intensity.

And the smile tipping about his mouth…

She'd seen it before.

Three nights ago…

In his bedroom.

He wasn't speaking of his stables.

He was speaking of…

Her.

His voice went low and gravelly. "I can't help but wonder if…"

"*If?*" somehow emerged from her in a breathless exhalation.

"If I've sufficiently proven it to *you.*"

Opposite her, not ten feet away, he sat propped against the stone casement, looking so arrogant and vital and assured.

Magnificent.

Her tongue nervously swiped across her bottom lip to wet it, and his gaze followed the movement.

Oh, no good could come of this feeling tracing through her…

She wanted him.

Really, she had to have him.

"You could prove it now," she said.

Oh, that was bold.

"Would you like to test me?"

She did.

Very much.

She reached out and planted her hands before her, coming to all fours, her knees digging into cool stone, as she crawled forward across the foot-wide window casement.

And he simply sat back and waited for her to come to him.

Arrogant man…

Irresistible man.

It seemed, for her, the one only enhanced the other.

She inched closer. His legs fell to either side of the ledge, as she moved forward until, at last, she was between them…close enough that all she had to do was tip her head back and shift to touch her lips to his.

He tucked his thumb beneath her chin, as they each angled forward, his scent of sandalwood and man surrounding her, intoxicating her. So close was she now that his breath whispered warm across her parted mouth, sending shivers rippling through her, lifting the downy hairs at the nape of her neck, puckering her nipples into ripe cherries.

Their lips touched—*firm...unyielding...tender*—catching Gemma by surprise, for there was little doubt where this kiss would lead. But he took his time and kissed her thoroughly, with intention. She would've thought she wanted a hot, lusty kiss bursting to get on with what came next, but, really, her body—and a place deeper within her—wanted *this* kiss. A tender, thorough kiss could be hot and lusty, too, for it touched places within her deeper than surfaces.

He tugged, and she swayed forward, her body pleading *more*. Tender thoroughness was all well and good, but her body had aches and needs that demanded attention.

Her hands found his broad shoulders, the muscles tensing beneath her touch as he grabbed her waist and pulled her onto him so her knees fell to either side of his thick thighs.

Carnal.

That was the word for how her body felt pressed against his—even through layers of clothes. Her arms around his neck. His manhood, rigid and thick, against her sex. His hands cupped her bottom and ground her against his length, her hips instinctively angling.

"Oh, Rake," she cooed.

This feeling... It was delicious.

His mouth found her neck, and she tipped her head to the side, his kisses and the scratch of his stubbled chin blazing a trail of pleasure down her throat. Her fingers fumbled for his cravat and began unknotting it, his shirt falling open to reveal his chest and those defined muscles. He shrugged off his coat and waist-coat, granting her greedy mouth and hands freedom to explore his shoulders and chest, even as she continued to press against *him*...and ached for these layers of clothing to vanish and for him to be inside her.

He chuckled and pulled back enough to meet her gaze. "You know dresses do have their uses."

"Like?" Gemma couldn't think of one.

And, honestly, who was thinking about dresses in this moment?

"Like for an easy tup."

Oh. In that case, she would much rather be wearing a dress right now. But her mind caught on a single word. "Would you like it if I were easier?"

His gaze searched hers for a heavy beat of time. The question could've been interpreted lightly. But it wasn't a light question—and they both knew it.

"I like you as you are."

And something incremental, but vital, shifted between them. Something she would think about later. But not now. Not when her body was demanding she figure out some way to get these layers of clothing out from between them.

But Rake's fingers were already working her trouser buttons. "I've never unbuttoned the falls of a woman's trousers."

"To be entirely accurate," she said into the sensitive skin of his neck. Her mouth couldn't keep off him. "They're a man's trousers."

Rake's fingers faltered, and he groaned.

Gemma couldn't help a laugh. There was so much seriousness and intensity in this act, but also so much delight.

Falls released, and Rake's fingers feathered across the sensitive skin of her stomach, and lower, until they were slipping inside her trousers...sliding along her slit. "So wet for me," he rumbled against her mouth.

His fingers glided across the magical patch of skin that made stars appear behind her eyes. When he found the entrance of her sex and pressed inside, she gasped.

With intention, as he slid in and out of her, his thumb touching *that* place. "Oh, Rake," she groaned.

But—*oh*—she wanted *more.*

She only realized she'd spoken her desire aloud when he pulled away. She opened her mouth to voice a serious objection, but he pressed a light fingertip to her mouth. "Do you trust me?"

A word wanted to fall from her lips, but it wasn't one easily spoken.

So, she nodded.

But it was enough. He swung them around so they faced the interior of the room. "Let's work on getting you more, shall we?"

His feet touched dusty stones, and hers followed. He pulled her close for one more kiss before setting her away. She just caught a glimpse of his wicked smile before he turned her. She reached for the window casement to steady herself, palms digging into rough stone, the valley spread below, the sun shining above, the rain shower gone.

Behind her, Rake bent and removed one of her boots, then the other. "I'm not sure that's strictly necessary," she said over her shoulder.

"It is for what I want to do."

Well.

A bead of heat purled up her spine, slid through her veins, pooled in her sex. She felt vulnerable and open—*nervous...thrilled*—as if she were careening around a bend, blind.

And only this man could see her safely through.

Boots tossed aside, her trousers were sliding down her legs, and he had them flung away too. Capable hands slid beneath her shirt, bared her bottom to the cool air.

"Gemma," he said, and she met his gaze over her shoulder. "Your sweet arse might've become my obsession."

Even as a laugh escaped her—there it was, that delight again—he remained utterly serious as he lowered to his knees behind her.

He took her bottom in both hands and bit lightly. "Just as I thought," he said, his warm breath sending goosebumps racing across her skin.

He licked, and Gemma's hands tightened on the window casement. Her knees threatened to give way.

"Spread your legs," he instructed.

Shock traced through her—even as she did as told. Because here was that feeling again.

A thrilling uncertainty.

And yet, through shock and uncertainty, *trust.*

She very much wanted to know what would appear around this blind bend.

And she trusted this man to show her.

Then she felt it…his lips…his tongue…trailing kisses across her bottom…the backs of her legs. She throbbed… She ached… Though he was giving her *more*, to her body it felt like less, as if a void had opened in her very center that pleaded and demanded to be filled. Surely, it was the only way she would ever feel whole again.

He took a thigh in each hand, and her legs instinctively spread wider. His tongue…oh, his slippery, naughty tongue found…*her*…sliding along her slit, her back arching to grant him more access to that sensitive—*magical*—cluster of nerve endings that demanded—*oh*—just a touch…just the slightest bit of pressure. He held her hips steady, and he gave her a long, slow stroke, and a groan poured from her that sounded more animal than human. The tip of his tongue firmed, and he flicked it against her.

Oh.

And again.

Her legs went wobbly and every cell in her body strained toward the place where he touched *her*. Her entire being felt lit from within as sensation rushed through veins, stilling the breath in her lungs. A whirlwind caught her in its wild orbit, taking her higher and higher, teasing her with release...taunting her... pushing her to a height that surely led to oblivion. If only...*oh*...if only she could...

On the next smooth flick of his talented tongue, the whirlwind let go and she came apart, all the substance of her given permission to leave her corporal form and disintegrate into light and air. She wasn't simply lit from within. She shimmered... She sparkled... As if she'd become one with the ether beyond the stars.

Inevitably, by slow increments, she began a return to Earth, to this room, to the substance of herself, and glanced over her shoulder to find him settled onto his haunches. That wicked smile on his lips, he shifted forward and bussed a parting kiss on each of her arse cheeks, stealing a giggle from her.

A *giggle*.

Was she the sort of woman who giggled now?

But that wasn't the question at the top of her mind right now.

Right now, she had a question of more pressing urgency to ask of this man...

"You don't think you're finished, do you?"

"Aren't I?" he asked, rising smoothly to his feet, his long, capable fingers working the falls of his trousers. Wickedness glinted in his eyes, belying the question.

"You haven't sufficiently proven yourself a rake just yet," she said, coy and breathless.

The falls released, and his length—thick...turgid...*ready*—fell forward, and Gemma sucked in a breath. She should feel silly, but she cared not.

There was no *should feel* in this moment.

There was only *feel*.

And what she felt was a wave of desire for this man so strong it might topple her over.

His eyes dark with intention, he stepped closer so his heavy length brushed against her bottom. *Oh...* the feeling of emptiness inside her... "I need you inside me," she said...pleaded...*begged.* "*Please.*"

That delicious, wicked smile on his mouth, he took a hip in one hand and guided himself to her before entering her in one long, claiming stroke.

Oh, the moan that poured from her as she adjusted to the hard, slick feel of him inside her.

From behind like this felt so *naughty.*

And so...*good.*

Hands masculine and slightly calloused from years of riding moved across her body, one settled at the base of her spine, the other on her shoulder. Masterfully, his hips moved, stroking in and out of her.

Oh, the fullness of him. It was as if her body had been incomplete all this time, and she hadn't known it.

And now she did.

Her back arched, her body wanting—*demanding*—*more.*

"Oh, yes," he growled.

Perspiration pinpricked her skin, as he squeezed her bottom and penetrated her with deep intention—*harder...faster*—and she was moving against him, unable to get enough of this pleasure and pain of union...of *him.*

She sensed his release building, his manhood somehow —*impossibly*—growing thicker and harder. The whirlwind caught her up again—it hadn't quite finished with her, it seemed—and her body went light and variable as she strained against him, demanding more of what he offered...demanding *everything...*

Sudden release expanded and broke within her—*somehow... impossibly*—and she was thrown to the elements—soul and spirit fracturing into sparks of lightning as her body came apart, her sex pulsing around his manhood, its demand unrelenting.

"Gemma," he muttered. "I can't..."

Then he was pulling from her, and she was crying out from the loss. She turned and collapsed back against the wall. His long fingers wrapped around his thick shaft as he took himself in hand and caught her gaze, holding it in his dark grip. Her mouth went dry as she watched him stroke himself, the sight strangely erotic and even more strangely intimate as he brought himself to release and spent onto the ground with a muted shout.

He reached out with his other hand and cupped the back of her head before pulling her toward him. Their lips met, not in headlong lust, but in…

Again, she felt it.

Tenderness.

This man and his contradictions. As if he spent his days fighting his true nature and here it was, revealed only to her. Not the cold, controlling duke he presented. Nothing ran cold inside this man. He was all heat and passion and…*tenderness.*

The kiss was over—*too soon.*

She pulled away only enough to hold his gaze. "Does anyone else know this about you?" she found herself asking.

His eyebrows crinkled together in puzzlement. "What about me?"

She shook her head, already regretting the question, choosing to keep the observation to herself.

Reality had begun to crowd in. This man—this *duke*—didn't want to be called tender.

In silence, they dressed.

Once fully clothed, Gemma watched him knot his cravat and realized she could say something else to him. Something he needed to hear. And if she didn't speak it now, the opportunity might never arise again… "You deserve better than you're allowing yourself."

His fingers froze, and surprised eyes lifted. "I'm a duke. I deny myself nothing."

She wasn't put off. "But don't you?"

This belief of his needed to be challenged, for it wasn't true.

He propped a shoulder against a stone archway and crossed his arms over his chest, waiting for her to continue, all dukely tolerance.

"The marriage you described with the Duchess of Acaster won't make you unhappy," she ventured.

Still, he waited. But she noticed his jaw had gone tight.

Now for the part he needed to hear... "But it won't make you happy, either."

Her words sank, leaden, into the air between them.

"And have you any ideas about the sort of marriage that *would* make me happy?" he asked.

The question was an instinctive riposte, but also a challenge, and strange answers occurred to her. Ones she wouldn't give voice to.

Even to herself.

Perhaps a braver Gemma would speak them.

"That's for you to decide."

She wasn't a braver Gemma.

Opaque emotion flashed behind his eyes and was gone the next instant, so elusive it could've been a trick of the light.

And that was the end of it, as within minutes, they were mounted and riding back to Somerton.

Still, Gemma's mind raced.

What was she thinking by carrying on with Rake—*The Duke of Rakesley*, she reminded herself—in this manner?

She wasn't at Somerton to concern herself with the state of his happiness—or unhappiness.

She was here to spy on a duke's horseracing operation.

A certainty crept in—one she'd been denying to herself but couldn't any longer. If Rake discovered she was a spy, he would come to hate her. He would compare her betrayal to Felicity's, and he wouldn't be half wrong—except it was worse. He would believe she was using her body—and his—to gain access to his secrets.

Guilt grabbed her stomach and twisted it into knots. His hatred and anger she could bear, but it was the hurt she would cause that was more difficult to face.

No.

Guilt was a distraction. It was imperative she regather her focus and intention.

If life had taught her nothing else, it was that one must ever maintain vigilance—or one could lose everything.

All it took was the blinking of an eye for a future to go from bright to bleak.

And she was finished with bleak.

She'd been presented a different future—one that was nearly hers for the taking. All she had to do was hold her nerve and her focus.

It was no small irony that the very man upon whom she was spying was the distraction.

A dangerous, tempting distraction.

For he'd presented a different future.

One with him.

As his mistress.

The future her mother had with the earl.

But, her mind countered, *Rake is a different sort of man.*

A better man.

No.

It mattered not.

To embrace that sort of future would be letting her brother down.

But, most of all, it would be letting herself down.

CHAPTER SEVENTEEN

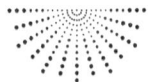

THREE DAYS LATER

*R*ake made his way inside Somerton's small dining room—the one used for family and friends—not the one used for large supper parties and royal visits.

That dining room had more in common with a sumptuously decorated cavern, all echoes and cold drafts.

This room was more akin to a small, sparkling jewel, all done in amethyst silk on the walls and chairs. Rich mahogany graced the floor, its shine reflecting the white coffered ceiling, while in the center stood a large round dining table constructed from walnut with inlays of various exotic woods. A two-tiered crystal chandelier hung above the center and threw sparkling, prismatic light onto every surface.

Rake had taken his evening meal here when in residence at Somerton since he'd become the duke. Mother had wanted him to dine at the more formal table, but his insistence on dining here had been one of his first dukely demands—at age eight. Mother could've overridden him but hadn't. This was around the time she'd started calling him Rake, and of course, that was no coincidence.

He was the duke; he would have his way.

Now, he strode into the room, the table's four occupants engaged in smiling conversation. Julian, the Duchess of Acaster, Artemis, and her bosom friend, Lady Beatrix, who had only arrived this afternoon. As Rake took his seat, he found his sister and Lady Beatrix teasing Julian about the name of the colt he planned to run in the Derby.

"But, Julian," said Artemis. *"Filthy Habit?"*

Julian spread his hands wide. "I didn't name him. You know how it goes with these racehorse names. Everyone tries to outdo everyone else to see what they can get away with."

"Sir Peter Teazle is a particular favorite of mine," said the Duchess of Acaster—*Celia*, she kept insisting.

And Rake kept trying.

"My filly is called Light Skirt."

"But it's a fact well established," said Lady Beatrix in her matter-of-fact manner, "that the Marquess of Ormonde is one of the most virtuous lords in the land. A single glance at his angelic looks will tell you as much. He possesses not one single, solitary filthy habit."

The duchess took a sip of her champagne and canted her head. "I'm afraid I'll have to disagree with you there, Lady Beatrix."

Artemis gasped. "Is there something you know about Julian that the rest of us don't?"

"Not particularly," said the duchess. "But in the general sense, yes. I've become convinced over the years that there isn't a man on this Earth who isn't possessed of at least one filthy habit." She shrugged, helpless against the rules of the universe. "My apologies, Lord Ormonde if I've put you under pressure," she finished on a laugh and another gulp of champagne.

"Not at all," said Julian, an amused smile about his mouth that didn't quite reach his eyes. Only Rake would notice that last bit about his friend.

As for the Duchess of—*Celia*, Rake had rather come to like her. She was intelligent, beautiful, serious about her stables, and possessed of a sense of levity. He could appreciate such a woman.

In fact, such a woman was exactly the sort he should take to wife.

While the conversation flowed around him, his gaze slid over to the empty place to his right. One supper guest hadn't yet arrived.

Gemma.

Tomorrow, they all would begin walking their colts and fillies to Newmarket, which would take a few days as the process was slow so as not to wear out the horses. As tonight was their last night at Somerton, Rake had decided to hold a small supper and invite his jockey. Such things were done. No matter that she wasn't an aristocrat; he was a duke, and if he wanted to invite his jockey to supper, that was entirely his prerogative.

Now, he could only hope his jockey would grace the gathering with her presence.

He'd only seen her on the practice course or in passing these last three days. Each time, however fleeting, he experienced a jolt in his body—and a pull.

But he'd resisted it and had satisfied himself with daily reports from Wilson, as most owners did.

If that could be called satisfaction.

It wasn't.

He shouldn't have invited her tonight for two simple reasons.

First, he should be staying away from her. After their last encounter, he'd realized he'd gone too far.

In more ways than one.

He needed to rein himself in. It wasn't as much about the physical act as it was about the words voiced—and the ones left unvoiced.

The marriage to the Duchess of Acaster won't make you happy.

That wasn't the worst of it. He'd followed her words with some of his own—more of a challenge, really.

And have you any ideas about the sort of marriage that would make me happy?

He could hardly warrant it.

Nay.

It wasn't his words he couldn't warrant. It was momentary impulse—one barely contained—to follow those words to a different conclusion.

One that would have him either rejected outright or...

Engaged to wed his jockey.

An idea that defied belief.

But does it, came the small voice that wouldn't leave him be.

He'd made a laughingstock of himself a decade ago with Felicity. Three days ago, he'd found himself on the verge of making a fool of himself, again—with his jockey.

And there was the second reason he shouldn't have invited her to dine with them tonight.

He'd given her the power of refusal.

Truly, he couldn't be trusted around women.

Horses were an altogether safer bet.

As were duchesses who flashed sparkling eyes full of invitation his way.

Celia held up her champagne coupe in a silent toast intended for only the two of them. Rake raised his coupe and drank, thankful he'd had her seated opposite him and not beside him in the guest of honor's chair. That chair was reserved for his jockey —*Gemma*—and remained stubbornly empty.

"Brother, what's your opinion?" asked Artemis. The mischievous look in her eyes told him she'd seen him not heeding the conversation and had purposely caught him out. It had been a favorite game of hers since childhood.

"About...?" He asked, unbothered.

"The ladies have been discussing the Earl of Bridgewater," supplied Julian.

Rake gave an indifferent shrug. "I don't have much of an opinion on Bridgewater beyond what everyone knows. He runs his horses into the ground and does the same with his women."

"He's just married," supplied Lady Beatrix. It was little wonder she and Artemis were bosom friends. Both ladies were inquisitive to a fault and unafraid to voice it. "And his new bride is thirty years younger."

That was quite a disparity in age, even by *ton* standards.

"Thirty years?" scoffed Celia. "Why, that's nothing. Try fifty-six."

An uncomfortable silence stretched. Rake had known the years between Acaster and his duchess had been great, but fifty-six... It was unconscionable, really.

Needless to say, Celia had surely more than earned the freedom afforded her by widowhood. And yet...here she was, presumably anxious to shackle herself to Rake a year after the duke's death.

Curious, that.

He cleared his throat and held up his refreshed champagne coupe. "I wish Bridgewater's countess the very best of luck." A beat. "She's going to need it."

"Why is that?" asked Celia. "Beyond the usual reasons, of course," she added, the lightness of her words belied by the seriousness in her eyes.

Marriage certainly hadn't been kind to the Duchess of Acaster.

"Bridgewater is more known for his stable of mistresses than horses."

"Ah, but you're making quite the assumption."

"Which is?"

"That his countess made a love match on her side."

That got a few amused waggles of eyebrows around the table,

and Rake realized he had, indeed, made that assumption. Even after Felicity—and even with his own intentions toward this very duchess—he'd made the assumption of a love match on the part of the lady.

What was becoming of him?

"You see," continued Celia, her gaze steadily holding his, "I would be the sort of bride who would welcome an understanding with my husband."

Mistresses. Rake would be free to have mistresses.

A potential prospect came to mind... The woman for whom he might've formed a bit of an obsession.

He would never feel thusly for the duchess, which left little doubt that she was the perfect wife for him.

Yet Rake did doubt.

Why else hadn't he proposed marriage these last three days? He'd been given ample opportunity.

And still he hadn't been able to bring himself to the point.

You deserve better than you're allowing yourself.

What match would be better than an understanding duchess with a stable full of racehorses?

The small voice inside him opened its mouth to reply—it seemed to harbor notions of a different match—and he quashed it.

No good could come of that reply.

As if his thoughts had the power to conjure the woman, a figure appeared in the doorway.

Gemma, hesitating as she glanced around uncertainly, dressed in the new set of clothes he'd had delivered to her room today. Not a silk dress and satin slippers, as he'd been tempted to send, but a man's ensemble, from black leather boots buffed to a mirror shine to gray trousers and matching coat to pure white silk cravat and moss-green waistcoat intended to pull the color from her eyes. Hair tied back into its customary queue at the nape of her neck, she looked quite dashing.

But what she didn't look like was a man.

A cleaned-up Gem bore a striking resemblance to a Gemma.

Julian caught Rake's gaze and lifted a single, inquiring eyebrow.

In fact, as Rake glanced around the table, he saw from the cant of everyone's heads they'd all arrived at the same conclusion.

"Ah, Gem," said Rake, "delighted you deigned to join us."

That got a curious shift of everyone's gazes toward Rake. No matter. This was between him and Gemma. He indicated the chair to his right. "For the guest of honor."

She didn't immediately take him up on his offer, looking poised to pivot on her heel and flee. Instead, she drew herself upright and entered the room as if she belonged here as much as the duke, duchess, marquess, daughter of a duke, and daughter of a marquess populating it.

If she'd been born on the correct side of the blanket, the fact was she would.

The table conversation moved on, but Rake paid no mind to it. His mind only had room for Gemma.

A footman pulled her chair from the table, and she slipped into it. Separated by no more than two feet, Rake imagined he could feel her heat.

Except it wasn't her heat he felt. It was his own.

The reason?

Simply that the blood rushed faster in his veins when she was near.

Though the soup course had arrived, it was her scent that he caught. Clean and fresh from the lye washing she'd surely given herself. He wouldn't think about the sight of her administering to such ablutions to herself, or he would give himself a cockstand here at the supper table.

Oh, blast it, he was already halfway there.

But she smelled of Gemma too—of woman and hay and faintly of horse.

She ever would smell faintly of horse.

He liked that about her.

From beneath her golden lashes, her gaze darted about the table, taking in the others and reaching her own conclusions about them all.

Nobs.

That would be her conclusion.

Lady Beatrix swallowed a sip of soup and directed a question at Celia. "Has the new Duke of Acaster yet been located?"

A long-suffering sigh poured from the duchess. "Not that I've been made aware of. Really, I've stopped bothering with checking. Rumors, of course, persist, but nothing of substance. The Crown will give it another six years before they either find someone else or allow the title to go extinct." She shrugged an ivory shoulder. "In the meantime, I shall carry on as dowager duchess." Her gaze met Rake's. "Anyway, the main thing is the horses in the duke's stables are mine outright. Acaster left them to me in his will."

A fact she reminded Rake of at every opportunity—and that she was, objectively, the perfect match for him.

And the woman to his right, trying to decide which spoon to use for her soup... She wasn't.

He slid his hand over and discreetly tapped the outer spoon.

"Speaking of horses, Celia," said Artemis, angling back in her chair to allow the footman to take her empty soup bowl. "Your Light Skirt is a sweet goer, if I ever saw one."

"Isn't she just?" Celia allowed the fish course to be placed before her.

"She'll take the One Thousand Guineas," said Artemis with her usual certainty. She sliced into her fillet of trout. "Mark my words."

Rake dragged his attention away from Gemma, who'd taken a bite of the trout and was chewing the fish slowly as if savoring it flavor by individual flavor. The woman appreciated good food. "Artemis," he said, "you should enter Dido in the One Thousand."

As expected, she rolled her eyes toward the ceiling. "I suppose I can't blame you for trying, brother," she scoffed. "I've no doubt she could take the One Thousand Guineas—"

"She could try," inserted Celia. "But with all due respect, she would have to get past my Light Skirt—and that won't be easy."

"Of course," Artemis allowed, like the good sporting woman she was. "But it's my Dido who will be besting Hannibal and taking the Two Thousand in one week's time." She held up her wineglass, cheekily toasted Rake, and downed the contents in one go.

"Are you trying for a place in the Race of the Century, duchess?" asked Julian.

Rake noted Gemma had moved forward in her seat, food forgotten. She was watching the conversation with the keen awareness of a competitor taking the measure of her rivals. Perhaps a useful morsel of information would escape that would give her an edge.

Celia gave the room her bright laugh intended to charm all it met. "Aren't we all?"

"I still say it's a ridiculous name for the race," said Artemis. "The century isn't even—"

"Half over yet," Rake finished for her, pulling a chuckle from Julian.

"Well," Artemis sniffed, "it isn't."

"Any word yet on the mysterious investors?" asked Julian with an off-hand smile.

All eyes shifted toward Lady Beatrix, who moved forward ever so slightly, eyes brimming with knowledge. "Rumors abound, of course," said the lady. "But I have it on good authority that the Duke of Richmond is one investor, and the other is…" Her mouth curled into a smile—the sort of smile comfortable with making a room hang on her words.

"Beatrix!" exclaimed Artemis, utterly put out with her friend.

"Gabriel Siren," relented Lady Beatrix, at last.

Artemis's eyebrows crinkled. "Who?"

"Owner of the Archangel," supplied Julian.

"The *Archangel?*" asked Artemis, no more enlightened than she'd been before.

"How would you describe the Archangel, Rake?" asked Julian. "It's not really a gaming hell."

"It's where those with money go to make more money," said Rake.

The duchess laughed. "Oh, is that all?"

"And this Gabriel Siren," said Artemis. "Who is he?"

"A young buck who only left Cambridge a few years ago, well behind Julian and me."

During the conversation, Rake felt Gemma beside him, attentive, taking it all in, forming her own impressions of the revelations and those who spoke them.

"Has the Midas touch," said Lady Beatrix. "At least, that's his reputation. Known as a maths prodigy, I believe."

"Well, if I were to lay odds on the Newmarket races," said Julian, "the Archangel is where I'd do it. Best chance of not getting cheated."

The duchess's gaze cut across the table and landed to the right of Rake—on Gemma. A sharp glint lit within her luminous amber depths. Gemma didn't seem to notice as she was presently scraping the cream sauce off her plate. As she sucked the last of it from the tines of her fork, Rake watched, transfixed.

"And you, Mr…" began Celia.

All gazes swung toward Gemma. It took a few beats of time for her to realize she was *Mr…*

Her fork clattered onto the plate, and she gave her mouth a hasty swipe of her napkin. "*Erm.*" She cleared her throat. "Cassidy," she said. "Gem Cassidy."

Celia's mouth lifted into a smile that didn't reach her eyes.

The glint had sharpened into a point. "Mr. Cassidy," she began, "are you a recent acquisition of the duke's?"

Gemma froze in place. All except for her eyes, which blinked, as if not quite sure she'd heard what she thought she'd heard.

Then a shift occurred—one only Rake would recognize. Gemma's jaw clenched and a responding glint sparked within her eye.

And here she was.

The Gemma he knew.

The woman who'd tamed an untamable horse and rode him fearlessly. The woman unafraid to mouth off to a duke when he needed it.

With this Gemma, the duchess with the butter-wouldn't-melt-in-her-mouth smile didn't stand a chance.

Rake braced himself.

"I'm afraid that isn't possible," she said, low and sure.

She was speaking not as Gem, but as Gemma. Rake doubted she realized.

"And why is that?" asked Celia with all the arch hauteur of a duchess.

"I cannot be *acquired*, because I'm neither object nor slave nor horse."

How Rake had missed this woman these last three days.

CHAPTER EIGHTEEN

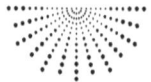

*S*tunned silence expanded through the room, filling it to bursting.

Gemma had even stunned herself.

The Duchess of Acaster's perfectly shaped eyebrows creased and released.

"Your Grace," Gemma only remembered to add five seconds later.

Five of the longest seconds of her life.

She dared not look at Rake, though she felt the heat of his gaze on the side of her face.

Just when the stunned silence threatened to extend into the next century, the duchess broke it. "And neither are you a lady," she said, holding up her recently refreshed coupe of champagne. "And you can trust me on this, *erm*, *Mr.* Cassidy, you're the better off for it." She downed the contents of her glass in a single swallow.

Not only did the woman look genuinely apologetic, but also thoroughly unconvinced of the *mister* portion of her words. She didn't believe for a moment that *Mr.* Gem Cassidy was a lad.

Gemma stole a glance around the table. It was likely no one in this room thought her a *mister*.

She was too clean. That was the problem. She lacked the concealing layer of grime that made Gem possible.

As it stood, she must've looked more akin to an eccentric woman.

Blessedly, talk returned to turf gossip, and Gemma considered the plate of sliced beef smothered in a luscious brown sauce and the creamed potatoes before her. She experienced a pang of longing for Mam, who could've easily prepared this meal. That was how tasty tonight's fare was. It was Gemma's highest praise.

Just now, a name was spoken... A name that pulled Gemma from her gustatory reverie and froze every muscle in her body. Her gaze fixed on her plate, she listened. Surely the name had been a trick of the ear...

"Where does the Deverill name hail from, anyway?" asked Lady Artemis.

"Ireland?" replied Lord Ormonde on an indifferent shrug.

"They call him Lord Devil," supplied Lady Beatrix, who bore a striking resemblance to a fox with her quick eyes that missed nothing. "Word has it that he has spies in every excellent racing stable in England. You might even have one in yours, Rake," she finished with a little waggle of her eyebrows.

Rake snorted, dismissive.

He would be.

To his detriment.

"Not at Somerton," he said, so certain. "Wilson keeps the lads in line and the stables clean. He's already routed two spies this year."

A ringing started in Gemma's ears, and a flare of heat struck through her. It was ever so when she became distressed. The beef turned to bland dust in her mouth.

"Anyway, there's always some such fellow with more money

than sense," he continued. "Gets a goer in his stables and thinks he'll sweep the season. But a single horse doesn't a stable make. There's no depth."

Lady Artemis smiled, teasingly. "I've heard this Deverill looks like Lucifer himself."

Lord Ormonde snorted. "Pointy horns and all?"

Lady Beatrix's expression went from vulpine to feline. "She's saying he's the most beautiful of all God's creations."

"Too beautiful to behold directly is what I've heard," corrected Lady Artemis. "'Tis said his blue eyes are so striking, they pierce to the quick of a lady's soul."

Rake snorted again.

Gemma held her peace.

What was there to say, really? Beyond the fact that she was a spy for Lord Devil, of course, and had been sending him two reports a week on Somerton's operation.

"What folderol." Rake pointed a faux-serious finger toward Lady Artemis. "And I forbid you from marrying him."

Sudden laughter burst from the lady. "I shall marry precisely no one, so don't concern yourself there, brother. Our dear, sweet mother taught me young about the consequences of ill-advised, unsuitable matches." An uncharacteristic edge of bitterness ran along her next laugh.

Rake didn't seem to notice. "The fact of the matter is that a filly with Little Wicked's lineage has no business in the stable of a man like Deverill."

Lady Beatrix's eyes narrowed. "And what is a man *like Deverill*? Not an aristocrat like yourself?"

"Not a man of the turf," returned Rake. "Racing is a lark to someone like him. And last time I checked, *Lady* Beatrix, you were the daughter of a marquess."

Lady Beatrix pursed her mouth and nodded, conceding the point. "Touché."

"And Bolton?" asked Lord Ormonde.

The ringing in Gemma's ears turned into the panicky clanging of an alarm bell.

Bolton.

Surely, he was speaking of a different Bolton.

"I heard he's entering a colt in the Two Thousand Guineas," continued the marquess as if he hadn't just flipped the room upside down. "Bloody Hell is his name, I believe."

It was.

Gemma had been present in the foaling box when Bloody Hell had been born.

Her heart threatened to break through her ribs, so hard and fast it banged about.

Lord Ormonde wasn't speaking of a different Bolton.

"Lord Bolton is the most unpleasant man I've ever encountered," said the duchess, her forkful of potatoes halfway to her mouth. "And that's saying something, because—" She took her bite, chewed, and swallowed, all in her own time. The room waited. "I was married to the Duke of Acaster," she finished on a laugh wholly composed of spiky points.

Though she surely shared nothing in common with the duchess—well, the woman did love her horses, Gemma would concede that—Gemma sensed something familiar in this beautiful, closely guarded woman.

She'd endured harm…

From a man.

It was an experience Gemma was particularly attuned to.

Rake flicked a piece of lint off his evening jacket. "He isn't competition. He hasn't entered a horse in a race in years."

"Anyone know why?" asked Lady Artemis.

Gemma felt sick.

All eyes turned toward Lady Beatrix—*again.* The lady did seem mightily knowledgeable on matters of society and turf gossip. "Strange whisperings about him persist."

"*Like?*" prodded Lady Artemis.

"Like he's gone half mad with grief."

"*Grief?*"

"I wasn't aware the countess was deceased," said Rake.

He glanced down at Gemma's hands, which had twisted her napkin into a knot, then lifted to meet her gaze, a question in his eyes.

"Not the countess," said Lady Beatrix.

It was the way she spoke the words that made the message clear. *Not the countess*, but a different woman in his life. No one had to say, "Ah," for that *ah* to echo off the four walls of this dining room.

"Word has it she was his cook—and there's more."

Everyone waited with bated breath until Lady Artemis exclaimed on a huff of frustration, "Out with it, Beatrix."

"Children."

Yet another *ah* that didn't need to be voiced. *Children*...on the other side of the blanket.

"*Children?*" scoffed Lord Ormonde. "One is an accident. Two is simply poor management."

Before Gemma could properly think through her actions, her chair was scraping across the floor, and she was shooting to her feet. She had to leave.

Now.

Before the walls crowded in and suffocated her. Her feet already on the move, she mumbled a few indistinct words and fled the room...

The house...

Through the stables and into her bedroom, all those footsteps a blur as she collapsed back against the closed door, her breath a sharp, ragged rasp in her throat and lungs.

Bolton.

He would be present at the Two Thousand Guineas. Of course, he would. And if the conditions were favorable, she had no doubt Bloody Hell could win it. The colt had been of sweet, solid temperament from the moment of his birth. When she and Liam had made the decision to leave Bolton's estate, it had been Bloody Hell to whom she'd spoken her final goodbyes.

But seeing him again meant seeing Bolton.

She set about tearing off all the fine, borrowed clothes sent by Rake and immediately donned her old, familiar rags. Instinct had her rushing across the room and jerking open the wardrobe, grabbing the rest of her belongings and stuffing them into her valise.

The fact was she could leave—*tonight...now.*

She'd collected enough information on the Somerton operation for Deverill.

And she didn't have to ride in the Two Thousand Guineas.

A pang of anguish struck through her at the very thought. She wanted to see the race through with Hannibal. With her on his back, he would show England what he could do.

No. She couldn't let such thoughts slow her.

She would ask Deverill for payment, then she and Liam would be on their way to New York.

It was that simple.

And that painful.

Here was something precious, lost.

But had it—the something precious she'd lost—had it ever been hers in the first place?

Two light taps sounded on the door. She stopped mid-step, and silence prevailed.

He was waiting.

That was the thing about the Duke of Rakesley. He was a patient man. He could wait and wait and wait. He was a stubborn man too.

If she wanted to flee Somerton, she would have to go through him.

That was what his presence at her door said.

She recovered the remaining frayed bits of her nerve and jerked the door open. She avoided his gaze and silently stood aside. He was going to come in. She might as well invite him.

As he stepped past, she inhaled. She couldn't help herself. He was the most delicious-smelling man she'd ever come across. Of course, most men she came across labored in stables. Still...

He gave the room a quick scan. "Going somewhere?"

Gemma glanced away from his too-insightful gaze. "It might be best if I..."

She couldn't finish the sentence. Every part of her mutinied against leaving.

And yet she must.

He crossed the small room in two quick strides, pulled a chair out from the beneath the rickety wooden table, and sat, settling back and resting an ankle on his thigh. He looked utterly at ease and utterly in command.

Gemma wasn't going anywhere just yet. That was what Rake was telling her without saying a word. She set her valise on the bed.

"It's Bolton, isn't it?" he said, getting straight to it in the way only he could.

"Bolton?" she asked. It emerged more squeak than word.

"*Bolton,*" he enunciated slowly.

Knowledge.

That was what shone in his eyes.

She gave a tight nod.

Silently, he dared her to look away—and waited.

She didn't have to explain herself to this man.

But she found she wanted to. She cleared her throat. "You know bits and pieces already. Liam's and my—"

"Your brother?"

"Aye." A truth revealed. Already, she felt lighter.

Rake nodded.

"Our Mam was a country lass from County Cork who went into service for a local lord."

Unshed tears clogged Gemma's throat, even as it felt good to speak of her mother, to acknowledge her. To bring her into the light when she'd spent so many years in the shadow of Bolton. A few angry tears mixed in with the grieving ones.

She moved to the foot of the bed and perched on its edge. "A visiting lord—Bolton—got a taste of her cooking and lured her away to England with the promise of adventure. He had an Irish mother and missed the flavors of the country. And Mam was beautiful. Wild red curls that glowed orange in the light. I suppose matters between them led where such matters between men and women lead, and Mam gave birth to boy and girl twins within the first year."

"And the Countess of Bolton had nothing to say about this arrangement?" Skepticism etched Rake's features.

Oh, there was so much this man didn't understand, because he simply couldn't conceive of it.

"The countess was childless, and Bolton took Mam's pregnancy and the birth of, not one, but two children as proof that something was fundamentally wrong with his wife. She wasn't of much use to him after that."

"Still," protested Rake, "she's the Countess of Bolton. She has a few rights."

"I think she would've been too embarrassed to pursue any rights through the law."

Rake held his silence. They both knew it for the truth.

"The thing about Bolton is…" Gemma couldn't quite articulate how to say what needed to be said.

"Yes?"

"No one can say anything contrary to his wishes."

"So, you all lived under one roof as one big, happy family?" scoffed Rake, disbelieving.

"Under one roof, yes, but *happy* would be overstating matters."

"He did have you and Liam educated."

"He brought in a tutor, yes," she said carefully.

"But you didn't leave the estate." He seemed to be catching on. "He made sure no one knew about you and Liam."

"We were never acknowledged openly, especially by the countess. We were his shadow children." That was how Gemma had felt for most of her life—like a shadow. "We belonged to him. All of us. The countess. Mam. Liam. Me."

Rake's brow creased. The next instant his face became thunderous. "What do you mean you *belonged* to him? Did he restrain you physically?"

This was the difficult part to explain—even to herself. "No."

"Your mother could've left with you and Liam."

"Growing up, I didn't understand her choice, either, until I realized it wasn't a choice."

"I'm afraid I don't understand."

"Bolton shaped her world. He shaped all our worlds." Gemma spoke words and ideas aloud that had never been given voice. "We existed to be in service to him. There were no thoughts or dreams beyond him. He knew of the affinity Liam and I had toward horses, so he planned that Liam would someday manage the stables."

"It does sound reasonable for an illegitimate son."

"It does," said Gemma. "I know it does."

"And he knows that, doesn't he," said Rake.

Here was understanding that made the burden lighter. "Then Mam got sick. At first, she was tired. Then she started coughing and was hardly able to get out of bed. This went on for a year."

"And Bolton?" asked Rake. "I can't imagine he took it well."

"The further Mam declined, the more controlling he became. Before Mam's sickness, Liam and I had already discussed a plan to leave. But once we realized she wouldn't be recovering, we stayed. And then—" A sudden sob took Gemma's remaining words.

Rake unhooked his ankle from his thigh and crossed the distance between them, settling beside her on the bed and taking her hand. This man…so impressive and capable and…*tender*. She might be the only person on Earth who knew this about him.

"She passed away," he said for her.

The sob receded. "Bolton became unpredictable. One moment, he was almost affectionate, and the next he couldn't stand the sight of our faces because we reminded him of his lost Maeve. So…"

"You and Liam left."

Gemma nodded. "First to Chester, then to Manchester, but those cities were too small."

"He pursued you?"

"Strange men would appear and follow us around, hanging about, making sure we saw them."

"Men hired by Bolton."

"We believed so."

"He was letting you know he still held all the power, and he would use it in his own time."

"Until we made the journey to London."

"A city big enough to get lost in."

"We didn't stay in one lodging for more than a few months, bouncing around from stable to stable."

Rake cocked his head. "How long have you been living this way?"

"More than a year now."

"You can't run forever."

"No."

And here was where Gemma knew the story must end. She and Liam couldn't run forever—which was why they'd accepted Deverill's offer.

Which was why she was betraying the tender, impressive man sitting beside her.

"I still don't understand it," said Rake.

Gemma braced herself. Here was where she would have to start lying again.

"How did you come to be in The Drunken Piebald's stable?"

Gemma found enough truth to draw upon. "Liam planned on seeking employment at Somerton."

"Ah," said Rake. "Which explains your boldness that first night. But, still, why?"

"Liam is quite a talented jockey. Word had reached London that you were experiencing jockey trouble, so he decided to throw his hat in the ring."

"And Liam, where is he, anyway?"

"At The Drunken Piebald, nursing a broken leg."

A beat of time passed. "So, you decided to take his place."

"Liam was none too keen on the idea."

"And the rest is history."

"Something like that."

"But not truly, is it?"

Panic streaked through her. Had he read the rest of the truth between the lines of what she'd said?

"Bolton won't have stopped pursuing the two of you."

"Aye."

"And now you know he'll be at the Two Thousand Guineas."

"Are you trying to make me feel worse?"

Rake tucked a thumb beneath her chin and turned her head so she was left with no choice but to meet his gaze. "Here's the thing, Gemma. You don't belong to Bolton. You belong only to yourself."

To hear those words spoken aloud—words she'd never been brave enough to speak herself—shifted something inside Gemma.

Because this man believed them.

And if he believed them, then perhaps she could as well.

"I can help you, Gemma."

His words set off a contradictory storm of emotions within

her. If he knew what she'd been doing to be free of Bolton, he wouldn't be speaking them.

And yet... How seductive was his offer—the idea of it.

Of him and her being on the same side.

A seductive fantasy was all it was.

"Stay, Gemma," he said.

CHAPTER NINETEEN

*S*tay…

The word not a command, but a plea.

One Gemma was powerless against.

She would stay, she knew, because it was he who asked.

She nodded, and a flash of relief passed behind his eyes.

What was happening between them?

Or was the correct question…what had already happened between them?

Past tense.

That was the feeling behind this feeling—both as if newly sprung into existence and as if it had always been there. As if it had snuck in when she wasn't looking and become part of her—now integral.

If she left, a core part of her would cease to exist entirely.

So, she would stay.

Tonight.

Then in a week, once she'd ridden Hannibal to certain victory, she would cut off this integral part of herself and go.

But, tonight yet remained.

She touched his face, the day's growth of stubble rough

beneath her fingertips. "Won't your guests wonder at your absence?" Even as she asked the question, her gaze fell to his lips.

She needed them upon her again.

"Perhaps." His eyes told her he cared, not about his guests, but about…

Her.

Her hand slid around his neck, her fingers weaving through thick, silky hair that curled at the ends. His head angled down, and her face tipped up. His breath skated across her mouth and their lips met.

Her body pulled—*begged*—to deepen the kiss, to descend directly into the carnal.

But other parts of her wanted something more.

She pulled away and met a question in his eyes. But he left it at that. This powerful, impressive man was ceding control and letting her take the reins. He could easily have all the power in this moment, but he was acknowledging her power.

Now, what to do with it?

What did she want?

Him.

An easy enough answer.

The real question was…

How?

How did she want this powerful, caring man?

She slipped her hands beneath his coat and pushed it off his shoulders. She wasn't sure exactly how she wanted him, but it was certainly with fewer articles of clothing. She unknotted his cravat and flung it away. As white silk fluttered to the floor, a smile twitched about his mouth, but his gaze remained serious and centered entirely on her.

She found the short row of buttons on his midnight blue waistcoat and made fumbly work of them. Then it was tossed aside, and his white muslin shirt flopped open in a V, revealing the dark fuzz of hair on his chest and the dense muscles beneath.

So...*male.*

A molten feeling slipped through her veins, pooling in her sex, making her thighs squeeze together. She could take him like this, the thick bulge straining against his trousers told her as much. Only a few flicks of the buttons of his falls separated her from what she wanted...*craved.*

But she hadn't yet arrived at *how.*

She tugged his shirt from the waistband and lifted it over his head. He planted his palms on the bed behind him and leaned back, curiosity and challenge in his eyes. Her gaze feasted on him —his broad shoulders, muscled chest, ridged stomach, dark hair that narrowed and pulled her eye down...

A shiver of anticipation traced through her. His manhood looked as if it were about to burst through his trousers, and an idea about *how* she wanted him came to her.

"I've never been had quite like this," rumbled from his chest.

And it hit her.

Just as she'd never been allowed this sort of control, he'd never ceded it. They were each venturing into a new sort of place.

A place of freedom for both of them.

"I know," she said.

She placed a hand on each of his thick, muscled thighs and pushed them wide enough to step between. This man was hers to take.

Exactly *how* she wanted.

She took one boot in hand, then the other, removing them with a few efficient tugs. Socks quickly followed.

With slow intention, she sank to her knees between his muscled thighs. Down the length of his half-clad body, he watched her, his eyes gone impenetrably dark. His pulse throbbed visibly in the column of his throat.

Her fingers traced up his thighs, squeezing those dense muscles, making their way deliberately up...up...up... They found the hard ridge of his manhood and her touch went light, feathering along his length, grazing her fingernails across fabric. He sucked in a sharp breath. She increased the pressure of her hand, rubbing him through gray superfine.

"I'm not sure how much of this I can take."

She'd begun to wonder the same about herself.

Fingers gone trembly, she slipped one button free, then another, and another, until she had *him* bared to her gaze.

A word returned to her.

Feast.

The man splayed before her was a feast.

And, oh, how she wanted a taste.

Her fingers wrapped around his hard, velvet length and stroked. A long groan escaped him. She shifted forward, enveloped in his musky, masculine scent, before her tongue reached out and tasted him. *Salt.* Her hand wrapped around his base as her tongue slid up his long shaft.

But she wanted more than a taste.

She took him into her mouth, inch by thick inch, her hand still gripping him, stroking him, as he and she found a rhythm.

"Oh, Gemma," poured from him.

Deeper, she took him in yet another inch, and his dark gaze met hers across his body. Gemma had never experienced the intimacy she was feeling in this moment. That this man was making himself vulnerable to her was a gift.

One she didn't deserve.

But that thought was for later.

For now…

With her mouth, she took him…savored him…drove him wild.

If this was power, she wanted more of it.

But, oh, how her sex ached. It needed *him* inside her.

He reached out and stroked her hair, weaving long, capable

fingers through her curls. "Gemma, I don't want to spend this way."

And she understood. Just as he'd brought her to release with his mouth, she'd brought him to the brink with hers.

She shifted back and, slowly, he slipped from her mouth.

On legs trembly with desire, she came to her feet.

Over her head went her shirt, down her legs her trousers. And still he watched with his dark, inscrutable gaze as she stood bared to him, body and, perhaps, soul too.

Perhaps, in this moment, it was safe to be so.

"Gemma, you're a beauty all the way through."

Her gaze wanted to slide away, to elide his words—her natural response to praise. To be noticed had never been good in her world.

But she wanted to be found beautiful by this man. From his mouth it wasn't a lie or flattery. It was the truth.

He saw her as beautiful.

He hooked a hand around her waist and tugged her forward. On instinct, she straddled his thighs and wound her arms around his neck, chest to chest, her taut nipples pressing into him, muscles unyielding.

Oh, he was all hard man, wasn't he?

With his other hand, he positioned the crown of his shaft against her sex. Then, inch by deliberate inch, she lowered onto him, impaling herself on his thick, heavy length.

Oh, the feel of him inside her—*hot...substantial...*

His fingers slid around to cup her bottom, and she hooked one ankle over the other around his waist as she adjusted to the feel of *him*. His lips on hers, she exhaled a long groan into his mouth, no doubt in her mind that she was having this man exactly *how* she wanted him.

There was—*oh*—simply so much of him.

With slow intention, he began to move her on his thick length, her hips responding intuitively to the rhythm he set. A thin sheen of perspiration coated their bodies, skin flushed with it.

At the center of this act was a tenderness, but also a demand. A push and a pull. An act full of contradictions. An act so very full of all that was human—the pleasure… the pain… the want… the need… the drive… the greed—all of it in one act…

With the right person.

And as her body gave in to its very humanity—*the pleasure… the pain… the want… the need… the drive… the greed*—she understood this man was the right person.

A feeling began to coil in her sex—one that had been made so very familiar to her by this man. She sensed the same in him as he began to drive into her with more focused intention. Though they were two separate people with their own ideas, ambitions, and drives, in this moment, she was one with him.

She caught his gaze and held it. *There.* That same feeling…that connection…the vulnerability that made such connection possible.

A feeling sank deep and unfurled inside her.

One she would carry with her long after she'd left him.

A feeling that would surely break her heart in two.

But the feeling, in this moment, only amplified what their bodies were experiencing.

She felt herself begin to tense on top of him, her body making demands that felt impossible to satisfy and yet…

Greedy fingers squeezed tighter around her bottom as he drove her onto him, stroke after stroke, relentless.

"Oh, Rake," she gasped.

"Too much?" he asked into her neck, his lips sliding against damp skin.

"No," she said, breathless, pleasure and pain spiking through her, mingling, one inseparable from the other.

It was so much. *He* was so much. Surely *too* much. But somehow…*improbably*—she took all of him…*demanded* all of him.

Pleasured to within an inch of its life, her sex held for an uncertain moment, teetering on an edge before it tumbled over and broke, a ragged cry pouring from her as she held on tight, the sensation of lightness blossoming inside her, tingling through her veins to the very tips of fingers and toes.

"*Gemma*," he groaned into her neck as he continued to move her on him, impossibly deeper, the promise of his own release drawing him inward.

At the very last moment, he pulled from her and took himself in hand. Instinctively, her fingers pushed his aside and wrapped around him. "Like this?" she asked, giving his length a testing stroke, an unexpected feeling of power slipping through her.

"Oh, yes," he rasped, his voice a crushed-velvet scrape, his dark gaze watching her bring him to the edge, then over it, as he shouted his climax toward the ceiling, his seed pulsing onto his stomach. He collapsed back onto an elbow, utterly spent.

Gemma reached for a cloth on the washbasin. With a few quick swipes, she had him cleaned up and was collapsing beside him.

He slid an arm beneath her head and turned onto his side, so he faced her. His gaze brimmed with words unspoken.

Words he looked determined to speak.

Not yet, came a plea from deep inside her.

With words, reality would steal into the moment.

And she wasn't yet ready for reality.

"Gemma," he said.

She touched a fingertip to his lips. "Not yet."

He took her hand in his and lowered it to his chest. Beneath her palm beat his heart, steady and sure.

"You're safe."

And there was reality landed square in the moment.

"Rake—"

Now it was him touching a silencing fingertip to her mouth.

"With me," he said. "You're safe with me."

"I know."

And it was true.

She did know it.

But she knew something else.

It couldn't last.

But he didn't know that.

A week from now, the rest of her life would begin—without him.

She swallowed back sudden emotion that wanted release. "I leave with Hannibal at dawn." The change of subject was utterly necessary.

"You don't have to go just yet," he countered. "Wilson and Blankenship can walk him with a few lads. You could go later in the week."

Temptation pulled at her.

Temptation to stay a few more days.

Temptation for more nights like this one.

But if she gave in to temptation, she wouldn't be able to leave.

And she couldn't stay.

Not after having betrayed him.

How she wished she could take it all back.

But it was too late for that.

"I must go."

They both knew she was speaking of more than getting Hannibal settled at Newmarket.

Rake had the air of a man who wasn't done fighting.

A man who didn't know the fight was already lost before it had begun.

"You'll be sleeping in the stall with Hannibal all week, won't you?"

"Aye," she said. "Or the blacklegs and touts will get at him. He will only drink water and eat food provided by me."

Rake nodded. It was a sad fact of the sport of horseracing that tactics like poison were used to stop the best horses from winning, if they weren't the pick of the blacklegs.

"Not the night before the race," he said, firm.

"That's the most important night that I sleep with him."

"I'll tell Wilson to do it," said Rake. "You need to be fresh and rested on race day."

Reluctantly, Gemma saw the wisdom and nodded.

"And you're not coming up until race day?" she asked.

"I have other matters to attend over the next few days."

Every so often, Gemma was able to forget he was a duke.

But he was one—to his very core. A man supremely aware of his duties and responsibilities.

And the way he was looking at her...

As if he now viewed her as part of his world. Perhaps not as a responsibility, but beneath his wing, like so many others in his orbit.

It felt good here. Like a place she could stay...

Forever.

Right.

She rolled away and ignored the pang of longing once her body was no longer touching his. She picked up her shirt and slipped it over her head. Trousers quickly followed.

And all the while, he watched her quietly, thoughts tucked behind his dark eyes, until she finished dressing. Then he said, "I suppose that's my cue to leave?"

Without haste, he pushed off the bed and came to his bare feet. Gemma tried not to watch from beneath her eyelashes, truly she did, but here he was—all naked, magnificent man. Article by article of clothing, he hid himself away, and she had no one to blame but herself.

Once he was dressed, his gaze shifted and met hers directly. Within shone knowledge. He'd known she'd been furtively watching, and he'd let himself be watched. He'd let her see what she would be missing.

The heat of mortification flared through her, and she cleared her throat. "Until race day."

A slow tick of time beat by before he gave a single nod and turned toward the door. He placed his hand on the handle, but he didn't twist it. Instead, he pivoted, determination in his eyes and in his step as he closed the few feet between them. Gemma only comprehended his intention the instant before he took her in his arms and kissed her as if with the entirety of his being.

Kissed her until her legs wobbled beneath her and threatened to give way.

Then he released her, jerked the door open, and was gone.

Leaving her standing in the middle of the bedroom, dazed, fingertips pressed lightly to kiss-crushed lips.

Leaving her kissed silly.

Leaving her with the urge to chase him down and grab him and kiss *him* silly.

An urge she suppressed.

She should leave, came a more reasonable thought.

But that thought, too, she suppressed.

She couldn't be reasonable when it came to Rake. That was what she was coming to understand about herself.

Increasingly, she felt herself pulled toward the unreasonable.

She wanted him, and it had begun occurring to her that she might want him more than she wanted her freedom.

No.

Her mother had been a lord's mistress, and her entire being had centered around pleasing that man. Over time, it had broken her mother down.

Gemma had long vowed she wouldn't live that way.

She mustn't give in to the fantasy of a future with the Duke of Rakesley.

The reality was she'd nearly attained all she'd been striving for to secure a future for herself and for Liam.

The reality was she'd betrayed the man who tempted her into fantasies.

And if—*when*—he ever found out, he would come to despise her and want naught more to do with her.

That was reality—her reality.

She mustn't forget.

CHAPTER TWENTY

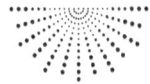

*G*emma stood before the full-length mirror and gave her scrubbed-up self a final once-over, her cheeks flushed from the rough washcloth and eyes still bright from Hannibal's training runs this afternoon.

It had taken a few days for Hannibal to become accustomed to Newmarket's Rowley Mile, as he didn't like change, but today had gone well. Where he'd been tight in the shoulders yesterday, he'd stretched out freely and hit his stride at pace today.

He was ready.

And judging from the looks she'd caught from the blacklegs observing the course, they understood they needed to be ready for him. She was certain the odds on Hannibal had already dropped. But if the odds didn't improve, that would tell her something—the blacklegs had a plan to stop Hannibal from winning.

Tonight, they would have to get through Wilson, who was also keeping guard over Dido. Knife balanced on his knee as he kept watch through the night, the man wasn't in any mood for shenanigans.

"They'll know what they're in for, if they try to enter Hannibal or Dido's stalls, that's all," he'd explained, matter-of-fact. "I'm a fair man."

Fair enough, indeed.

Gemma wasn't a gambling woman, but at supper tonight, she would tell Liam to lay a few bob on Hannibal tomorrow. Liam's leg had improved to the point that he could now hobble about on his own steam with a walking stick, so her twin had taken the post coach ahead to Newmarket while Gemma walked Hannibal.

She squinted at her image in the mirror. Though she'd bound her breasts, tied her hair back, and slouched her hat low over her forehead, she looked less and less like a lad every day.

Her heart had gone out of the ruse. That was the main issue.

No matter.

Tonight was the night before the Two Thousand Guineas—and her last as a lad.

She wasn't certain what the future held, but she was ready to start living life out from under the shadows.

And that began with being entirely herself.

Which meant life as a woman.

Except…she hadn't been living *entirely* as a lad these last few weeks, had she?

In fact, for a few nights she'd been *entirely* a woman with…

Rake.

It was as well that he hadn't come to Newmarket this week. If he'd been here, she doubted her ability to resist him—or her own desires, both carnal and…deeper.

And resist, she must.

That much she knew.

A tenderness had developed between them, one she couldn't have foreseen.

And that tenderness couldn't stand.

She'd spied on him. She'd deceived him. There were certain lines she hadn't crossed in her reporting on the racing operation at Somerton, but it was her first deception that made any sort of future with him impossible.

She couldn't continue with him and keep the truth from him.

And yet...what if...

What if she told him the truth?

What if...he forgave her?

The question warranted nothing more than immediate dismissal. In his eyes, she would be no better than Felicity and even worse—a spy...

An enemy.

She was left with no choice but to stick with the plan and walk away at the end of the day tomorrow.

Downstairs in the taproom of The Running Horse, Liam and Deverill waited for one final report. Then she and her brother would be free to start their new lives.

One more day.

Except she didn't feel on the verge of freedom—but rather the opposite.

She felt bound.

To her duplicity.

Impossibly, to Rake.

The dull ache in her chest told her as much twenty times a day.

And as she did twenty times a day, she pushed past it and shrugged on her overlarge coat.

A few minutes later, she was making her way downstairs to the taproom. The atmosphere of The Running Horse had been raucous from the moment she'd set foot in it a few days ago, and the party showed no signs of abating as more spectators, blacklegs, touts, owners, jockeys, and all London poured into Newmarket. With the Two Thousand Guineas, then the One

Thousand Guineas the following day, this was the biggest week of the year for the town.

Tucked behind a table in a relatively quiet corner, Liam waved.

Liam. Her family…her *only* family—or, more accurately, her only family that mattered.

Though spying on the Somerton stables wasn't exactly right, it wasn't exactly wrong, either.

She wouldn't take any of it back.

Not when it meant keeping Liam and herself safe.

Even if she hadn't succeeded in keeping her heart safe.

As she wound through the taproom haphazard with revelers who were roaring into life for another round, Gemma's gaze shifted from Liam to the raven-haired man seated adjacent to him at the small table. As only Liam had direct dealings with Deverill, this was her first time viewing the man in the flesh.

Where Liam was long and lanky, this man was large beyond his physical form. He had a *presence.* Of a sudden, his head angled, and piercing eyes the blue of a glacier shifted and made their own up-and-down assessment of her.

Lord Devil.

Even without having exchanged a word between them, Gemma understood the nickname.

The man was almost too handsome to gaze upon directly.

She took the chair next to Liam, opposite Deverill, and signaled for an ale she wouldn't drink.

"*Gem,*" said Liam, half ironic.

Gemma nodded, tight. Deverill sat back in his chair and openly watched her, all but demanding she meet his gaze.

A wry smile had settled about his mouth—a mouth almost at odds with the rest of his face. Where his features were all hard, sharp angles, his lips were pillowy and soft.

Lord Devil had a pretty mouth.

He opened that pretty mouth. "And everyone believes you a man?"

From the disbelieving tone in his voice to the skeptical look in his eye, he was clearly flummoxed.

Liam snorted.

"A *lad*," corrected Gemma. It was an important distinction.

Deverill cocked his head, unconvinced. "How old?"

"Seventeen years."

He nodded slowly, consideringly, and the moment stretched to the breaking point. Gemma didn't like this man. She decided it on the spot.

He shook his head and lifted his straight black eyebrows. "I suppose you're passable enough."

"In the general sense," said Gemma, "people believe what you present them."

Not the Duke of Rakesley, though, she left off. She'd never told Liam that Rake had seen through her disguise—or what had followed.

Her brother didn't need to know all that.

Anyway, why was she arguing with Deverill?

Habit, she supposed. Really, all she wanted from him was payment for services rendered and never to see him again.

"Dirt helps," she added.

Deverill pursed that pretty mouth of his and nodded, allowing it.

"It's what people fix on."

"Even so, Rakesley must be a fool," said Deverill, unbothered by the fact. "Like most nobs." He took a long pull from his ale.

Gemma slid a glance toward Liam. She only now noticed he was avoiding her eye. Something was happening beneath the surface here...

Deverill swiped foam from his upper lip. "A stroke of good luck that he made you jockey for Hannibal."

Gemma wouldn't have gone so far as to say that.

Deverill's gaze narrowed on her. "And tomorrow…"

"*Tomorrow?*" Gemma's hackles rose. Here it was. The something she'd sensed. "For us, there is no tomorrow. I've done all you asked by reporting back on the operation at Somerton."

"You have, but—"

She shifted forward and planted her forefinger into the center of the table. "I've earned the money promised."

What if… What if he decided to walk away without paying? What sort of recourse did she and Liam have?

The answer was easy.

None.

Still, Liam wouldn't meet her gaze.

"But what I'm wondering is…" Deverill refused to release her gaze. "Would you like to earn more?"

Liam shifted in his chair. He had the look of a brother who knew his sister wouldn't like what she was about to hear.

"And how exactly would I go about earning *more?*" she asked, low, a feeling of dread snaking through her.

Deverill shrugged a shoulder. "A little clover mixed into a horse's hay. That's all. Nothing that would do lasting injury."

Outrage surged through Gemma. "You want to best Rakesley so badly that you would have me harm Hannibal?"

Deverill looked genuinely taken aback. "What does this have to do with Rakesley?"

Gemma's eyebrows crinkled together in confusion. "What hasn't it to do with Rakesley?"

"Everything."

"But Hannibal—"

"Not Hannibal."

"And Rakesley—"

"Not Rakesley."

The blasted man looked as if he might be taking delight in confounding her.

Gemma sat back, baffled. "What has all this been about if not Rakesley and Hannibal?"

Deverill spread his hands wide. "Rakesley has the best horseracing operation in England."

"Established fact," she said, curt.

"*I* want to have the best horseracing operation in England."

"But why?" Gemma found herself asking. "Aren't you a manufacturer of steam engines?" She recalled the fact from Rakesley's supper party a week ago.

"Been doing your research?" he asked, sardonic. Here was a man who didn't like to be known. "Isn't it enough that I enjoy being the best at everything I set my hand to?"

Gemma gave her head a slow shake. "I don't think so."

A heavy beat of time loped past. "How does one fit into their world if one doesn't become *of* their world?" Deverill spoke the words with a lightness that didn't match the gravity in his glacial eyes. "Someone took something precious from me, and I want it back."

Oh... "This has never been about Rakesley, has it?"

"Not the man himself, no."

A strange sort of relief struck through Gemma. The information she'd provided on Somerton had been a means to an end—not the end itself. Still, one thing needed to be clear. "I'll not harm a horse."

"I'm not asking for any real or lasting harm."

"What they say about you is true."

"*They?*" Deverill scoffed. "I've never given a toss about what *they* think."

"You don't belong in this sport."

He shifted forward, humor replaced by utter seriousness. "I'll belong anywhere I damn well please." Now, it was his finger stabbing into the center of the table. "And *they* can put *that* in their collective pipe and smoke it."

Gemma's gaze flashed toward Liam. "And you're alright with going along with this?"

He shifted uncomfortably. "Ah, Gemma, a little clover is all. Nothing of import would come of it."

"Nothing of import can turn deadly serious with a horse very quickly. You know that." Her attention returned to Deverill. What she was about to say could mean the end of all her and Liam's ambitions. But one must draw a line somewhere and hold it. Here was her line. "I won't do it. Once you pay us—*now*—our dealings are finished."

A moment of time beat by, and fear settled deep in Gemma's gut. He could refuse to honor their deal, and she and Liam would have no recourse.

And then what?

It would've all been for naught.

And if she and Hannibal didn't win tomorrow, she and Liam would be back exactly where they'd started.

At last, Deverill's hand slipped inside a coat pocket and emerged holding a leather pouch that clanked when it hit the table. "Fifty pounds, as agreed."

Relief soared through Gemma. She saw it in Liam's eyes, too, as he snatched the pouch and tucked it away.

If she and Hannibal took the Two Thousand Guineas tomorrow, that additional £200 would make her future real—make it secure.

But...

A little voice wanted to speak, and she couldn't allow it.

She could only focus on what she'd gained—not on who she was about to lose.

No.

Rake wasn't hers to lose. He'd never been hers in the first place.

Tomorrow she would win Rakesley his trophy, and that would be the end of it.

Of *them*.

Now wasn't the time for her nerve to fail.

Deverill's chair scraped back across rough pine floorboards. "I believe our business is at an end."

Liam gave a nod of farewell, and Gemma glared at the man as he strode through the taproom and out the door, relieved to see back of him.

"Off to bed with you, sister," said Liam. "Big day tomorrow."

But Gemma had something to say to her brother. "Were you agreeing with that man?"

"Of course not," he returned. "But it's you in the trenches tomorrow, not me. I don't go deciding matters for you."

He was right. It was better Deverill asked her—and that she'd told him off.

She stood. "I'll poke my head into Hannibal's stall one last time for the night. And you?"

Liam's gaze landed on the swaying backside of a lady up from Town. "I'll take in the sights of Newmarket a little longer."

Gemma snorted and tugged the brim of her slouch hat low over her forehead. As she shouldered her way through the intensifying crowd, she made a vow to set fire to this hat and all the clothes on her back tomorrow. No remnant of this life would accompany her into her future.

She tamped down the tiny seed of doubt that she was only deceiving herself.

That she would, indeed, carry a remnant.

But if she gave that seed no light or air, it would surely wither away and stop causing such a deep ache.

Surely.

CHAPTER TWENTY-ONE

*R*ake stepped boot inside The Running Horse, hoping for a bit of reprieve from the rowdy atmosphere of Newmarket's streets, and quickly found his hopes dashed.

The crowd was as boisterous indoors as it was out of them.

That was race weekend.

The race lasted for all of a few minutes, but the bacchanalia went on for days.

He'd never much minded the festivities before, but tonight he couldn't help glancing around, looking for someone. Of course, Gemma had no reason to expect him. But he'd wanted to see for himself that all was right with Hannibal and, if he was being dead honest, to check that all was right with Gemma.

Their last night together...

He hadn't been able to stop thinking about it.

There was more he wanted to tell her—that he *needed* to tell her.

She wasn't alone in the world.

She was now under his protection—and not in the way Bolton had gone about it with her mother.

The fact was Gemma didn't have to be his mistress.

He needed to tell her that too.

But if not as a mistress, then as what?

That was the question. The one he hadn't an answer for, truth told. Because the answer was…complex.

The answer, he suspected, would require him to upend every plan he'd made for the future.

It was an answer not arrived at easily. And yet…

Perhaps he already had.

He'd taken two steps into the taproom when his gaze caught on a familiar glint of red-gold hair peeking out from beneath a slouch hat.

Gemma.

She occupied a small table in the farthest corner of the room, engaged in intense conversation with two men. The one with the same hue of red-gold hair, Rake knew in an instant as her twin brother. *Liam.* But the other…

Dark of hair, he was dressed in clothes as fine as any dandy of the *ton.* Bespoke clothes, to accommodate the width of shoulders that looked as if they belonged on a boxer.

Rake's brow furrowed. What in the hellfire was going on?

Why was Gemma meeting such a man in a Newmarket taproom the night before the Two Thousand Guineas? A location and timing too close not to be suspect.

Perhaps the man was an owner and had seen Gemma on the track with Hannibal and was attempting to woo her away. Such goings-on happened the night before races all the time.

Or, perhaps, he was a friend of Liam's.

Perhaps.

Rake should let it lie. It was none of his business. Except…

It couldn't not be.

To lose Gemma the night before the race would be an unmitigated disaster. There was no time to try another rider with Hannibal.

Rake pivoted on his heel and jostled his way to the front desk through a newly arrived gaggle of young lordlings. He caught the innkeeper's eye. The man immediately dropped what he was doing, which was handing a room key to another guest, and attended Rake. The Duke of Rakesley was known in all the racing towns.

"Your Grace," said the man on a bow that bordered on the obsequious.

Rake gave an impatient nod of acknowledgement. "I need to know the room number for one of your guests."

The man shuffled his feet and wrung his hands together. "It's just that," he began meekly, clearly fearing the ire of a duke. "I'm not supposed to—"

"Gem is his name. The—" *Woman*, Rake just stopped himself from saying. "The man is my jockey, and I need to give him some last-minute instructions."

It was a lie close enough to a truth.

Rake plunked a guinea onto the countertop, as to assuage any remaining scruples.

"Of course, Your Grace," said the man, sliding the coin across oak and pocketing it before Rake could change his mind. "That'll be Room 5."

"And can you direct me toward the servants' stairs?" It wouldn't do to stride through the taproom to the main staircase in full view of all, including Gemma.

Confusion writ plain upon the innkeeper's face, the man silently pointed Rake toward a short corridor.

And Rake was off, quickly locating the stairs and taking them two at a time to the second floor. He propped a shoulder against Room 5's doorframe, crossed his arms over his chest, and waited.

Gemma would eventually need to sleep—and Rake was patient.

Several parties came and went, a few recognizing the Duke of Rakesley, but none possessing the temerity to ask a duke what he was doing loitering in a public corridor. Still, it wasn't long before the light tread of familiar footsteps sounded on the stairs. A figure wearing a slouch hat appeared above the landing.

Gemma's gaze lifted, and her step stuttered to a stop. "You're not supposed to be here."

Rake snorted. "Missed me that much?" he asked across the distance. His heart felt as if it would lift out of his chest at the very sight of her.

Oh, he was deep in it, wasn't he?

The furrow of her brow deepened. "You came to check on Hannibal, I suppose."

"Aye," said Rake. "Amongst other things."

Like you, he left unspoken.

The look in her gold-flecked, green eyes seemed to know it, anyway.

As she neared, he held his place in the doorway, not precisely blocking it, but not making it easy for her, either. Making it so she had to come within a few feet of him and meet his gaze. She held up the room key. "May I?"

"By all means," he said, unmoving.

It was all very ungentlemanly of him, which he felt perfectly at peace with. She twisted the key in the lock, and the door swung open. Still, he blocked the way. If she wanted inside the room, he would have to move.

She snorted and shook her head. "You could ask to come inside."

"May I come inside?"

"What if I said no?"

"Are you going to say no?"

She hesitated, a war in her eyes. "No."

He stood aside, and she shouldered past him. He might've detected a roll of her eyes.

The door clicked shut behind him, and Rake took in his surroundings. "It's a nice room."

Gemma lifted a single eyebrow. "Under your instructions, I presume."

"Nothing but the best for my jockey."

He set his hat on a table, pulled out a chair, and sat. With its cozy fire burning in the hearth and a bed rounded with downy pillows and coverlet, the room gave a warm, settled feeling.

A feeling very at odds with what he'd witnessed downstairs.

"Is there something you would like to discuss?" asked Gemma, taking the chair on the opposite side of the table. She ignored the bed as she took one boot in hand and tugged it off, then the other. The slouch hat followed, red-gold tendrils escaping the queue at the nape of her neck and curling about her shoulders.

Delectably mussed. That was how he would describe her.

"I saw you in the taproom." Best to cut directly to it.

Not a hint of surprise registered in her eyes. "And?"

"You were with two men."

"There's no law against that."

"One of them was your brother, correct?"

She nodded. "Aye, Liam."

"And the other?" Rake asked, low.

A tetchiness glittered about her. Though she'd known the question was coming, she didn't want to answer it. "A friend of Liam's."

The words emerged as if dragged from her mouth.

"A *friend*?" Rake couldn't keep the disbelief out of his voice.

"Aye," she said. "Liam makes friends wherever he goes."

Though the words held the ring of truth, they weren't the entire truth. He could sense it.

He could sense something else.

She didn't like lying to him.

"Have you been to the Rowley Mile today?" she asked, clumsily attempting to change the subject.

He let her.

For now.

"Aye," he said. "Best it's looked in years."

"The turf has some spring to it."

"It'll be a good ride."

"Aye."

He wanted to have a discussion with her that she wasn't going to like. "About tomorrow…"

Suspicion entered her eyes. "What about it?"

"I want you to race from the front." Before she could refuse, Rake continued, "Get Hannibal off to a fast start and let him hold. He can do it."

Gemma shook her head, adamant. "I spotted several blacklegs at the Mile today."

"Those scoundrels are always hanging about the courses."

"They had their eye on Dido, in particular. She ran well." A beat. "Too well."

Rake began to understand. "You think there will be several false starts tomorrow."

Gemma nodded. "She's high-spirited, and they're going to try to rattle her." Her gaze held his. "I won't start Hannibal fast. He has heart. He'll earn it."

"Then what's your race strategy?" he asked, but his brow was already furrowing with understanding. "You're not suggesting the Chifney Rush."

She didn't flinch. "As it happens—"

"*No.*"

"You can't tell me no."

"I can, and I do. It's too dangerous."

"It's becoming more and more popular with jockeys."

"Those jockeys are all men." When she opened her mouth to mount another protest, he continued, "In case you haven't noticed, you're all woman, Gemma." He ran an annoyed hand through his hair. "You're simply too small to ride it safely with all the muscling for position that's involved." He spread his hands before him. "So, the answer is *no.*"

Her back teeth ground together. "If you want to win the Two Thousand Guineas...if you want a chance at the Race of the Century..." She shifted forward. She wanted him to know she was serious and utterly undaunted. "I ride the way I ride. *I* choose. No one else."

Rake didn't want to agree. But he heard *need* in her voice. A need she'd rarely had satisfied in her life.

Choice.

She needed to choose her own way—and he needed to stand aside and not challenge her. She was the most skilled rider he'd ever seen. If he wanted her to trust him, he needed to trust her.

So, he nodded, and a measure of tension released from her shoulders.

Still, a question wanted to be asked. "And September?"

"What about September?" Her eyes told him she knew what he was asking.

He shifted back in his chair and held her gaze. "You could ride Hannibal in the Race of the Century," he said. "You could stay."

Cloudy emotion passed behind her eyes. If pressed to put a name to it, Rake would say it looked suspiciously close to longing.

She blinked, and it was gone. She shook her head.

"I would double...*triple* your pay." He wasn't giving up so easily.

Gemma shook her head. "My disguise as Gem won't hold for more than one race. I'm surprised it's held this long. If we win—"

"*When* we win," Rake cut in.

"*When* we win, I must immediately disappear."

"There's no official rule that says a woman can't be a jockey."

Her eyebrows lifted with incredulity. "You're being willful."

He shrugged. "I don't know any other way to be."

"You are such a duke," she scoffed. "Has anyone ever told you that?"

"Artemis may have mentioned it in passing."

A laugh sprang up from Gemma, and it felt good to have drawn it out of her.

Still, he went as serious as he'd ever been about anything in his life. "You're not planning on disappearing tomorrow because you might be exposed as Gem."

Her smile fell away by slow increments. "No."

"This is about Bolton."

A streak of panic flashed behind her eyes. "He'll be there tomorrow," she said, words carefully measured.

"Aye." He expected as much.

"He will recognize me," she said. "I've no doubt of it."

Rake nodded. "He will."

"I must go."

The desperation in the break of her voice was clear, and all Rake wanted was to take it away.

As a duke.

As a man.

As the man who—

The breath stopped in his chest—the world might've stopped spinning on its axis—as a truth, immutable and sure, sank into him and revealed itself.

As the man who loved her.

But he couldn't speak that truth so bluntly.

She needed to be eased into the idea.

"If you stayed," he began.

"I can't stay," she said, so certain of her words.

"But, if you stayed"—he wouldn't be deterred—"you wouldn't have to stay as my jockey."

Her head canted, but she remained silent.

"And you wouldn't have to stay as my mistress, either."

Still, she didn't speak.

Yet words insisted on falling from his mouth. Words not guided by his mind, but by his heart.

"You could stay as my—"

Her eyes went wide, and her hand shot across the table, touching a staying fingertip to his lips. "Don't say anything you'll regret on the morrow."

Rake reached up, his fingers gently curling about her delicate wrist. He turned her hand and pressed his mouth to her palm. "We'll have it your way, Gemma," he spoke against her warm skin, his gaze holding hers steady. "For tonight." A beat. "But on the morrow, I shall finish that sentence."

A promise.

"Tonight, however…" He stood and tugged her hand, inviting her to follow him. "I want to show you something."

He led her to the dressing mirror, his larger body behind her smaller one. Their gazes found each other in the reflection. Within he met connection—but also a question.

He took her baggy coat in hand and slid it off her shoulders. Within her eyes, he also saw knowledge. She knew what he was about.

But not all of it.

There was something he wanted to show her.

Something she needed to see.

About herself.

He tugged her shirt loose from the waistband of her trousers. "You don't have to live in the shadows any longer, Gemma." He pulled the shirt over her head, exposing another article of clothing—if it could be called that. The length of linen that bound her breasts. That hid Gemma from the world.

His fingers found the tucked-under end and began unraveling. "Here, in the light, with me, you can be entirely yourself."

In her eyes he detected a desire to believe him.

But she couldn't quite.

At least, not yet.

She would get there.

He was determined.

"You are a diamond, Gemma. You are not a spot of shame or blight on the world."

The last bit of the cloth fell away and fluttered to the floor, leaving her chest bared to his gaze. Pink nipples taut, her breasts stood high and proud on her chest. Lightly, he feathered his fingers around her waist, both their gazes following the trail as they moved over her stomach and up to cup those small, perfectly formed breasts.

She sucked in her breath and watched as he lightly squeezed her nipples.

He angled his mouth to her ear. "Perfection," he murmured.

He loosened the strip of leather that only just reined in her hair. "I'd like to see your hair in long curls down your back."

Emotion flickered in her eyes. She might've wanted the same thing, but she said, "I won't be here to—"

He touched a light fingertip to her mouth. "Let's not speak in absolutes tonight."

His hands moved across the ivory skin of her shoulders, again drawing her gaze. Together they watched where his fingers trailed. Below the flat of her stomach, they found the waistband of her trousers, just above the falls.

Here, Rake hesitated.

From here, there was no return.

Her gaze lifted. "What are you waiting for?" she asked, her cheeks flushed suggestive pink.

A smile tipped at the corner of his mouth. "For you to ask precisely that."

His fingers made slow work of the buttons—*one...at...a...time*—her eyes dark with desire, and anticipation roared through him. Carnality pulled and demanded that he make quick work of it, drag her trousers to her knees, bend her over, and enter her in one swift, satisfying stroke. His cock throbbed with the need.

But that wasn't the sort of coupling the rest of him needed.

He needed connection of a different sort with Gemma. Most

of all, he needed her to feel that connection—not just his cock inside her.

The falls dropped, and his fingers found her fiery mound of curls. A moan poured from her, and she melted back against him, her arms reaching up and winding around his neck...her ivory torso stretched yet languid...her pink nipples taut, as his fingers slid along her slit, now deliciously wet with desire.

"Perhaps your name does suit you," she muttered. *"Rake."*

"I have my moments," rumbled from him.

Goosebumps raced across her skin, as her head arched back and dug into his shoulder. With one finger he entered her, and with his thumb, he stroked her sweet, sensitive nub. She inhaled a quick gasp, then exhaled a long, breathy groan, her round, fetching bottom arcing back against his rigid manhood, as she watched him pleasure her in their reflection.

"Oh, Gemma," he growled into her ear, holding her gaze captive.

Here was connection. Here, they were bare to one another, no shadows...no place to hide. Their wants, desires, and aches unguarded and undisguised.

Here was intimacy.

Her hips found a rhythm with his fingers. He could sense her impatience. She wanted release—*now*—and he wanted to give it to her.

Only with great force of will was he able to move his hand to her waist and turn her to face him, stepping her backward toward the bed.

He would bind her to him by means fair or foul.

All was fair in love and war, no?

She perched on the edge of the bed, propped onto her elbows, a smile curling about her mouth.

And she thought she was leaving him tomorrow?

He pulled her trousers off and flung them away. Her delighted laugh followed. "In a hurry, Your Grace?"

He grunted and tugged at his boots, hopping on one foot, then the other. Next went all the other articles of clothing in hasty succession as she watched from the bed, her body arrayed like the most delectable feast—created to be devoured.

He took a leg in each hand, and she bit her bottom lip between her teeth, eyes burning bright, as he bussed a kiss onto the arch of a foot. He stepped between creamy thighs, his rigid length leading the way.

Again, base carnality beckoned him to take her, but it was another feeling twining alongside it that he heeded.

Tenderness.

He knew it wouldn't hold as their bodies succumbed to lust. But it could be a beginning. A way for his heart to express itself.

He angled forward and continued his trail of kisses—the arch of her foot...the turn of her slender ankle...the dimple above her knee...the stretch of skin just inside her hipbone...the taut tip of her nipple...the indent at the base of her throat... He was a man in worship to this woman, and he would have her understand it.

He planted one forearm to the side of her head, the length of his body heavy against hers and met her lust-glazed eyes. "Rake," she whispered, "what has happened between us?"

"Tomorrow, remember?" he spoke low.

Her brow furrowed for an instant and released.

He reached between them and took himself in hand. Her legs spread wide to accommodate him, one foot sliding down and hooking around the back of his leg, as the crown of his manhood pressed against her cunny, smooth and slick and swollen with desire.

Ready, that was what she was for him.

His mouth found the curve of her neck, and trailed around to take her mouth, the kiss sweet and demanding as he entered her slowly, filling her inch by deliberate inch. Her hips swiveled, greedy for more, but he held steady. This coupling wasn't simply about what their bodies wanted, but about what their souls needed.

In and out of her, he moved, pulling gasps and sighs and moans and groans from her. Delivering all the pleasure his body could give hers.

He reached beneath and cupped her bottom, controlling not just his movement, but also hers. Her arms twined about his neck as his thrusts intensified, perhaps tipping into the pain of pleasure for her—the way he knew she liked it.

There was a time for tenderness.

But in every coupling the time inevitably arrived when the carnal took over.

Yet with Gemma, it was different.

With Gemma, he couldn't give enough of himself.

Because of the feeling that beat within his heart for her.

And he knew.

Though he'd convinced himself otherwise, he'd never experienced this feeling before.

Not like this.

Not as if he wanted to pour all of himself inside another person.

And like this, together, their bodies moving in unison and abandon, she began to tense beneath him. A whimper of ache escaped her as they reached the edge, oblivion beckoning. As one, they tipped over that crest, her cry of release joined by his shout, their bodies mere mortal vessels for another sort of expression— that of their souls.

The bounds of Earth fell away and it was only him and her, here.

Awash in the glow of satiety, he gathered her into his arms, willing her not to speak, but let this one perfect moment be.

Her breath became soft in the cadence of sleep, and Rake felt the twin strums of elation and determination resonate through him.

For the rest of his life, it would be only him and her.

Now to convince her of it.

Nay, not now.

Tomorrow.

Tomorrow, he would have everything he'd ever wanted.

CHAPTER TWENTY-TWO

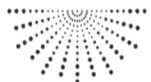

NEXT DAY

*R*ace day at Newmarket dawned perfect—the bluebird sky cloudless, not a whisper of breeze in the air.

It was the sort of day that all but guaranteed a flawless run.

Gemma ran the brush along Hannibal's shiny black coat and held that last thought in reserve, lest she get ahead of herself and transfer the feeling to him.

Which wouldn't do.

He needed calm.

Though this wasn't a usual day in his usual box at Somerton, she'd done all she could to keep to his usual routines at the usual times. It was as important for her as it was for Hannibal.

Nerves pulled and strummed through her body at a high vibration—anxiety, fear, excitement, and anticipation all having their way with her.

But she was Hannibal's jockey.

She was the one in control.

She must hold tight.

Today, she even looked like a jockey. Gone were Gem's dirt-encrusted clothes and slouch hat. In their place shone Rake's colors of spring green and midnight blue, the striped silk shirt pressed and sharp, matching silk cap, and gray riding breeches perfectly fitted. Hair tied back in a tight queue, she was clean and presentable.

Anyone who looked at Gem closely enough today would easily be able to see Gemma.

She didn't give a toss. She was no longer Deverill's spy, and today was her first and final professional race as a jockey.

She smoothed her palm along Hannibal's velvety nose and brought her forehead to touch his. Together, they would go one for one.

Not long from now, they would be at the starting line, bodies packed in...the sweat, the determination, the panic, the elation... the gun would sound...

And they would be off to their destinies.

The blood charged hard through her veins at the very thought.

A head poked into the stall. "Everything as it should be?" asked Wilson, the twitch of one eye giving his anxiety away.

Gemma nodded. "Any trouble last night?" She couldn't help asking.

He snorted. "Not a whiff of it." His knife was out of view, which didn't mean it wasn't near at hand. Horses, money, and trouble made familiar bedfellows, and Wilson was having none of it.

And Wilson was off. He understood not to break into Gemma's routine with Hannibal. Wilson wasn't the most likeable fellow, but Gemma respected him. He ran a fine stable.

One she would never see again.

A pang of regret for something she hadn't quite yet lost sliced through her.

A slight figure passed the open gate and gave a playful salute.

Cal. Though she'd only seen him for the split of a second, his eyes shone bright with the energy of Newmarket on race day. One couldn't help being infected by it. She would miss him, as well.

Yet there was one she would miss above all...

Rake.

Through the night, they'd slept entwined. Again this morning, they'd made love, in silence, their bodies speaking to each other in the language only they knew.

Even as she tried to keep her mind clear and concentrate on Hannibal, words from last night kept returning to her. The words he'd spoken—and the words he hadn't.

The words she hadn't allowed him to speak. Words he would've surely regretted today.

As were the words she'd left unspoken.

Words that ached for release.

Words she tamped down and hoped would eventually go quiet.

It was too much to ask that they disappear entirely, unexpressed.

These words had burrowed deep inside her heart.

They would never disappear.

You don't have to live in the shadows any longer, Gemma.

More words that yet resonated through her. She wanted them to be true with every fiber of her being.

The irony wasn't lost on her. A life out from beneath the shadows was the very life she'd been striving and deceiving for. A life where she could be entirely herself.

An honest life founded upon dishonesty.

To Rake...to the world...to herself.

And yet, even through the layers of deceit—so many layers she'd lost track—he saw the truest her. The *her* she could be only when they were alone together.

But it was the untruths that made any sort of relationship—jockey...mistress...that other unspoken word—impossible. He'd offered her protection, and what a temptation to accept it and shelter beneath his wing.

But that life would always be a lie.

And while she mightn't deserve better, he did.

A throat cleared at the gate. Clad from head to toe in saffron yellow, Lady Artemis stood watching her with a little smile. "Obsessing over race strategy, are we?"

"Something like that," replied Gemma, attending to the braid she was plaiting in Hannibal's mane. She silently hoped Lady Artemis would go away. While she'd come to admire the woman, and even like her, she needed to keep her distance from Rake's too-perceptive sister.

But the lady remained, smiling and unmoving. "You won't be returning to Somerton after today, will you?"

Gemma continued braiding. "I won't."

"I figured as much," said Lady Artemis in her usual breezy manner.

And still, she didn't move along.

"How is Dido this morning?" asked Gemma, for something to say.

"High of spirits," said Lady Artemis on a little laugh. Gemma detected nerves in that laugh. "But aren't we all?"

"Aye," said Gemma, sensing Lady Artemis needed her to say as much to allay her own high spirits.

Lady Artemis stepped inside the stall and stroked Hannibal's nose. He gave a whicker of approval. "This fellow looks to be his usual stalwart self."

Gemma noted a flicker of doubt within Lady Artemis. "Dido doesn't have to race today," said Gemma, conversationally, so as not to spook the idea away. "She could run in the fillies' race tomorrow, or the Derby next month."

"She can win today, you know," said Lady Artemis with an uncharacteristically brittle snap.

Intuitively, Gemma treated her like a skittish horse who needed calming. "Aye. But…"

Lady Artemis's eyebrows crinkled. *"But?"*

"They all can, Lady Artemis," said Gemma. "They're all beautiful, strong animals bred for this day. But only one *will* win."

The one with the most heart, she couldn't bring herself to say.

A few beats of silence ticked by while Gemma's words settled into the air. Lady Artemis gave Hannibal a parting kiss on his velvety nose and a good-luck wish. "I don't know where you're going after today," she said to Gemma, "and I don't need to know. But if you're serious about helping horses in the way you described, I have an estate in Yorkshire that I think would be fit for the purpose. Endcliffe Grange, it's called. If you ever find yourself up that way, there will always be a place for you."

Sudden emotion clogged Gemma's throat. "That's a very kind offer, Lady Artemis."

And one impossible to accept.

Laughter returned to Lady Artemis's eyes. "And a selfish one. Rake would turn positively green with envy if I stole you off him."

Oh, if Lady Artemis only knew the half of it. But something in the lady's eyes told Gemma that perhaps she already did.

Right.

And with that, Lady Artemis issued a parting may-the-best-woman-win farewell and set about her day. Within three seconds, Wilson took her place in the gate opening. "It's Hannibal's turn for the weigh-in."

The time had arrived to walk Hannibal to the Rubbing House to be weighed, then it was on to the starting line of the Rowley Mile where the best horse would prevail.

Her palms went damp with a fresh round of nerves and excitement.

Gemma and Hannibal emerged from the stables, squinting against the sunshine-bright sky. Newmarket on race day was a spectacle to behold. Banners flying overhead, the odd strain of fiddle twirling through the air, along with the savory scent of pasties and pies—the odd ribbon of expensive ladies' perfume too. Though this was the sport of kings, it was also the entertainment of the masses, low mingling with high.

In fact, all sorts of industries sprang up around the racing season. Blacklegs and bettors. Turf journalists and papers. Horse painters, capturing the action of the day. Jockeys, trainers, grooms, and stable lads. Seamstresses who sewed the jockeys' silks. Saddleries and blacksmiths who made riding even possible.

This sport of kings was serious business for many, and to be here, at Newmarket on race day, was to be human and alive.

The murmur of voices turned into a roar as spectators got their first good look at Hannibal, his black coat gleaming in the sun, the pull and release, the power and might, of dense muscles visible for all to see. The crowd parted like the Red Sea before them as they walked toward the weight slab. Already, she saw blacklegs running through the crowd toward the betting post, where a large, rowdy crowd was gathered round. The very sight of Hannibal would already have the laying and taking of odds shifting.

At the weight slab, Hannibal's feet were placed in marked positions so his true height and weight could be measured. It was meant to be a fair system, but every year a few old tricksters still devised ways to cheat it. Whether it was training the horse to stand with his feet splayed wide so as to redistribute his height and weight or training him to "shrink" down. This was achieved by trainers who routinely rapped the horses on the withers during training. So, on race day, any time the horses were touched on the withers, the animals instinctively shrank down, thereby losing an inch or two in height. Many would do anything —including mistreatment of an animal—to carry less weight and gain an edge. It disgusted Gemma to the marrow of her bones.

As Wilson and Blankenship handled the dealings of the

weigh-in, Gemma stood aside and surveyed the crowd. Her gaze came up empty, and disappointment pinged through her. She'd been looking for Rake. She couldn't help herself.

Her eye, however, did happen upon a very different—and familiar—figure.

Bloody Hell.

Not the exclamation.

The horse.

An instinctive smile spread across her face. With his rich chestnut coat, black mane, and strong bearing he was the beauty he'd ever promised to be.

A sudden shear of panic struck through her. If Bloody Hell was here, then...

Her gaze shifted and unerringly located Bloody Hell's owner a hundred or so yards away, up on the Heath.

Bolton.

Seated on a chestnut hack, his reptilian gaze was already upon her. As he showed no surprise, she intuited he'd been watching her all this time. He tipped his hat, his mouth curved into the outer semblance of a smile, and dread ran cold through Gemma's veins.

Of course he'd found her.

It had been inevitable.

Which only reinforced precisely how vulnerable she was to him.

For now, however, she had a measure of protection. As long as she stayed in plain sight. Which couldn't last forever. The cruel pinch of his smile told her that much.

A plan driven by panic and too-familiar necessity formed in an instant. Directly after the race, she would head straight for The Running Horse, and she and Liam would set out for London. There, they could disappear into its shadowy, labyrinthine alleyways and snickets where a person couldn't be found, if they didn't want to be. They'd done it all before.

A small voice proffered an alternate option.

Accept the protection promised by Rake.

She gave a mental shake.

It wasn't an option.

It never had been.

He would want nothing to do with her if he knew of her deception.

Now, Cal returned Hannibal to the mounting block where Gemma had been waiting. She swung a leg over the saddle, her hand clasped tight onto the pommel as she settled. With the firing of the starting gun imminent, the air of Newmarket ratcheted into the wild and untamable. Necessity demanded Gemma cast aside the concerns of her life and concentrate on Hannibal, who stamped his foot and whinnied fractiously.

Cal took the reins and began leading them through the crowd. Gemma bent forward and began a steady stream of patter in Hannibal's ear, which had stopped flicking at the low, familiar sound of her voice. "They're all here to see you run, my friend."

At the starting line, the scrum of horses pranced, their jockeys in various stages of calm and chaos. At a glance, Gemma was able to connect the horses with their owners by their colors. There was Filthy Habit in Lord's Ormonde's sky blue and white silks, serenely surveying the scene around him as if he was about to go for an afternoon's trot. Bolton's Bloody Hell in forest green and drab tan. Her gaze settled on Deverill's Little Wicked in aubergine and charcoal gray.

Deverill was here—of course.

Though it seemed he had no personal grievance with Rake, the men would see each other, possibly even be introduced, and Rake would know Deverill for the man he'd seen with her last night at The Running Horse. In less than a beat of time, he would put the pieces of the puzzle together and know that Gemma had been one of Deverill's many spies all this time.

And he would know her betrayal.

A pang of regret pierced her gut.

Regret that she must tamp down.

There would be time for that later.

Cal handed Hannibal's reins up to Gemma. "Me and the other lads got a guinea on yer old boy here."

Gemma didn't flinch. "The odds?"

"Four to one."

That sounded right. Hannibal wasn't the Ring's pick, but they'd lowered the odds, acknowledging him as a contender. "And Dido?"

"Twenty to one."

Though the filly was fast as lightning, the Ring hadn't ranked her as a possible winner.

Which meant one thing—the Ring was going to stop her from winning.

The dark look in Cal's eyes told Gemma he'd reckoned as much.

The lad tipped his cap before disappearing into the crowd.

Gemma gave the field a wide berth as she began to walk Hannibal to the far side. When they reached the center of the scrum, she spotted saffron yellow and dove gray. *Dido*. She needed to leave it be. The race strategy for Dido was none of her concern, but the filly was clearly miserable, her ears flicking and eyes flashing with anxiety. Deeds seemed to think the only solution was use of the crop.

A bad feeling settled into Gemma's gut.

Without thinking, she redirected Hannibal and called out to Deeds. "You'll not get the best out of her that way."

The other jockey flashed her a cold glare. "Mind yer own, eh?"

Left with no other option, Gemma continued walking Hannibal to the far outside edge of the starting line, following through with her own strategy. Her first responsibility was to her mount.

A voice called out for the horses to take their places. As all assumed the position for the sounding of the starting gun, the crowd's roar lowered to a whirring buzz. Gemma's heart became a hammer in her chest, and anticipation streaked through her as she leaned forward into riding position, light on her haunches, feet secure in stirrups. Hannibal sensed the subtle shift in his rider and went still, even as all the muscles in his body tensed.

He was ready.

The time had arrived to see what sort of heart beat within Hannibal's chest—and within hers.

CHAPTER TWENTY-THREE

From atop Moonraker up on the Heath, Rake greeted lords, ladies, and long-time acquaintances of the turf, all the while keeping half an eye on the weigh-in proceeding a few hundred yards below.

Among all the colors denoting horses royal, aristocratic, and even a few from the middling class, he sought out the striped flash of light green and blue silk. Gemma and Hannibal, his coat shining black in the sun, mane braided, his chest high and proud. But it was Gemma who held Rake's attention, his heart lifting in his chest so it felt entirely possible it might carry him away.

Perhaps it already had, considering all the poetic nonsense that garbled his mind when he so much as looked at the woman.

Seeing her clad in his livery and colors spurred a visceral reaction in his body and a single word.

Mine.

Of course, he didn't own her. Yet part of him—a part not controlled by reason or logic—responded to this public claiming of her as his.

For now, it was as his jockey.

Soon he would claim her as more.

This morning, in the in-between time betwixt night and dawn, he'd awakened with her in his arms, and with slow deliberation, he'd made love to her once again. Then he'd left without speaking another word.

He knew what his next words to her would be—and they needed to wait.

Though he'd never thought it possible to feel this way, he didn't much care if Hannibal won the Two Thousand Guineas, as long as Gemma was his at the end of this day.

But Gemma cared. She'd been working with single-minded diligence to bring Hannibal to victory. Rake wouldn't do anything to distract her from it.

A figure mounted on a chestnut hack appeared at the periphery of Rake's vision, horse and rider ambling to a stop ten or so feet away. Rake cut the lord a glance—and recognized him half a heartbeat later.

Bolton.

Instinctively, Rake's hands clenched into fists, then with great reluctance, released. No matter how Rake might feel about the man, he needed to keep the conversation civil.

Bolton cleared his throat. "A fine piece of horseflesh you have down there."

Rake nodded—and waited. Bolton wasn't here to talk about Hannibal.

"From the Darley line?"

"Byerley," Rake corrected.

Bolton crossed his arms over his chest. Gemma had a bit of the look of the man. Red-gold hair and straight, narrow nose. Which was where the resemblance ended. Where Bolton's mouth held a cruel twist, Gemma's tipped with kindness. Where Bolton emitted cold severity, Gemma radiated warm generosity.

Bolton sought to possess.

Gemma sought to understand.

Firsthand, Rake saw the matter as it stood—Gemma needed to be protected from this man.

"And your lad?" asked Bolton, mildly, as if making idle conversation. "Where did you find him?"

Rake had a choice. He could continue to stare out in parallel to Bolton and pretend indifference—or he could cut straight to the point.

For Rake, there was but one option.

He turned to face Bolton square and met the man straight in the eye. "The *lad* is under my protection."

Bolton's mouth pinched at the corners, and his gaze narrowed an assessing sliver. "You mean in your employ, of course."

Rake wasn't playing this man's game. "You will stay away from the lad," he stated, each word clear and deliberate. "You will have no contact with the lad."

Bolton glittered with barely contained affront. Earls weren't spoken to thusly. "And what's the lad to you?"

Since Bolton only understood the world in terms of possession and subjugation, Rake spoke in the language the man knew. "*Mine.*" It was possible he'd growled.

Though it felt slightly wrong to speak such a word about another human being, it felt mostly *right* to speak it of Gemma.

She was his.

Not his possession.

But *his.*

Bolton's brow lifted and understanding lit within his eyes. He scoffed in disbelief. When Rake didn't flinch, he blinked. Then scoffed again. But Rake could see the man was beginning to understand.

Good. He had more to say. "Neither you nor your toadies are to come within a mile of Gemma or her brother."

Bolton puffed out his chest, like a pigeon attempting to make itself appear larger and more fearsome than he really was. "You have a no right—"

Rake smiled, and the rest of the sentence died in Bolton's mouth. His skin turned the shade of spoiled milk. "I am the Duke of Rakesley," spoke Rake, low and implacable. "I have every right. More than most, in fact."

As a duke, it was only the truth, and they both knew it.

Bright scarlet flushed up Bolton's neck, making his cravat appear suddenly too tight. "More fool you, then," he spat. Now the man was making his true self known—and what a nasty piece of work he was. "A willful pair of ingrates from the moment of their birth. Their mother was practically a whore."

Rake wasn't having it. "She was the mother of your only children." There was yet more he would say. "The way you treated her...did you think it love?"

Bolton's mouth snapped shut, and he swallowed the lump that had surely formed in his throat.

"Here's what someone like you doesn't and can't understand," continued Rake. "That's not love. It's power and control. Anything that hurts another isn't love."

"I protected them," proclaimed Bolton. "All of them."

Rake gave his head a slow shake. "As a gaol protects its prisoners from the outside elements?"

"You...you..." stammered Bolton. "You go beyond the pale, Rakesley."

Rake wasn't deterred. "That's not protection. That's captivity." He wasn't quite finished. "If you ever contact Gemma, I won't rest until I've ruined everything you hold dear."

With that, he squeezed his knees, stirring Moonraker into motion, and they rode down the gentle slope of the Heath, leaving behind a blustering Bolton. Rake had neither the time nor inclination to explain love to someone who would never understand it.

He'd only begun comprehending it himself.

But the main objective had been achieved. Bolton would no longer be a source of concern for Gemma.

After greeting various lords and ladies on the short ride to the grandstand, Rake left Moonraker with a groom and jostled his way inside the structure reserved for spectators of the aristocratic variety. While he and Artemis had agreed to meet here before the race, they would watch outside, from their mounts, as did many spectators at Newmarket. The Jockey Club had been trying to put an end to the practice for years, but there was no better way to view a race on the Rowley Mile than by horseback.

Rake scanned the overcrowded room. Artemis would be here, socializing with peers, listening to and spreading turf gossip. Then relaying it all tomorrow morning to Rake over the breakfast table.

Ahead, hip cocked against a wood railing, a figure just caught Rake's eye. A man—large, immaculately dressed, raven-haired. A man not known to Rake by name, but one he knew by sight.

Not *a* man, but rather *the* man he'd spotted in the taproom of The Running Horse last night, seated at a corner table with Gemma.

A voice came at Rake from behind. "And how do you like your chances today, Your Grace?"

He glanced around to find Lady Beatrix staring up at him, mischievous, vulpine smile affixed to her mouth. "That man," he said, jutting his chin to indicate the man from last night. The one with piercing blue eyes and presently surrounded by no fewer than five ladies—all married. "Who is he?"

A feeling churned in Rake's gut.

He wouldn't like the answer.

He knew that much.

"Ah," began Lady Beatrix, clearly drawing out the moment for her own amusement. It was no wonder she and Artemis were the best of friends. Birds of a feather, those two. "That would be the notorious Lord Devil."

Rake's stomach plummeted to his feet.

Deverill.

The light of interest entered Lady Beatrix's eye. "Are you so well acquainted to warrant a face like thunder?"

"I've never met the man." Rake needed to get himself under control, but it felt an impossibility. He didn't know Deverill, but…

Gemma did.

Gemma knew this man who attracted every woman within a ten-mile radius…

This man with a newfound interest in horseracing…

This man with a spy in every stable in England.

"Well, I'll leave you to it, then," said Lady Beatrix. "Best of luck to Hannibal." She tossed the words over her shoulder before disappearing into the crowd.

Others moved to fill her place and have a jolly word with the Duke of Rakesley. But after a single glance at his face, they pivoted in the opposite direction.

Gemma knew the man who had a spy in every stable in London.

Gemma had been in that man's company only last night.

Gemma…

Was Deverill's spy.

The knowledge sank deep inside Rake and sprouted tangled roots.

Breath refused to enter or leave his lungs. Stunned, that was how he felt.

He felt something more, as well.

He'd been a fool for a woman.

Again.

Of their own volition, his feet took a determined step forward, then another, as an idea seized him. He was going to confront Deverill.

"Brother," came a voice behind him.

Rake twisted at the waist and registered his sister moving toward him, a broad, happy smile on her face.

She stepped in front of him and stopped him in place, a single eyebrow lifted in question. "You have a face like a thunderstorm, Rake," she said, entirely unbothered. "That concerned Dido is going to best your Hannibal?"

Rake grunted. If there ever was a time he wasn't in the mood for his sister, this would be it. Deverill had moved from his place at the railing and was presently walking with his harem of married ladies toward a row of seating.

As quickly as it had come, the impulse to confront the man faded. He hadn't the faintest interest in talking to Deverill. The man wouldn't be telling Rake anything he didn't already know.

Gemma was his spy.

And, like that, the last of her puzzle pieces had fallen into place.

Artemis grabbed his upper arm and tugged. "Come, let's get to our horses. The man with the starting gun is walking toward the line."

Outside, they jostled through the dense crowd to the stretch of railing where the groom waited with their hunters. Julian and the Duchess of Acaster were just riding up to meet them.

For the first time, Rake looked at the duchess—really looked at her—and, at last, saw her for who she truly was.

Perfection.

The Duchess of Acaster was perfect.

He understood it to his bones.

Even as other parts of him—namely, the part beating in the center of his chest—soundly rejected the notion.

Hearts could be slow to catch up.

Mounted on her horse, wearing Ashcote Hall's colors of ivory and pink in the form of an ivory riding habit and dashing pink sash, sat a woman who would never make a fool of him.

This was the woman he was supposed to marry.

The order of the universe all but demanded it. And yet...

Until ten minutes ago, he'd been determined to turn the universe topsy-turvy for a different woman.

Perhaps…

His heart, it seemed, still held out hope.

Perhaps there was an explanation.

Perhaps she'd spoken the truth and Deverill was only a friend of her brother's.

At that moment, the man emerged from the grandstand. There strode a chancer who had climbed into the upper echelon of society through hard work and tireless scheming. He wasn't a man who collected friends.

He was the sort of man who collected enemies.

Rake certainly considered him so.

"Oh, Rake," Artemis called out in a sing-song voice. "Get a move on, will you?"

He tore his gaze from Deverill and found Artemis, Julian, and Celia staring down at him from their mounts with varying expressions of curiosity. Julian looked the most concerned, while the duchess looked the most assessing. Artemis simply wanted to get a move on, and, in fact, was already doing so.

Rake mounted Moonraker and set off toward the midpoint of the Rowley Mile. For this course, the first two furlongs ran flat, followed by the downhill penultimate furlong that bottomed at "The Dip," leaving the horses to race uphill for the final furlong stretch and finish.

The Two Thousand Guineas was a tough, thrilling race, and only the horse with the most heart went the distance to a win.

As they passed the starting line, he caught a glimpse of his colors. *Gemma.* She appeared to be exchanging words with Dido's jockey. Artemis noticed. "Do you know what that's all about?" she called out.

Rake shook his head, but he knew. The man held a crop in his hand. Gemma wouldn't like that.

But that wasn't his main concern.

Gemma... A riot of emotions flooded him at the sight of her. *Joy... anger... uncertainty...*

Was she a spy? Or...

Was she his?

A silken rainbow of colors shone on horses and jockeys in the sunlight, reckless exhilaration charging through the air. The moment they'd all been waiting for was nigh.

Gemma and Hannibal took their place to the outside, as the others found their preferred spots. With Thoroughbreds being a particularly high-spirited breed, most didn't take kindly to close quarters. He understood Gemma's wisdom in taking Hannibal to the outside, but they would have their work cut for them. This was a fast group of horses.

A few minutes later, Rake held a spyglass to his eye, awaiting the starting gun with bated breath and racing heart, like everyone else. From this distance, one couldn't hear the commands being issued, but it was clear to see—the next command would be the firing of the gun.

A thought strayed in—if Gemma was Deverill's spy, would she throw the race?

After all, she'd offered him her body and used it to gain access to his secrets. What lengths wouldn't she go to?

Quick on the heels of those questions came a certainty.

No.

Her love for Hannibal was real—even if everything else had been a sham.

Sudden smoke plumed the air gray, followed an instant later by the sound of the gun.

The race was off.

Except, it wasn't.

A second firing quickly followed, signaling a false start.

"Oh, here we go," said the duchess on a resigned sigh.

Artemis met Rake's gaze. "Do you think the blacklegs caught wind of Dido and bribed the starter?"

"Not necessarily," supplied Julian. "They always bribe the starter. I predict at least two more false starts before we're off."

A small, worried frown pulled at Artemis's mouth.

"They're trying to see who they can rattle, that's all," said Rake to ease her nerves.

But his words did nothing to calm his own.

Dido would be rattled.

He shifted the angle of his spyglass and found Gemma, leaning over Hannibal, murmuring into his ear, keeping him steady. She would see him through to the finish.

He found it hard to believe such a woman could contain an ounce of duplicity.

It had to be a misunderstanding.

One they would clear up after the race.

Julian, it turned out, had been correct. Two more false starts were fired. Then it wasn't only horses and riders becoming increasingly fractious, but also the crowd. With all the money that swirled around racing meetings, the blacklegs seized control where they could, usually through bribes, poisonings, lamings, fraudulent betting...and the list went on. They found the shadowy spaces between the Jockey Club's lines of control, keeping one step ahead of the laws, until they were eventually caught out.

Then they reassessed and started a new connivance from a fresh angle, ruthless in their pursuit of a shilling.

The fellow with the starting gun was replaced—hopefully by a man who wasn't also in the pockets of the blacklegs. A new seriousness filled the air, as everyone sensed the next firing of the gun could see the race well and truly started.

Hannibal was ready to run, and so was Gemma. Even from here, Rake could see as much.

All they'd been working toward came down to this moment.

The gun fired, and the horses lurched into motion.

The crowd held its collective breath.

No second firing of the gun…

The crowd roared.

The race was on.

Dido and Filthy Habit stretched out to an early lead, with Little Wicked and Bloody Hell half a length behind. Gemma and Hannibal were well in the back, not even contenders.

Rake's jaw clenched, his heart an unsteady gallop in his chest.

Anticipation exploded into exhilaration as he watched her begin to overtake one horse, then another, allowing Hannibal to stretch fully into his stride, his action free and smooth and so deceptively fast on the flat. Aggressively and methodically, Gemma worked them through the field, without crop or spur, employing, instead, strategy and skill and the complete trust Hannibal had in her.

A trust shared by Rake.

Now in the lead by a full length over Filthy Habit, Dido's speed was lightning. The Ring hadn't gotten it right in trying to rattle her. Working and muscling through the scrum of other horses and riders, Gemma would have a hell of a time catching up to her.

Yet, still, she came on.

"Did you instruct Deeds to give Dido the crop and spur?" Rake called over to Artemis.

She gave her head a tight shake. "No."

Dido wouldn't be accustomed to such treatment, as she'd never experienced it at Somerton. It wasn't necessary for Deeds to push her so hard, so soon in the race. After one furlong, she'd extended her lead over the field by two lengths. The early success only had her jockey using his crop more. Artemis went quiet, her mouth pinched as she watched, her knuckles white around the reins of her chestnut hunter.

And still Hannibal came on. He was a brawler, that horse. Unafraid and bold in his pursuit of Dido. He'd now pulled abreast of Filthy Habit, whose jockey was attempting to crowd

Gemma and Hannibal off the straight line. It was a common practice, but Rake could hardly bear to watch. Gemma was slight of frame, but determined and wily. Hannibal, however, had the bigger body of the two horses and wasn't ceding any ground as they finished the second furlong and galloped into the fast downhill section of the race toward The Dip.

Dido only gained speed and created more space between herself and the other horses, the outcome of this race already a foregone conclusion. Hannibal had overtaken the rest of the field, but he gained no ground on Dido, who was a good four lengths ahead, her pace blistering—and hard won, as her jockey kept at the crop and spur.

They bottomed at The Dip and were now galloping uphill for the final furlong.

Of a sudden, Hannibal began to gain ground on Dido. At first, Rake thought his eyes were deceiving him, but no, he and Gemma were, indeed, pulling farther away from the rest of the field and closing in on Dido.

"Rake," said Artemis, a slight tremor in her voice.

It wasn't so much that Hannibal was gaining ground on Dido, but rather that she was losing it…quickly. Not knowing what else to do, her jockey employed crop and spur. But to no avail. Dido was dropping speed at an alarming rate.

Three-quarters of a furlong to the finish, Hannibal streaked past Dido and took the lead.

Without a word, Artemis gave a few clicks, urging her hunter into a sudden gallop, and she was off.

Rake followed in fast pursuit. Whatever was happening, it wasn't good. Artemis wouldn't be facing it alone.

Dido stumbled, and the rest of the field galloped past her as she collapsed to the turf, throwing her jockey, who was experienced enough to jump clear before he found himself between a fallen horse and the unforgiving ground.

Within seconds, Artemis was at the fence, dismounted, and

running on the track. As Rake jumped from his horse, a roar went up from the crowd, and he caught the finish of the race. Gemma and Hannibal were across the line, the winners.

But now wasn't the time for celebration.

He hopped the course fence and was running on the track, in pursuit of Artemis. This wouldn't be good. Horses collapsed during and after races all the time, a tragic fact of the sport. The cause was usually related to the heart.

Ahead, Artemis dropped to the ground beside Dido, whose wind was labored and rough. "Rake," his sister called over her shoulder. She cast him a pleading look, one that asked him to do something, anything. He was her older brother who always knew what to do…how to make any situation come out all right.

As a small crowd of gawkers and otherwise useless people began to gather around, a figure appeared in the distance, running toward them. *Gemma*, cheeks flushed crimson from the ride, sweat beading down the sides of her face, her chest heaving with exertion.

"Help her, Gem," sobbed Artemis.

Gemma didn't hesitate as she made straight for Dido and kneeled over her, ear pressed to Dido's chest, which had gone eerily still. A few beats of time later, she lifted her head, and her bright eyes met Rake's. She gave her head a small shake, which Artemis caught.

Artemis threw a sob of pure, inconsolable grief and disbelief to the sky, and Rake was wrapping his arms around his sister.

A few seconds later, when he glanced up, Gemma had disappeared into the crowd.

Swirled in to all the other emotions of the last few minutes, Rake experienced the pang of loss.

Nothing would be the same after this day.

He understood it with certainty.

He'd won.

But he'd lost so much more.

Lady Beatrix pushed through the intensifying crowd, shouting at them all to, "Back the blazes away," and threw her arms around Artemis, who began sobbing into her friend's shoulder.

For now, his sister was attended to.

Rake had another matter to settle.

Gemma.

Before this terrible day was done, he would know the truth about her.

He suspected he already did.

But he needed to hear it directly from her own mouth.

Grimly, he set out.

CHAPTER TWENTY-FOUR

hroat scratched raw from thanking well-wishers and back sore from accepting claps of congratulation, Gemma walked Hannibal into the stables and out of Newmarket's festivities, which had gone from rambunctious to riotous now that the race was finished. A full-on bacchanalia would be following the setting of the sun, to be sure.

What she and Hannibal needed was calm and routine. She'd finished cooling him down, and now he needed a bit of food, a bucket of water, and a good, long grooming session. She reckoned she had time for that as her farewell.

But with the relative calm of the stable—it was only a hair more subdued than the course grounds—came the image she'd been pushing from her mind this last hour.

Dido.

Gemma still couldn't grasp it. One instant Dido and Hannibal had been neck and neck, then the next, she'd faded back. In that moment, the thrill of elation had burst through Gemma. She and Hannibal were going to win the race. It wasn't until they'd crossed the finish line, and Filthy Habit had come in two lengths behind that Gemma looked back.

The rest was a blur.

Ignoring the crowd that had been rushing in with roars of cheers and jeers, she'd dismounted and handed off Hannibal's reins to Wilson. Then she'd been running, her feet pounding against the turf as hard as the beat of her heart against her ribs. It wasn't a clear run. She'd had to dodge and weave through horses and riders and crowds of gawkers, hoping against hope she'd been mistaken about what she'd glimpsed.

Then she'd shouldered through the final layer of the crowd, who had drawn as close as they dared, and her feet had come to a sudden stop, her mind only registering images. Dido on her side, unmoving. Lady Artemis bent over her beloved horse, inconsolable. Rake's arm draped over his sister's back. Then Lady Artemis pleading with Gemma to do something. Though she already knew what the outcome would be, she'd pressed her ear to Dido's chest, which had gone too still. She'd not heard the beat of the filly's intrepid heart.

She'd met Rake's gaze. Perhaps he, like his sister, had held on to the hope that she would be able to do something. Her first instinct had been to go to him. But she'd stopped herself, instead giving a small shake of her head.

There was the time before the race—and the time *after*.

The time for her to go.

To separate herself from his world.

To let them heal.

Without her.

Starting now.

She cut a glance toward Hannibal. "You're quite the handsome lad with that flower garland gracing your neck."

He gave a soft whicker as if acknowledging the truth of her words.

They arrived at his box, and Gemma stopped dead in the center of the gate opening. There, propped against one of the stall walls, was Rake, arms crossed over his chest, waiting.

Magnificent.

As ever, that was the first word that came to mind at the sight of him. Her heart gave a hard thump in her chest.

As ever too.

Yet a look glinted in his eyes—one she didn't particularly want to read. It wasn't concern or grief or elation at having won the Two Thousand Guineas. An impenetrable, closed-off look.

Anger. Not the hot, blustery sort, but rather cold and clear-eyed.

He knew.

Right.

Gemma walked Hannibal into the box, threaded his reins through the tie ring, and set about removing his saddle before she rubbed him down.

All the while, she felt those angry eyes upon her.

She hefted the saddle over the box wall and heard a voice, low and steady, at her back. "Shall we do this here, then?"

Gemma froze. She'd hoped he would allow her to groom and feed Hannibal first. She shook her head. "Not here with Hannibal," she said, knowing it was the right thing. "He needs calm."

Gemma couldn't be certain she would be able to maintain her composure through the coming conversation.

"Wilson," Rake called out.

He was such a duke. But, really, how on earth could Wilson hear—

A head poked around the corner. "Need something, Your Grace?"

"Get a lad in here to groom and feed Hannibal."

Gemma couldn't remain silent. "But I'm already here. I can take care of—"

Rake gave his head a curt shake. Gemma's mouth snapped shut. "Not you."

If Wilson detected anything untoward, he gave no indication as he set about his master's orders.

"After you," said Rake.

But Gemma couldn't go just yet. She stepped around to face Hannibal and stroke his nose. "You showed your heart today, my friend," she said, low, for his ears only. "I'll never forget you." He lowered his head, and she angled forward so her forehead met his. "Goodbye."

She swiped away inevitable tears, Rake watching her. For an instant, she might've glimpsed an emotion other than anger. Then he blinked, and it was gone, and he was gesturing that she lead the way.

They emerged from the stable, squinting against the warm afternoon light, to a roar of cheers and more claps on the back. Gemma would be black and blue tomorrow.

"That was the stuff, old chap," came a congratulation.

"You could've let me know you had a goer," came a grouse.

"Where did you come across the lad?"

"Been keeping mum on this one, have you?"

Gemma couldn't keep track of all the words being tossed their way, mostly from lords in varying states of drunkenness. All the while, Rake had a face like a storm about to break. But Newmarket's habitués must've been accustomed to such from the Duke of Rakesley, for it didn't put them off one bit. Gemma kept her gaze pointed toward the ground and followed where Rake led.

For the reckoning coming.

Though she was utterly worn to the bone, both emotionally and physically, and her back threatened to seize up any second, this needed to happen.

So much lay expressed between them.

But so much more lay unexpressed.

It was only when they arrived that Gemma saw that he'd led them to his carriage. He jerked the door open and stood aside, making it obvious she was to precede him inside.

She hesitated, cutting him a glance before entering, catching his gaze. There it was again—that opaque flash of emotion. And it hit her—the other emotion that ran alongside the anger in his eyes…

Hurt.

Somehow, it was worse than the anger.

She cut the contact and hefted herself inside the carriage with a pained grunt, wincing before lowering herself to a seat. Her back wasn't pleased that she would be sitting inside a carriage, no matter how sumptuous. Really, though, the interior of a duke's carriage was more comfortable than most people's beds.

She shook that last word loose. It wouldn't do to think about beds—or what she'd done in them with this man.

He seated himself on the bench opposite her and stretched his long legs in a sprawl that suggested power. He gave the ceiling two sharp raps, and the carriage lurched into motion.

Gemma wanted to stare out the window…at her hands presently clutched together on her lap…anywhere but at the gorgeous, angry man sprawled across from her, but she wasn't that much of a coward, so she lifted her gaze and met his.

She detected an emotion utterly unexpected within those depths. *Concern.*

"Did you suffer injury during the ride?"

"Just my, *erm*…" She hesitated. "My back."

My back.

It didn't bear thinking about what this man had done not so long ago to make her back—and other parts of her—feel better.

She detected the same knowledge within his eyes.

The concern didn't fade.

Even now, knowing what she'd done, he wanted to protect.

It was his nature.

"I'll be alright."

A moment passed before he gave a brief nod of acceptance. As the carriage made slow progress through the racecourse grounds, he said, "I had a few interesting sightings today. Would you like to hear about them?"

That look in his eyes... "I'm not sure."

A laugh, bitter and hard, erupted from the firm line of his mouth. "Ah, Gem, ever the honest lad." The ugly laugh fell away, and Gemma was glad for the small mercy. "Except that isn't true, is it?"

Gemma possessed enough good sense to stay quiet—even as parts of her clamored to be heard.

Clamored to say there were truths about her that only he knew—that only they knew about each other.

But the time had passed for those truths to be expressed.

In reality, that time had never existed.

"I finally beheld the notorious Lord Devil."

Gemma braced herself.

"Except that isn't quite true, is it? Because I saw him last night." A beat. "With you."

"Aye."

"Funny you didn't mention his name then," said Rake, conversationally. "It's almost as if you were hiding something."

Oh, Rake was good and het up. A fact he wasn't trying to hide. And what she would say next would only make him more so.

"You didn't need to know."

His black eyebrows lifted, incredulous. "You certainly don't lack for audacity," he scoffed, half admiringly.

After so much secret keeping, the time for the whole truth had arrived. "My work for Deverill is finished. I met with him last night for payment."

"And, presumably, your work for Deverill was to spy on *me*."

"Not *you*." Gemma wanted this to be clear. "Your stable operation."

It had been a vital distinction in her mind—and still was. Not that she expected the angry man seated across from her to see or understand.

He shifted forward, forearm braced against muscled thigh. "And what did Deverill receive for his blunt?" he asked, each word a sharp point designed to inflict pain. "Does he know the lengths to which his *stable lad* went to secure information?"

Sudden anger sparked through Gemma. Her back went rigid with indignation, and she instantly regretted it, grimacing against its protest. "Are you...are you..." she stammered. "Are you calling me a doxy?"

Rake's eyes became glittering black diamonds. "If the word fits."

He was wounded, and he was out to wound. Horses in pain struck out thusly. Though Gemma understood, she still felt the pain inflicted. "You know that wasn't how it is...*was*...between us."

He wouldn't relent. "I know nothing."

"Then know this, Your Grace." She spoke the last two words with particular emphasis. "Year after year, I watched my mother work herself to the bone for a man who gave her no choice but to be his chattel. That was how he treated her. How he treated Liam and me." A beat. "It's something you can't understand."

"Oh, I understand betrayal quite well."

Clearly, her words had not penetrated one bit.

Gemma felt her anger double in force. "Because a woman who didn't love you in the first place left you for another man?" she scoffed.

He went very still.

"Confess, Your Grace," she charged on, heedless around a blind bend. "You didn't truly love her either. It was your pride that was wounded all those years ago—not your heart."

"You know nothing of my heart."

She knew there was now a fortress around it that would remain forever impenetrable.

And that she'd put it there.

"Here's what I do know," she said. It was time someone laid out a few facts for the duke. "I know need. You only know want.

What you want, you have. When Felicity left you, was that the first time you were ever denied a want?"

His jaw clenched. He didn't appreciate being cast in this particular light.

Too bad.

Truth hurt.

"Some of us never have the luxury of attaining a want," she continued, unrelenting. "We're too busy taking care of needs. Yes, I spied on Somerton." She let the statement sit for a moment. "So Liam and I could leave behind a life of constant need and have the future we want."

Rake cocked his head, gaze narrowed, assessing both her words and her. "And what future is that?"

"Liam and I have made plans."

His brow furrowed. "What plans?"

She shouldn't tell him. She was no longer any concern of his. That was clear. Yet… "We're going to New York."

And she knew—she didn't want to go.

Though she wouldn't be spending any more of her life with this man than what time remained in this carriage ride, the idea of putting an ocean between them caused a black chasm to expand within her.

"*America?*" he asked, utterly perplexed.

"Liam's already purchased our passage for the 30th."

"That's within the fortnight."

"And you'll never have to see me again." Still, a question found itself spilling from her mouth. A question she didn't have to ask… "Have you asked the Duchess of Acaster to marry you?"

His jaw clenched and released. "Not yet."

Not…*yet.*

"Once you do," Gemma spoke around the lump that had formed in her throat, "you and the Duchess of Acaster can live happily ever after."

Of a sudden, the words he'd left unspoken last night and vowed to speak today filled the air between them.

"She'll no longer be the Duchess of Acaster," he said. "She'll be the Duchess of Rakesley."

"I'm sure the two of you will be very happy together." The words tasted like bitter quince in Gemma's mouth.

"Of course, we'll be happy. All our interests align perfectly."

Gemma wasn't sure what was worse—the words themselves… or the fact that he spoke them so coldly.

"You know," she began. Oh, why was she talking? Why couldn't she leave it be? This man had his future all mapped out before him. She didn't need to say anything more… "You could stand to let a little chaos into your life."

Rake blinked, astonished. A lengthy bout of laughter followed. "I would counter that I already have in the form of one slight woman who was once my stable lad."

A fact Gemma couldn't deny. Still… "You don't have to hold the reins of control so tightly all the time. Like, when I ride Hannibal, it isn't about controlling him. It's about setting free and seeing where it takes us. It's in the in-between space that the magic in life happens."

His condescending smile fell by slow increments.

Once, they'd set free and found that magic—together.

He wanted to doubt it, but truth was truth. It existed and couldn't be denied into nothingness.

He reached into an interior pocket of his greatcoat, his hand emerging with a fat leather pouch, which he tossed across the footwell. Gemma caught it and tested its heavy, jangly weight. The £200 purse for winning the Two Thousand Guineas.

"Your thirty pieces of silver."

Gemma wasn't about to let him get away with those words. "Oh, Deverill paid me those last night." She held up the leather purse. "*This*, I earned today for a job well done. You've got Hannibal through to the Race of the Century."

She wasn't done provoking him. "We both got what we wanted."

She hadn't intended the words to emerge as an irony, but rather as a cheap provocation.

It felt like the opposite was true.

While both of them had gained what they'd wanted in the beginning, wants had shifted over the last few weeks and possibly changed. The possibility existed that for a fleeting moment, they'd wanted an entirely different outcome.

An outcome that might've been a possibility.

In another life.

The carriage rolled into the stable yard of The Running Horse. The time had arrived for Gemma to vacate this carriage.

And never see this man again.

Even as the conveyance slowed to a stop, neither of them moved to open the door.

"You don't have to worry about Bolton anymore," said Rake, offhand, as if the words didn't mean very much.

Gemma blinked. "What do you mean?"

"He understands that you're now under my protection."

Her brow furrowed. "When did you—"

"I spoke to him today."

"But…" Oh, this needed to be said. "I'm not under your protection."

"Bolton doesn't have to know that."

A long moment stretched between them as the implications of Rake's words penetrated. She couldn't leave this carriage without saying something. Even with all that had been said, two words yet remained. "Thank you."

Rake's jaw clenched. He didn't want to accept her thanks, that was apparent. Still, he nodded. Then he reached for the handle and pushed the door open.

Gemma willed stiff muscles into motion, and somehow, she got herself out of the carriage. The door clicked shut behind her.

She didn't expect to meet his gaze through the window. So much yet pulsed and pulled between them.

All of it impossible.

The chasm between them was too wide...*unbridgeable*.

He gave the ceiling two sharp raps, and the carriage lurched into motion.

Alone in the stable yard, Gemma watched it roll out of view. But she wasn't alone. Rake had left her with a gift.

The gift of freedom.

He was angry with her. He wanted nothing more to do with her—and yet he wasn't vengeful. He was generous. At the end of it all, he was a good man—an honorable man.

He was the man she loved.

For here was the gift—she and Liam were not only free of Bolton, but they no longer had to leave England. Not as long as Bolton believed them under the protection of the Duke of Rakesley. And Gemma knew Rake would never disabuse Bolton of that belief.

Of a sudden, her future spread wide open before her. Not because of the money she'd earned from Deverill and from winning the Two Thousand Guineas. But because of Rake—his generosity...his protection.

That was the man she loved.

That was the man she couldn't have.

The man she could've had in a different life.

If...

If she'd been born on the correct side of the blanket.

If she'd not betrayed him.

If she was a wholly different person.

And that she couldn't be.

She could only be herself, making the best of the lot in life she'd been born into.

Even so, she understood all the *ifs* would haunt her for the rest of her days.

And one more *if*.

If...she could've been Rake's.

What would this life that she was free to fashion for herself be worth without him?

CHAPTER TWENTY-FIVE

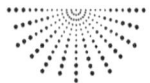

LONDON, ONE WEEK LATER

*I*t wasn't until the third occurrence of muted footsteps scurrying past his closed bedroom door that Rake willed his eyes open.

And even then, it was one eye that squinted to check the time on his bedside clock.

Half past seven.

He noted the sun peeking around the edges of velvet curtains shut tight against the outside world. He lay back and rubbed the sleep from his eyes. The sixth day in succession he'd lain abed past daybreak. He could try to convince himself he was keeping London hours—and he was, if drinking and gaming his evenings away at Brooks's counted as London hours. But the simple truth was, every morning he lay in his bed and struggled to find a good reason to remove himself from it.

He shouldn't be in London, anyway. But Artemis hadn't been able to return to Somerton after the Two Thousand Guineas, and Rake couldn't allow her to ramble about his Grosvenor Square mansion alone with only Mother for company—not that their parent was of any use. She strictly kept to her own hours and calendar, and since her children weren't scheduled, they weren't seen.

Which was a blessing.

She'd listened attentively to the tragedy that had befallen Dido and at the end of it had said, "It's a horse, Artemis."

And that was the end of it for Mother.

But Rake sensed he had a deeper, truer motivation for having accompanied his sister to London.

Gemma.

She would be in London.

Her ship was to set sail from the London Docks.

Today.

Outside his bedroom door, the continuous sound of feet shuffling about corridors, accompanied by voices lowered to a muted pitch didn't relent. Rake flung the blankets away and snatched up his dressing robe. As duke of this mansion, he supposed he needed to investigate what the blast was going on. It wouldn't be Mother, for her silk sleeping mask didn't leave her face a second before noon, which left but one other occupant.

Artemis.

What the blazes was his sister about?

He swung his bedroom door wide and asked the first servant who shuffled past exactly that. The servant swallowed, not too keen on further invoking the ire of the resident duke. Rake attempted to school his face into one less wrathful. "Perchance, my good man," he said, in a semblance of patience, "would you happen to know what all the hurly burly is about?"

"'Tis Lady Artemis, Your Grace," said the servant.

Rake only now noticed the man held a leather satchel clutched in each hand. "Is she going somewhere?"

This would be the first time she'd left her rooms since they'd arrived.

Rake didn't know if this was a good development.

Or a very bad one.

Before the servant could answer, Artemis emerged from her bedroom door at the far end of the corridor, dressed from head to toe in a lavender velvet travel costume. Rake's brow furrowed. "Going somewhere?" he called out.

She closed the distance between them. "I'm leaving, Rake."

"I'd gathered as much," he said. "But why?"

She swallowed, and her gaze shifted, presumably to supervise the servants hauling her belongings out of her rooms. "I can't be here," she said, the words simple, but weighed down by a burden of meaning.

"Shall I have the carriage made ready for our return to Somerton?" he asked.

He needed to get out of London. He didn't trust himself not to do something rash.

Like ride straight for the London Docks, when he had an appointment with a very different lady at ten o'clock.

Artemis met his gaze, hers unsteady, yet sure. "I'm leaving without you."

"Artemis," Rake began, "there was nothing anyone could do."

Grief held deep shimmered about her. "I know, Rake. Still, I can't bear to look at you right now." She swallowed. "I can't bear to look at myself either, for that matter."

"It's one of those things that happens on the racecourse, Artemis. No one can predict it. You know that." He was saying all the right words, but he could see none of them were sufficient to penetrate the cloak of mourning wrapped tightly about his sister. "It's not your fault."

"Oh?" Artemis shot back, anger swirling through the single syllable. "Then whose fault is it? You tried to warn me. Gem tried to warn me. I wouldn't listen to anyone." She closed her eyes and shook her head. When she opened them again, they were shining with unshed tears. "Dido trusted me, and now she is—" Artemis choked up, unable to speak that last word.

Rake tried a different angle. "At least tell me where you're going."

She drew herself up to her full, willowy height and regained her composure. "To West Riding."

"Endcliffe Grange?" he asked for clarity's sake.

She nodded tightly.

"Is it necessary to go all the way to Yorkshire?" He had to ask. He'd rather she go to Somerton, where he could keep an eye on her.

"I'm, *erm*, meeting a friend up there."

"A *friend*?"

"I do have a few of those, you know."

"In Yorkshire?"

"Besides," she began. Her jaw took on the pugnacious set that signaled staunch opposition to further argument. "I own the Grange outright, as Grandmama left it to me."

"What does that have to do with anything?"

She slid a purple kidskin glove onto one hand, then the other. "Do not follow or try to contact me, Rake," she said. "I'm quite serious."

A moment ticked past while Rake weighed his sister's resolve. The fact was he could hardly stop her. But if he thought she was in no condition to care for herself, he wouldn't allow her to go alone. She would hardly be able to stop him.

They knew as much about each other.

But the resolute glint that shone in her eyes told him she would be all right on her own.

So, when she brushed past him and practically flew down the stairs, he called after her, "Fare thee well, sister," and let her go.

Feet all but dragging across the floor, he returned to his bedroom and kicked the door shut behind him. The temptation to fall back into bed pulled at him, heavily.

But it was no use.

He needed to ready himself to pay a call to the Duchess of Acaster's St. James's Square mansion in a few hours. They were on each other's social calendars for ten o'clock.

Whereupon he would enter her drawing room and suggest they join their lots together in marriage.

It was the only reason for the call.

And they both knew it.

The marriage you described with the Duchess of Acaster won't make you unhappy... But it won't make you happy, either.

Gemma's words.

Happiness.

An idea better left to the lower classes.

Wasn't that how Mother had taught him to think about it?

Hadn't he, in fact, failed rather spectacularly every time he attempted to pursue the elusive ideal?

He wouldn't be happy with the Duchess of Acaster—but he wouldn't be unhappy, either.

With a wife like Celia, he wouldn't feel the utter wretchedness that had settled like a brick in his chest for the last week.

Nor would he ascend to the heights he'd achieved with Gemma.

There were wants, and there were needs.

Hadn't Gemma taught him about those?

Further, she'd been right.

In the moment, he'd been too blinded by his sense of betrayal to see the matter from her viewpoint. The fact was he'd never had to scramble or scrape for what he needed.

Not like Gemma.

Not as she'd been courageous enough to do.

But what did it matter now?

She was presently boarding a ship bound for New York.

And he was bound for a duchess's mansion to propose marriage.

They each had their own plans, and their own lives to lead.

Today was the beginning of his perfect, not-unhappy life.

* * *

Sᴛ. James's Square

10 o'clock

Rake shifted on the Duchess of Acaster's rose-silk drawing-room settee and attempted to make himself comfortable.

But no configuration of crossed or uncrossed legs—or recrossed, for that matter—would do for more than a ten-second stretch.

He simply couldn't be comfortable.

The Duchess of Acaster was about to make him the happiest —or not unhappiest—man in the world, and he couldn't settle in his own skin.

No matter.

He didn't need to be comfortable or settled.

He needed to get the question out of his mouth—and the rest of his life would follow.

The duchess walked into the room dressed in a coral pink of a hue different from the rest of this pink room. The woman certainly liked her pink. But that was beside the point. With her sable hair cascading over her shoulders in artful waves and the dress caressing her many curves in all the right places, she somehow managed to look both like a duchess and every man's fantasy of a woman—refined yet voluptuous.

He'd never seen Gemma in a dress.

The thought only struck him now.

She wouldn't fill out this dress like Celia—all luscious curves.

But she would look no less fetching in it.

He gave himself a mental shake. Gemma had no place in this room—particularly not in light of the question he was about to ask the woman approaching him.

"Rakesley," said Celia, a flirty smile about her mouth. Her pouty bottom lip glistened, moist as if she'd only just licked it, and her cheeks glowed bright and fresh, as if she'd pinched them the moment before entering the room.

When he took this woman to wife, he would be the envy of every man in England.

"Celia," he said, rising to his feet and only resuming his seat once she she'd settled onto the settee opposite him.

A not-uncomfortable beat of silence passed. It was the next beat of silence that caused the discomfort.

That made Rake want to begin crossing, uncrossing, and recrossing legs.

Which wouldn't do.

"Congratulations are in order, I believe," he said, for something to say.

She gave a satisfied smile. "You're speaking of Light Skirt, I presume."

"No small thing to win the One Thousand Guineas."

"She'll be up against your Hannibal in the Race of the Century," she returned with no small amount of challenge in her eyes.

Here, with talk of horses, they stood on safe ground.

An expression of sympathy entered her luminous amber eyes. "How is Lady Artemis bearing up after the loss of Dido?"

"As well as can be expected."

Rake supposed platitudes were for acquaintances and strangers, and certainly not for one's future wife, but he couldn't find it in him to speak to this woman any other way. Besides, he didn't want to talk about Artemis. If he talked about Artemis, he would think about Artemis, and then he would find himself on the road, making sure she arrived in Yorkshire safely.

Perhaps Gemma was right.

Perhaps he truly couldn't bear not to be the one in control all the time.

Gemma.

She had a way of stealing into his thoughts at every turn.

"Shall I have tea brought in?" asked Celia, a nearly imperceptible, questioning line knitted between her eyebrows.

Rake shook his head.

Another silence stretched between them.

He hadn't come here for tea, and they both knew it.

He'd come here to ask this woman a question.

And she'd come here to say yes.

It was all a foregone conclusion. And yet…

The question refused to dislodge from his mouth.

He cleared his throat. "Actually, I've come to…"

The words that would ask her to marry him were having a devil of a struggle.

He tried a different configuration of words. "I've come to the conclusion that I should ask…"

Her eyebrows crinkled together.

Should? As if it were an unsavory chore?

You to marry me, should've been emerging from his mouth.

It's in the in-between space that the magic in life happens.

More of Gemma's words.

And Rake realized something—he would never experience that magic with this perfect duchess who would make him not unhappy.

And he realized something more—he wanted that magic.

He *needed* that magic.

And there was only one woman with whom he could experience it.

Sudden urgency and impatience streaked through him.

He was in the wrong place—speaking to the wrong woman.

But first, he needed to make the attempt to smooth matters over with this wrong woman. She was regarding him as if he'd suddenly sprouted a pair of horns.

"It turns out," he began, "I've come to ask if you wouldn't mind very much if I *don't* ask you to marry me."

Startled silence met his question that wasn't really a question.

Then Celia's eyebrows released, and a stony laugh escaped her. It seemed he couldn't help provoking that response from every woman he came across today. Still, he hadn't been expecting it from this woman.

Now that he thought about it, he didn't know what response he'd expected.

He sat forward, when what he really wanted to do was shoot to his feet and leave this room. But he couldn't until the duchess rose first. He yet possessed a few of his manners. "Are you very disappointed?" he asked. It seemed like a natural question, given the circumstances.

Her gaze lifted toward the white coffered ceiling. "*Disappointed?*" she scoffed. "Oh, you haven't any idea."

"You aren't…*weren't*…in love with me, I hope," he said. Her response was setting him on the back foot, truth told, so use of the past tense only seemed sporting.

Another stony laugh burst from her. "Of course not."

Rake couldn't stem the tide of relief.

The duchess, however, wasn't finished. "Why ever would you suppose such a thing?"

"Your reaction for starters."

"Oh, it most definitely isn't the loss of *you* that'll have me crying into my pillow tonight," she said with no small amount of scorn. "It'll be the loss of your—" She bit off the rest of the sentence and shot to her feet, giving Rake the excuse he needed to rise.

"Stables," he finished for her.

Her eyes went utterly serious. "Something like that."

What was going on here, anyway?

But Rake hadn't the time or inclination to pursue the question.

For her part, the duchess snorted. Possibly the first snort to emerge from her ladylike nose in all her life. "Men," was all she said, as if that said it all. Her eyes, which had only ever gazed upon him softly, went hard. "And I'll be keeping Silky Sadie."

Rake's brow formed a deep furrow. "Now, let's not get carried away."

She lifted a single eyebrow. His protest had no chance of catching purchase on that stony ground.

"Of course," he groused. Damned dishonorable was what it was.

But he couldn't very well blame her.

She'd thought there would be no risk in using Silky Sadie as bait, because upon marriage, their stables would combine.

Then there was the fact that he intended to leave here and immediately pursue another woman.

The duchess could have her mare.

He would have something far more valuable.

A life with Gemma.

If she would have him.

He spoke a hasty, "I wish you all the best," and his feet were hastening across the room. Another stony scoff met his back as he exited.

Outside, he took the front steps down two at a time and called up to his coachman, "The London Docks."

He would catch Gemma before she set sail and proclaim his feelings—if he could find a way to gather them into coherent sentences.

And if she still wanted to leave after that, then…

Actually, he couldn't think of anything after *then*.

He wasn't sure he could go on without her.

It would sound like maudlin rot—if it didn't feel so true.

* * *

HALF AN HOUR later

What Rake hadn't counted on in his haste and hurry to the

London Docks was its hordes and hordes and *hordes* of people.

People of all sorts. Captains and crew...street vendors...soldiers...men and women of every social tier, from lowest to highest. They walked and ran, hurried and scurried, darted and dashed, paced and raced, strolled, scrambled, and scampered in every direction.

Then there were myriad ships of all sorts and sizes—barques, schooners, brigs, sloops... Oh, the variety and quantity of seafaring vessels went on and on.

Overwhelmed, Rake planted his feet and cast his gaze about. Had he thought to arrive and simply lay eyes on Gemma?

That certainly wasn't going to be the case.

Frantic, he began asking all and sundry who came within a ten-foot radius if they could point him in the direction of the ship bound for Falmouth today, then on to America. Most avoided his gaze and shoved past. Others gave him the courtesy of an indifferent shrug.

What if she'd already sailed?

He couldn't think about that *what if.*

He needed definite answers, and he wouldn't stop until he'd had them. He could think of only three possibilities.

Her ship had, indeed, sailed.

She was here—and would hear him out and answer him with a firm *no.*

Or...she would answer him with a *yes.*

A one in three chance she would be his forever.

With those odds, he had to keep searching.

He felt a tug and glanced down to find a small, grimy hand clutching his greatcoat. A street urchin squinted up at him, a canny glint in his eye. "Ye lookin' fer the *Morgana*?"

"I'm not sure," said Rake, slowly.

"The one goin' to Falmouth?"

Relief pulsed through Rake. Finally, he was getting somewhere. "That'll be the one."

The boy cocked his head and held out his hand.

A universal language, that one.

Rake searched pocket after pocket until, at last, his fingers found coin, emerging holding a bright, shiny guinea. Without a moment's hesitation, the lad snatched the coin from between Rake's forefinger and thumb. Rake could only be thankful the lad's feet were slower than his hands as Rake caught him by the collar before he could disappear into the crowd. "The ship?"

The boy pointed toward the river.

All Rake saw was water. "It sank?"

"'Course not," the little lad scoffed. He pointed again.

And Rake understood.

The lad wasn't pointing at the river—but at the ship sailing away upon it.

Unconsciously, Rake's hand released the lad's collar, and he seized the opportunity to vanish into the crowd.

The ship was a good hundred yards down the river. Too far away to do anything about.

Gemma was gone.

A hole, black and bottomless, opened up inside Rake, and he felt suddenly winded, even having to put his hands on his knees to support himself.

He'd lost her.

Truly lost her.

Strangely, he hadn't considered it a real possibility.

Her decision was made.

And he had no choice to respect it.

Respect it?

Nay, if she'd stayed in England, he wouldn't have been able to keep away from her.

But when a woman followed through on putting an ocean between her and a man, well, it sent a message.

One he would have to try to find a way to live with.

He had only himself to blame.

CHAPTER TWENTY-SIX

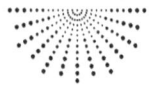

EPSOM DOWNS, TWO WEEKS LATER

*R*ake rested his forearms on the top runner of the track fence and watched alongside Julian as horse and rider blazed past, hooves pounding the earth with a muted *thud-thud... thud-thud.*

Julian glanced at his pocket watch. "Eight seconds faster than the last go."

"Filthy Habit will need a good gallop about an hour before the Derby to get his blood up," said Rake.

Julian nodded in agreement and slipped his watch into his pocket. Together, they watched the horses in their morning workouts. Though the Derby was still a week away, Epsom was already buzzing with the frenetic energy that possessed every course in England the week preceding a racing meeting.

"Little Wicked is in fine form for the Oaks," observed Julian.

"Aye, she's a sweet goer," returned Rake. "Good bottom."

He could barely speak the words through gritted teeth. It would always irk him that Little Wicked belonged to Deverill.

He flung thoughts of the man from his mind. All they did was lead to…

Gemma.

"I think we've got Filthy Habit's main issue sorted," continued Julian.

"What issue?"

"Not so much with Filthy Habit himself, as with his jockey."

"Too much crop?"

Julian shook his head. "Too little, actually."

A dry laugh sounded through Rake's nose. "Don't ever let—" The remainder of the sentence died in Rake's mouth.

Don't ever let Gemma hear you say that.

Of course, Gemma couldn't hear it. She wasn't here.

She wasn't even in England.

Or on this side of the Atlantic Ocean, for that matter.

"Not that he should be whipped," said Julian, oblivious to the endless circle of Rake's thoughts these last two weeks. "But Filthy Habit responds to a light tap of the crop at crucial moments. He can get distracted. It keeps his focus from drifting."

As if to illustrate the point, Filthy Habit trotted past, his jockey in the process of cooling the animal down. He was a beautiful, well-built colt. Rake had no doubt he would be taking the Derby crown in a week's time and giving Hannibal a run for his money come the end of September in the Race of the Century.

"I need to tell Smithwick to give him two more miles of cooldown," Julian called over his shoulder as he hopped the fence.

Rake watched his friend recede into the distance and thought of Artemis, who wouldn't be joining them at the Race of the Century. He still felt that loss keenly.

Unable to help himself, he'd sent a note to Endcliffe Grange a week ago, just to make sure she hadn't been beset by highwaymen on the Great North Road. Yesterday, he'd received a terse three-word reply.

Leave me be.

He was to stay away. She couldn't be any more clear.

Which was difficult to accept. His instinct was to try to fix the situation. But he understood control wasn't what was needed. Artemis needed time. Time was the great healer.

Or some rot like that.

He hadn't actually found it to be true for himself. Every day, it was a struggle for him not to book passage on a packet bound for America and scour every inch of New York until he found Gemma.

He would start with the stables.

A horse and jockey bolted past, catching Rake's eye.

But what held it was a hazy sense of recognition.

He knew the horse—*Good Sir Longshanks*—but not the jockey. Yet there was something familiar about the lad. The way he sat the horse lightly. The flame of red-gold hair curling from beneath his cap.

It wasn't Gemma, of course. This jockey was taller, lankier…a man.

Then he made a bend, and recognition streaked through Rake.

He was one of the two men Gemma had met at The Running Horse.

Not Deverill.

The other one.

Her brother.

Liam.

The sudden whirlwind of Rake's mind unloosed a gossamer thread of logic. Liam was *here*, which could only mean that Gemma was…

His heart hammering against his ribs, Rake spun in a slow circle, taking in every inch of course and grounds. He would recognize her in an instant, for he knew the lines and angles of her form better than he knew his own.

Nothing.

His brow creased into a deep furrow.

Liam was...*here*...

In England.

But...

Where the blazes was Gemma?

His feet were moving without him telling them to do so, making their way to the stables. Liam would eventually end up there with Good Sir Longshanks.

Half an hour later, Liam was at the mounting block and sliding off the horse. Once he'd finished conversing with the trainer and taking a few instructions, Rake stepped into his path. As Liam's feet stumbled to a stop, it was the widening of his eyes that gave him away. He knew Rake on sight.

Rake jutted his chin toward an area where they could speak without the intrusion of prying onlookers. In a low voice that wouldn't carry farther than Liam's ears, he cut straight to it. "Aren't you supposed to be in New York?"

Liam planted his feet wide and crossed his arms over his chest, eyes of the same gold-flecked green hue as his sister's staring out at Rake. The same look in those eyes, as well. *Stubborn... willful...* The man was digging his heels in. His head cocked. "What's it to you?"

"You know who I am?"

Liam was assessing Rake, that was for certain, and like his sister, he wasn't too impressed by the title of duke. "Aye."

Both men knew what Rake wasn't saying. He only had everything to lose by not asking... "And Gemma?"

"She isn't here."

Unaccountable anger surged through Rake. "You let her sail to New York without you?" He asked...*demanded.* "A young woman on her own in a place she doesn't know? This is how you repay everything she's done for you?" The words just kept pouring out.

Perhaps they weren't meant for Liam at all, but rather for himself. "What sort of brother are you, anyway?"

Liam watched Rake with a curious expression on his face, letting Rake's accusations wash right over him, not particularly bothered. "All finished?"

The question caught Rake on the backfoot. These Cassidy twins... They weren't like anyone Rake had ever known. "I'm not sure yet."

"What I said," began Liam, enunciating every word clearly, "was that Gemma wasn't *here*, at Epsom. I didn't say she was on the other side of the Atlantic."

A feeling began to expand within Rake—one he needed to tamp down...

Hope.

If she wasn't on the other side of the Atlantic, then...

Where was she?

Liam wasn't quite done. "Of course, I didn't abandon my sister. What sort of man do you take me for?"

Rake understood what he needed to say next, particularly if he wanted any useful information out of this man, who happened to be the brother of the love of his life. "My apologies," he said, sincere.

Liam took his measure before he gave a curt nod, reluctantly mollified.

"Where is she?" asked Rake with a telling rasp of emotion. "She knows she doesn't need to be in hiding anymore."

"Aye, she knows." Liam shifted on his feet. "And I'd like to thank you for that."

"Thank me?" Rake was at a loss. "For what?"

"For getting Bolton off our backs," said Liam. "For a chance at living the lives we want."

Rake saw his sincerity. "That's all I'm asking for, Liam." He wasn't sure he'd ever made himself so humble to another living soul. "A chance."

With Gemma, he didn't need to say.

They both heard it.

At last, Liam relented. "A lady made her an offer to work up in Yorkshire."

"And you let her?"

"*Let* her?" That got a good, long laugh. "You've met my sister. There's no *letting* her do anything. She doesn't wait for permission."

In fact, Rake did know this about Gemma.

It was one of his favorite things about her.

Liam snorted, and a knowing light entered his eyes. "I thought that might be the case."

Now, it was Rake's head cocking to the side. "What case?"

Again, Liam snorted.

Which was all the answer Rake needed. Were his intentions toward Gemma so obvious?

Likely.

Definitely.

"In Yorkshire, you say?" asked Rake, the words only now sinking in. "With a lady?"

Of course...

"What sort of work?" he demanded.

"Helping horses," said Liam. "What other work would tempt her all the way north?"

A friend...

Artemis said she and a friend were leaving for Endcliffe Grange.

Gemma was that friend.

He should've seen it sooner.

He needed to leave...

Now.

But, first, he had something to say. "Thank you."

Liam went dead serious. "And your intentions toward my sister?" he asked. "She won't settle for the life our mam had."

Liam was a good brother. Rake saw that. "I'll make her a duchess, if she'll allow me."

"That's not the title—or life—she cares about."

"I'll make her my wife...my partner...my love."

The moment stretched as Liam weighed Rake's sincerity. Then he nodded, satisfied.

Though his feet itched to be on their way, Rake had another question for Liam. "And you?"

A smile tipped about the other man's mouth. "Here, for now," he said. "Can't keep me away from a stable or a racecourse."

Rake snorted. "I figured as much." This was firm, companiable ground. "Do you have your sister's way with horses?"

"Aye."

"If you ever find yourself up near Somerton," said Rake. Now his feet were truly on the move. "You'll have a place."

Liam's chuckle met Rake's back. "I wish you all the luck."

Rake tossed a grunt over his shoulder and kept moving. He instructed a stable lad to deliver a parting message to Julian, and he was on his way north within minutes. He could be in Yorkshire in two days, if he started now.

Then he would speak all the words he should've already spoken to Gemma.

And ask the question he should've already asked.

And if she refused him...

Nay.

He would win her.

Loss was never an option—not without a fight.

And that wasn't about to change with the most important moment of his life.

* * *

ENDCLIFFE GRANGE

Two days later

Beneath a Yorkshire sky, gray with a dense cloak of clouds, Gemma led Snip—imaginatively named for the snip on his nose —to the far easterly field, where he could graze and laze the afternoon away. A sturdy gray Cleveland bay who had served as a post coach's off-side leader for three years, the fellow had certainly earned the rest.

A week ago, an innkeeper in the nearest village had put up a notice offering the animal to any interested farmer. Such was the life cycle of a coach horse. They were worked until they could no longer maintain the speed and stamina to pull passenger carriages across long distances, then they were sold to farmers for field toil. These animals were worked and worked until every last bit of work was squeezed from them and they eventually broke completely down.

Not this old coach horse, Gemma and Lady Artemis had decided when they saw the notice.

And so it was that they'd acquired their first horse at Endcliffe Grange.

Though the locals mostly observed the budding animal operation at the Grange from the side of their collective eye, animals of all sorts had begun appearing on the long drive up to the manor house. In addition to Snip, they'd also come into possession of an ill-tempered, one-horned billy goat, an orange tabby cat and her kittens, and a three-legged, one-eyed sheepdog Artemis immediately named Bathsheba, lady and dog instantly taking to each other. Bathsheba even slept in Artemis's room at night.

It was clear the locals all thought Gemma and Artemis a little mad, but they were accepting enough. After all, Artemis was a lady, and ladies had their own—*strange*—ways.

Gemma knew this was how Artemis was healing the damage in her own heart after the death of Dido. And Gemma couldn't think of a better way of going about it than to provide shelter and recovery to animals. She admired Lady Artemis for taking an approach that moved her forward, rather than allowing herself to wallow in sadness and guilt—feelings Gemma very much understood.

In fact, she'd been doing exactly that when a Bow Street Runner had appeared at her and Liam's London rooms—*hovel*, more accurately. Her first thought had been that the man was sent by Bolton—and her first instinct had been to run.

But the investigator hadn't been sent by Bolton, but rather by Lady Artemis Keating, with a message that she would be arriving at eight o'clock the next morning to transport Gemma to Yorkshire, if she was interested in starting an animal sanctuary together.

Gemma hadn't had to think about the instinctive *yes* she'd sent by way of return.

Yet she knew her days here were numbered.

It was only a matter of time before word reached Rake.

And she would have to go.

She'd just finished latching the pasture gate when Bathsheba raced over with her wobbly, three-legged stride, her nose nudging Gemma's hand for a pet. Artemis wasn't far behind. "How is our fellow today?" she called out. Gemma saw a bit of her former bloom returned to her cheeks.

Gemma propped an elbow on the fence and gazed out at Snip idly munching grass. "The sores on his withers are healing."

Artemis nodded. "No saddles or harnesses for him ever again."

"Aye."

Artemis held up a square of white paper. "I just received this."

"What is it?"

"An invitation to dine with Sir Abstrupus Bottomley. Actually, it isn't so much an invitation as a summons."

"That cannot possibly be the man's name."

"Oh, but it most certainly is," said Artemis, conversationally. "His lands adjoin Endcliffe Grange on the northern border. Grandmama couldn't stand the man. Called him an eccentric old nodcock." Artemis rolled her eyes skyward. "Grandmama was in her seventy-sixth year when she passed ten years ago. So, if she knew him—and thought him old—well, I don't see how he could have fewer than ninety years on him."

"You can't possibly refuse, if only to assuage your curiosity."

"True," said Artemis, thoughtfully. "I seem to remember he named all his horses after herbs and root vegetables. There was a Parsley and a Coriander. Carrot—or was that Turnip?—placed at Doncaster a few years ago, if memory serves. All descended from the Darley line."

"You sound like—" Gemma's mouth snapped shut.

Rake.

She couldn't trust herself to speak the name without her voice breaking in two.

Artemis didn't seem to notice. "My brother? Aye, I reckon I do." Her mouth curved in a small, faraway smile. The old Artemis would've laughed. But not *this* Artemis. This Artemis was somber and serious. Like the animals she took in, she needed time and careful handling to heal. That smile was, at least, a start.

Gemma's eye caught on a figure in the distance. *Tall...lean...*

A familiar figure...

A figure possessed of a specific magnificence.

She blinked. She was seeing phantoms. Except, not phantoms, for as far as she knew Rake was very much alive.

What he wasn't, however, was here at Endcliffe Grange.

Artemis took one look at the figure and reached a different conclusion, for her brow gathered and she immediately called out, "Rake!" an unmistakable note of fractiousness in her voice.

Gemma squinted, her eyes going wide the next instant.

The figure was, in fact, Rake.

A torrent of competing emotions buzzed straight through her.

Rake...here.

"I told you to stay away!" shouted Artemis. At her side, Bathsheba gave a loud, loyal bark.

Rake didn't break stride.

Now, he was close enough for Gemma to see where his focus was centered—directly upon her. And within those eyes that were once so inscrutable to her, she detected determination.

A warm shiver traced through her. She'd never much minded being the object of his determination, if she was being entirely truthful.

For her part, Artemis opened her mouth to say more to her brother, but Rake held up a hand, staying the words in her mouth. "I'm not here for you, sister."

Artemis glanced back and forth between Rake and Gemma, then once again for good measure, and her eyes went wide with sudden understanding. "Oh," she said. "Right."

And still Rake's gaze didn't once stray from Gemma. "Now, leave us."

Artemis didn't need to be told twice. "Bathsheba," she said with a light click, owner and dog striding away.

Which left Gemma with Rake.

Alone.

Several beats of time ticked past, the silence awkward until Rake said, "You're not in New York."

A statement of the obvious.

"No," she said. Another statement of the obvious. "I never really wanted to go." Her throat went thick with emotion. "Thank you for making it possible for me to stay in England."

He ran a hand through tousled hair, an air of frustration about him. "You can stop thanking me. I don't want your thanks or undying gratitude. I want your—" His mouth snapped shut.

"What is it you want?" Gemma was barely able to whisper, her heart beating a hard tattoo in her chest. It knew what it hoped he wanted.

"We can talk about that later."

More ticks of awkward silence crept past. Gemma had to stop herself from shuffling her feet. "How did you find me?" she asked, at last.

"I saw your brother at Epsom."

"Ah," she said on a slow nod. "His shock of red hair wouldn't be too difficult to spot."

Rake remained utterly serious. "He's a damn fine jockey."

"Aye."

"I offered him employment at Somerton."

Instinctively, Gemma scoffed. "You cannot offer my brother employment."

"I can." Rake shrugged. "I did."

Sometimes, she could forget what an arrogant duke he was.

Then she was reminded.

"Did you come all this way to tell me that?" she asked, irked.

"No."

Her irritation faded, a dizzying feeling of anticipation taking its place.

He glanced around their surroundings. "Do you like it up in Yorkshire?"

"It's a bit nippy, but aye."

His gaze shifted and seemed to really take her in. "You're doing what you always wanted."

"Aye."

"You look well."

"I am."

Though they were speaking about her life, it felt like a superficiality. As if another conversation were straining below the surface of this conversation, aching to get out.

Then it hit her—Rake's appearance. Three-day stubble on his face... His head hatless, hair wind-tossed... A scuff of muck on his greatcoat sleeve…

In short, he looked bedraggled.

Rake never looked bedraggled—not even when he'd just rolled out of bed.

A question came to her. A question she must ask—a question that required nerve.

Well, she'd never lacked for that.

"And the reason you've come all the way north?" she asked softly, nearly breathless.

Oh, the gallop of her heart… It would race straight out of her chest any second.

And Rake… He looked as intense and serious as she'd ever seen him—and something else. *Tetchy.* As if his nerves buzzed beneath his skin.

Nervous and bedraggled… Who was this Rake?

"I came in search of magic," he said, low and earnest.

The breath froze in Gemma's chest and refused to budge.

"I came in search of *you.*"

He reached out and took her cold hand in his. Warmth poured through her. *His* warmth. And, oh, how she wanted to enter it fully with him. But…

She must say something that might destroy this moment.

Yet if there was to be a future—if there was to be magic…if there was to be *them*—she must say it.

The only way out was through.

Horseracing had taught her that much.

"But I…" She drew in a bracing breath. "I betrayed you."

"You did what you had to do for your family. For you and Liam. You did it for your loved one."

"But I did it, Rake." She needed to say something else. "And I would do it again."

He needed to understand that about her.

The echo of a smile curved about his mouth. "That's what I love about you."

She blinked.

Love?

And it occurred to her that, yes, *love*.

Love was what they were speaking of.

"You love fiercely and protectively," he said. "I can think of no honor that would make me prouder than to be the man you love."

She swallowed and blinked away sudden tears, even as her heart threatened to burst.

This business of love certainly put a heart through its paces.

"Gemma, you can stop running now."

"But I have," she said. "Bolton no longer—"

Rake gave his head a slow shake. "Not from Bolton."

Her eyebrows crinkled together. "From who then?"

"From yourself."

It was possible she would never draw breath again. Such was the way those two simple words struck her. Though gently spoken, they hit like a blunt instrument.

As her mind wanted to reject them, every cell in her body knew them to be true.

"You've only seen love destroy, Gemma."

Oh.

"But what of a different sort of love?" He took her hand in his. "What of a love that builds? Love doesn't have to be destructive. Love can be...*is*...beautiful. Our love is—"

"*Magic*," she finished for him.

"You're a need and a want, Gemma, and I can't do without either. I'm asking you. I'm *begging* you."

And, like that, the clouds in her mind cleared.

It was safe to be mad with love for this magnificent, tender man.

He tugged, and all resistance fell away as she swayed into his embrace. Her head tipped back so she could hold his dark gaze. "I love you, Rake," she said. Her every want and desire began spilling out of her. "I want you to be my husband. I want you to be father to my children. I want you to be my lover. I want you to be mine. I *need* you to be mine."

A feeling novel and effervescent blossomed within her. It was safe to speak those wants and needs, because this man would honor every last one of them.

Because he was hers—and she was his.

He caressed her cheek and tucked an unruly curl behind her ear. "You'll never have to run again."

She wrapped her arms around his neck and lifted onto the tips of her toes. "Only into your arms," she spoke against his mouth.

And when his hands found the small of her back and pulled her in, she melted into his kiss. All the heat and desire and need and passion and love a swirl of emotion, lending a magic to the kiss in a way never before expressed.

What she and Rake shared…

It was special.

It was *them*.

No two other people on Earth shared *this*.

He pulled back a hairsbreadth. "That life we're going to build together?" he muttered against her mouth.

"Yes?" she asked, her arms tightening around his neck. She wasn't ready for the kiss to end. It had only gotten started.

"We can start building it tomorrow."

"I was thinking *now* would be more ideal."

She tugged his cravat loose with both playfulness and serious intention. It had been entirely too long since she'd run her hands across his bare chest.

A wicked smile curled about his mouth. "Gretna Green is but a day's ride away."

"Can we not live in sin for a few days first?"

He gave his head a slow shake. "You'll be my duchess when I have you next."

Frustration seared through Gemma when she looked properly into his eyes and saw her future husband was utterly, damnably serious.

It seemed he'd left her with no choice.

"If it means having you in my bed again," she sighed. "I suppose I'll become your duchess."

EPILOGUE

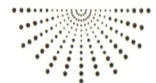

ONE MONTH LATER

*I*n the end, Rake had provided the *ton* with enough salacious gossip to keep their drawing rooms buzzing for a day or two.

Of course, the story of a duke who ran off to Gretna Green with his jockey and married her would, inevitably.

If he was a laughingstock, it was a fate he happily accepted.

After all, he'd won the prize—*Gemma*.

As they sat side by side on the folly's window casement, he reached for her hand and shifted slightly so he could observe her profile while she stared at the valley stretched below.

Utterly besotted.

That was how Artemis had described him with a mystified shake of the head when he and Gemma had asked her to serve as witness for their anvil marriage.

"Oh, how the mighty have fallen," laughed Artemis. "I never thought I'd see it, brother. Next, you'll be spouting poetry."

And Rake found his sister hadn't been half wrong. His heart

did seem to be in possession of a poetry both unexpected and strangely welcome.

He wouldn't fight it.

He was done fighting his heart.

To behold his wife was to feel poetry down to the essence of his soul.

The essence of his soul...

Here it was again—the poetry.

Her hair, the red-gold of autumn leaves, curls free to flow down her back.

Her green eyes flecked with amber—direct, intelligent, playful, compassionate...

Her eyes contained the world.

The only world that mattered.

Oh, how the mighty had fallen, indeed.

Gemma's head angled, and she met his gaze, a soft smile about her mouth, a question in her eyes. "Yes?"

She'd caught him staring. He didn't mind. He would have her know every minute of every day what she meant to him.

Which sounded rather close to poetry.

Again.

Actually, he did have a question grounded in the real world and not in the *la-di-da* one of poetry... "When was the last time you rode Hannibal on the practice course?"

She tapped a contemplative finger against her chin. "Two weeks ago?"

As he'd thought. "You know, you don't have to stop riding Hannibal simply because Liam has taken over as his jockey."

"Oh, but I took him out for a nice amble just this morning."

"I'm speaking of the racecourse."

"Ah," she replied, utterly unconcerned.

"I still think you should ride him in September. You and Hannibal would win," he pressed. "The Jockey Club has no rules explicitly stating a woman can't be a jockey."

"How about a duchess?" she asked, eyes sparkling with amusement. She wasn't taking this conversation as seriously as he wanted.

"A duchess can do what she damn well pleases."

"And what pleases her husband?" she asked, playfully stroking light fingers along his thigh, giving his cock ideas.

Though distraction pulled at him—he could take her here and now...*again*—he wouldn't give in...*yet*.

"Gemma..."

Her hand stopped, but didn't move from his thigh. *The minx.*

"It's just that September is so very far away," she began, breezily, "and by then I might be a bit wobbly in the saddle."

Rake shook his head, certain. "That's impossible. No one— neither man nor woman, not even Liam—sits a saddle as well as you."

She threw her head back and gave in to the laughter that had been shining in her eyes. "Oh, husband."

Husband.

Warmth stole through Rake every time his wife spoke that word. He was husband to her.

Of all his titles, this one was his favorite.

She took his hand in hers—oh, that it lifted from his thigh— and she set it low on her stomach. Within her eyes, he saw a smile both secret and telling. "*This* is why."

Only now, Rake noticed the soft, subtle rounding of her stomach. "Gemma..."

Sudden emotion flooded him, choking the words in his throat.

Her eyes brimmed bright with unshed tears. "I know."

He reached out with his other hand, his fingers finding the nape of her neck, weaving through loose curls, tugging her forward. In the instant before his mouth touched hers, he said, "You've made me the not unhappiest man on Earth."

As he pulled her into his embrace, he suspected a few unshed tears might be shining in his eyes too.

Julian had once called him intelligent for choosing those he loved.

But this life with Gemma wasn't one of mere choice. It had naught to do with anything as flimsy or shallow as a mind's choosing, but rather necessity of the heart.

The necessity that made a life worth its years on Earth.

Love.

Without love, a life could be no better than not *unhappy.*

And this life with Gemma was utterly, joyously, unabashedly *happy.*

The End

ALSO BY SOFIE DARLING

ABOUT THE AUTHOR

Sofie Darling is an award-winning author of historical romance. The third book in her Shadows and Silk series, Her Midnight Sin, won the 2020 RONE award for Best Historical Regency.

She spent much of her twenties raising two boys and reading every romance she could get her hands on. Once she realized she simply had to write the books she loved, she finished her English degree and embarked on her writing career. Mr. Darling and the boys gave her their wholehearted blessing.

When she's not writing heroes who make her swoon, she runs a marathon in a different state every year, visits crumbling medieval castles whenever she gets a chance, and enjoys a slightly codependent relationship with her beagle, Bosco. Visit her website.